Belanger Books presents

Not Forgetting Adèle

a sequel to
'Jane Eyre'
by Charlotte Bronte

Julia Harbour

Not Forgetting Adèle

Not Forgetting Adèle

By
Julia Harbour

Belanger Books
2020

Not Forgetting Adèle

For information contact:
Belanger Books, LLC
61 Theresa Ct.
Manchester, NH 03103
derrick@belangerbooks.com
www.belangerbooks.com

Cover and Back design by Brian Belanger
www.belangerbooks.com and *www.redbubble.com/people/zhahadun*

DEDICATION

To my husband Colin and two close
young relatives Mae and Adele

CHAPTER 1

"Name of Varens?"

It was almost dark. The steam from the engine coiled about me, catching the light from a single gas lamp above the platform and creating a confusion of changing images. I could just discern a tall figure, silhouetted against this dim illumination.

Madame Grevier's strictures on a young lady travelling alone and dealing with subordinates came to my mind. I drew myself up and declared, "I am Miss Adèle Varens. Who are you, sir?"

The figure strode forward, and I glimpsed curly chestnut hair escaping from underneath a shiny bowler hat. A hand touched the bowler's rim, and a Cockney voice exclaimed, "Jack Whitaker at your service, miss. Sent by Mr and Mrs. Rochester to drive you to Southlands."

Forgetting Madame Grevier and her Little Book of Etiquette, I clapped my hands excitedly "To Southlands! They've moved in then? How wonderful. I'm so looking forward to seeing their new house and spending Christmas there."

"You're Mr Rochester's ward aint ya?"

The question was asked in a tone which I found much too familiar. "And you, presumably are their servant? Well, Jack Whitaker, please conduct me to the carriage, without further delay, si'il vous plait. That is my valise."

Jack bent down and placed the case on his shoulder in one quick easy movement. "Follow me, Miss Adèle," he said, giving the last two words extra emphasis.

The familiar carriage stood in the station forecourt. Jack swung the valise up to the roof, opened the door, pulled down the step and held out his hand to help me enter. Ignoring his hand, I lifted my skirts and stepped into the carriage as gracefully as I could. Jack leapt up into the coachman's seat, and the coach raced off at such a speed that I was flung sideways and, to my annoyance, one of the plumes on my bonnet was bent. As I endeavoured to repair the damage, a wave of anger flooded through me. How dare he? I will certainly mention it to Tante Jane.

At the thought of Tante Jane, as I often called her, (although she wasn't really my aunt) my feelings softened. She was the angel in my life. The one who had always, unsparingly given me her love and care which I had so badly needed, when as a little child I had come to Thornfield. I had been a trifle frightened of Mr Rochester in those days and was still very wary of his uncertain temper and unpredictable moods. I had tried so hard to please him when he returned that time after Jane Eyre (as she was then) had arrived as my governess. But nothing I did could ever please him. I longed for his approbation and his love but it had always been denied me. He had thought of me as a little doll. No matter how I sang and danced for him, I would see that look of contempt in his dark eyes. I still longed for his love and respect. The greatest happiness in my life would be if I could prove that I really was his daughter, even though the 'child of an opera dancer', as he had said more than once in my hearing. Recently some information had come to me which had made me believe that this proof was possible. But I needed to get Tante Jane to help me.

I was deep in these thoughts when, after about twenty minutes, we reached two familiar stone gateposts surmounted by large stone eagles. I remembered this to be the entrance to

Ferndean where the Rochesters had lived for a short time after their marriage, and I had stayed there with them. The land surrounding the old house had once been a farm owned by Mr Rochester, and I knew from Tante's letters that their new house, Southlands, had been built on part of this land. They had selected an open site facing south, and I remembered Tante Jane telling me that this was the very field in which she and Mr Rochester had strolled after they had been reunited and where Mr Rochester proposed to her – for the second time. I knew also that they had taken great care to ensure that the new house in no way resembled either Thornfield, with its gloomy corridors and creepy third floor, nor Ferndean, dark and damp and buried in woodland.

Almost immediately on passing through the gates, the coach swung right, through two new brick gateposts with white gates standing open, and I saw in the dim light from the carriage the name Southlands inscribed in elegant lettering on a stone tablet on one of the posts. Beyond was a small lodge, and as we turned into the drive, the front door opened and an old man hobbled out.

The coach stopped and I pulled down the window and called out, "Hello, John, how are you?"

John looked up at me. "Well, if it isn't little Miss Adèle."

"How's Mary?"

"Oh, she's fine, Miss. Working at the new house now. I don't think they can do without 'er and 'er cooking."

"What are you doing here John?"

"Oh, I be retired now Miss. Mr Rochester has been very good to us. He 'ad this lodge built at the same time as the 'ouse and it's ours to live in for our lifetime. I 'elps out a bit with the garden and the new 'ot houses, but I can't do too much these days. It's me joints y'see. They be very stiff after all that long time in that damp old 'ouse, Ferndean. But I'm 'appy now. I keeps the gate and checks the visitors when they come."

It's good to see you, John," I called as the coach began to move away, "Happy Christmas."

"And the same to you, miss. We've missed your bright little face."

The new gravelled drive, pale against the dark grassland, climbed upwards and, straining my eyes, I could just make out a knot of tall trees on the hill's summit and, in front of them, the shape of a large building with many lighted windows. It was a clear, crisp night and above our heads the sky was sprinkled with stars. The coach had now entered a gravelled forecourt and stopped in front of an imposing entrance door approached by several wide semi-circular steps.

Jack leapt down to the ground, opened the carriage door and pulled down the step. This time he didn't offer me his hand. I began to descend when somehow my cloak got entangled with my feet, and I staggered. I would have fallen, but Jack's hand was there on my elbow to steady me. Shaken by this incident and very annoyed with myself for my clumsy and 'unladylike' descent, I felt the blood rush into my face.

He gave me a quizzical look "Better watch yerself there, miss."

"Thank you, Jack, but I could have managed perfectly well!" I shook off his hand, tossing my head.

However, all further words were swept away as the front door opened, letting out a flood of warm light and there, in a beautiful crimson velvet gown stood my dearest, my beloved Tante Jane with arms outstretched to receive me.

I ran lightly up the steps towards her and we embraced.

"Oh Tante, how wonderful to see you and to be spending Christmas at Southlands."

"My dear child, welcome," she murmured, kissing me.

But before we could say anything else, two little figures careered through the door and flung themselves on me, almost knocking me over.

"Adèle, Adèle, we're so excited to see you. Come and look at our lovely tree," they chorused.

"Now, Fairfax and Johnny," cried my laughing hostess, "pray be careful. You must be very tired after your long journey Adèle."

Turning to her little sons she explained, "Adèle has travelled a long, long distance. All the way from Switzerland."

"From Switzerland!" exclaimed Fairfax, looking at me with round dark eyes, just like Mr Rochester's.

"Well," I touched my damaged feather, trying to push it straight, so that it was less noticeable, "I should be grateful for a wash and a cup of tea."

"And those you shall have, my dear."

We had now entered a spacious hall where I noticed that everything which at
Thornfield had been in darkest oak, such as the stairs and wood panelling, were at Southlands in a light gold-coloured wood. At the bottom of the stairs stood a large sparkling Christmas tree covered with all sorts of pretty ornaments. These trees had recently become the rage in English households following Prince Albert's introduction of them at the Royal palaces.

A cheerful fire leapt in the large grate surrounded by polished brass twinkling in the blaze.

Then my heart missed a beat, for there was Mr Rochester beside the fireplace, leaning on his good hand, which rested on the mantelpiece.

Johnny and Fairfax raced across to him, "Papa, Papa, there's a beautiful lady to see you."

Mr Rochester's face brightened, as he ruffled little Johnny's hair, "A beautiful lady, eh? Who can it be?"

He turned his head towards me and I couldn't help noticing the change in his expression from cheerful to inscrutable. I hadn't seen him for two years and subconsciously noted that the scar on his forehead was less prominent. He wore a black patch over his blind eye and a padded leather glove concealed his missing hand. His hair was still the same ebony black but his dark brows had drawn together in a frown.

Trying to ignore all this, I tripped across the polished oak floor towards him.

"My dearest guardian, Mr Rochester. How are you?" I stopped in front of him.

He slowly extended his hand. "Well enough, my dear." He surveyed me from head to foot. "I see you haven't changed. You always did like to be fashionable. What an interesting bonnet. A broken feather, is that a symbol of something or just the latest style from Paris?"

I laughed self-consciously and felt the colour rising in my cheeks at his somewhat sardonic greeting.

Jane crossed to us quickly. "Edward, doesn't Adèle look beautiful? Quite the young lady now." She nodded at me encouragingly.

"Humph," returned her husband. "Fancy clothes and fine feathers, but have you learnt anything else at that finishing school of yours?"

Although trembling, I looked him steadily in the face and replied, "I have learnt many things about being a lady, sir, but the most important to me is a reinforcement of the conviction that I should continue to be grateful for the love and kindness I have received from yourself and Mrs Rochester, my dearest Aunt Jane, which will always mean that I hold you both in high regard and affection."

"Well, well," he gave me one of his rare flashing smiles and began to turn back to the fireplace. "Go with Mrs Rochester, she will show you to your room. We will be having tea in the library as soon as our other guests arrive."

Jane and I mounted the carpeted stairs. As we went, I noticed that everywhere was light and bright. From the top of the stairs a broad carpeted, well-lit corridor ran both ways leading to a series of bedrooms. Jane explained that there were only two floors to the house, with the servants' wing behind a green baize door to the rear. The house had been built on three sides of a courtyard.

"No third floor or any dark attics here," she said happily.

Opening a door, she ushered me into my bedroom, which was capacious with a separate dressing room; all comfortably and tastefully appointed. Velvet curtains obscured the windows but she confirmed that the room faced southwards and looked down the expanse of the garden and grounds to the river at the bottom of the hill.

I took off my bonnet and looked ruefully at my broken feather which I quickly plucked out and threw into a nearby waste paper basket. I then took off my pale blue fur-lined cloak to reveal my dress of darker blue trimmed with white lace at the collar and cuffs.

"I must say you do look very pretty, my dear. Have you enjoyed the last two years at Madame Grevier's?"

"I have, I have," I said quickly, "But Tante, there is something exciting I have to tell you."

There was a knock on the door. It was Jack Whitaker, now wearing the costume of a footman with dull green waistcoat, white shirt, and a neat bow tie.

"If you please madam, more visitors 'ave arrived…Captain and Mrs Fitzjames and the Reverend and Mrs Wharton with their children.

"Oh!" exclaimed Jane, hurrying towards the door. "Please excuse me Adèle. I must go down to greet them. Is everything organised for their reception Jack?"

"Yes, indeed madam. Mrs Tompkins 'as it all in 'and."

Turning to me, she said "You can tell me all your exciting news later, Adèle. Come down to the Library for tea when you are ready." She disappeared along the corridor with a swish of her crimson skirts.

Jack Whitaker still stood in the corridor looking at me. His expression carried a tremble of amusement, but his tone was very respectful as he said, "I 'ope everything is to your satisfaction, Miss Adèle. If there is anythink you need, the 'ousekeeper, Mrs Tompkins, will be 'appy to oblige." I nodded my head in acknowledgement.

As he turned to go, I couldn't resist commenting, "I thought you were the coachman but now I find you're the footman as well. A little unusual."

He laughed, "Yes I suppose it is, miss, but Mr Rochester doesn't like to have too many servants. The house is only staffed by Mary in the kitchen and scullery maid, Gladys, Mrs Tompkins, the housekeeper – you probably remember her as Leah, the maid at Thornfield, Daisy the housemaid and yours truly, who does treble duty as

Coachman, Footman and Mr Rochester's Valet. I don't mind, though, I like to be busy."

"No lady's maid for Mrs Rochester then?"

"No, she doesn't want anybody. She prefers to look after herself, although Mrs Tompkins sometimes helps out in that direction, if required."

"How long have you been working here?"

"I joined the household in mid-November, miss."

"Thank you, Jack," I said and he disappeared, with a little bow.

It was only afterwards that it struck me. Jack's Cockney accent seemed to come and go. In his last few utterances, he hadn't dropped his 'h's once. 'Strange,' I said to myself. I splashed my face and hands with water, tidied my hair and, leaving my room, walked down the corridor to the stairs. As I did so, I heard sounds of merriment echoing up from the hall. Looking down I saw several ladies and gentlemen sitting about the fire with Tante Jane and Mr Rochester, all talking and laughing as they watched children, of various sizes and ages running joyously around the Christmas tree, hands linked.

"Why don't you sing us a carol, children?" called one of the fathers whom I afterwards identified as Captain Fitzjames.

"Yes," cried his wife, Diana, "What about 'The First Noel?"

"We know the words to that, don't we Johnny?" exclaimed Fairfax and he and Johnny began to sing in unison with the others joining in including the party beside the fire.

I walked down a few more steps where I had a wider view of the hall and noticed Jack Whitaker had come forward. He had taken a child's little hand in each of his so that he could be part of the circle and began to sing in a melodious tenor.

"Come on children, sing up... "Noel, Noel, Noel, Noel Born is the King of Israel'"

Mr Rochester joined in with a powerful baritone, which I had often heard in past days.

This happy scene filled me with such delight that I just had to be part of it. I loved little children and singing came naturally to me. I clapped my hands and ran down the rest of the stairs to join in the circle and the carol. During my time at Madame Grevier's, I had taken singing lessons and had discovered that I had a pure clear soprano voice, with no trouble at all in reaching high notes. As I sang, I saw various heads turn to look at me, particularly when I reached the last top notes of the carol, which not everybody could manage, but Jack's voice and mine blended beautifully together. When we had finished, everyone clapped each other and us.

"Shall we sing another one Papa?" asked Fairfax eagerly.

"Not just now, dear. Our visitors are waiting for their tea," said Jane. She moved across the hall and, as she reached me, she smiled. "What a lovely voice Adèle. You must sing to us again over Christmas." Then, turning to her cousins, Diana and Mary, she said, "I'm sure you remember Mr Rochester's ward, Adèle Varens? She's been at Finishing School in Switzerland for the past two years and will be spending Christmas here with us."

Diana came forward, "Adèle, how delightful to see you," she said, giving me an affectionate embrace. Mary quickly followed her sister's welcoming gesture.

I was soon being introduced to their respective husbands. To Diana's spouse, Captain Fitzjames with his upright Naval bearing and dark moustache and beard and to

Mary's, the Reverend Stephen Wharton, bespectacled and studious in appearance. Both of them shook my hand warmly.

The children then ran up, Harriet Fitzjames, age six, and her little brother Henry, age four, and James and David Wharton who were seven and six respectively. I bent down and gave each of them a warm kiss.

"Come into the library everyone," called Jane throwing open double doors to reveal a comfortably furnished room, lined with books and another bright fire. Small tables were arranged for tea and there were plates of scones and cakes. Soon we were all a jolly party, sitting about the fire. I took it upon myself as, I liked to think, 'the daughter of the house' to help Tante Jane with the serving of tea and handing around of refreshments. I noticed Jack standing sentinel-like by the door but alert and ready to supply our needs for extra hot water or milk or more scones, as required.

Diana Fitzjames was particularly warm and friendly to me, wanting to know everything about my time at Madame Grevier's establishment and how I enjoyed my stay in Geneva. I made her laugh heartily when I told her about Madame Grevier's 'Petit Livre de l'Etiquette' and gave her some amusing examples. These began to be passed around to the rest of the company, and we all became very merry at poor Madame Grevier's expense.

Later, all the children were sent up to bed. To which they went very reluctantly, until told that Santa Claus only came to good children fast asleep. Even Fairfax, the eldest of the children had a sneaking belief in that jolly old gentleman with the scarlet cloak and white beard and Johnny was heard to remark to his mother that, as Southlands was a new house, the chimneys would be "nice and clean", so Santa wouldn't get dirty climbing down inside them.

There was an interval of quiet while everyone changed for dinner and then began to assemble in the Library again. I couldn't help feeling that happy, tingly thrill I had always had in anticipation of Christmas and that sense of a magic sparkle everywhere. The world weary would call this childish, but I don't think I could ever lose it. Particularly this year with such a happy, merry throng of people.

I had put on my pale pink satin dress trimmed with rosebuds which showed off my slender arms and shoulders to advantage, at least I thought so, and I arranged my golden-brown ringlets more becomingly and was soon down in the Library sitting on the sofa with Tante Jane. She had changed her crimson velvet for maroon silk shot with gold and a delicate necklace of gold filigree and pearls.

I couldn't help remembering her as she had been all those years ago, when I was a child of eight and she was my governess, Jane Eyre. I recalled that Mr Rochester had invited a group of fine ladies and gentlemen to Thornfield and Jane Eyre had been requested to be present. She sat quietly and I know pale and unhappy in the corner in that very plain grey silk dress with the little pearl ornament at her throat and bore so patiently and with apparent indifference the spiteful gibes of that horrible woman, Blanche Ingram, who had fancied herself Mr Rochester's chosen bride and her equally unpleasant mother. Although I had pretended to show off to them my childish talents in singing and dancing, I was conscious that Blanche viewed me with contempt, and I overheard her refer to me as "a little puppet" and ask Mr Rochester where he had "picked me up".

All the time I was thinking that I wanted to go to Jane and put my arms around her and comfort her and make her feel loved. I know now that Mr Rochester loved her too, and I've never really understood why he let her suffer such

18

humiliation. I contrasted her then with the self-assured attractive lady who now sat beside me, confident in the love of her adoring husband and her two little sons, the mistress of a comfortable and happy home. Then she had seemed so plain but now, at one and thirty, she was in the prime of a woman's life. Her figure had filled a little but not too much, just enough to be attractive and her complexion, no longer marked, glowed with good health and contentment.

That Christmas Eve dinner was everything I could have anticipated, and it will always stay in my memory as a very happy time. It was such a joyous occasion with plenty of good-humoured banter and laughter. Once again, I noticed Jack Whitaker in his customary place by the sideboard, observing everything and ready for any request or service. He had changed the green waistcoat for a black tailcoat and, to my mind, looked rather splendid. He could easily have been the butler. He saw my glance and, to my consternation, I definitely observed his right eyelid drop over a twinkling eye.

I hastily looked away and immediately started up an animated conversation with my neighbour, Captain Fitzjames. I found him a charming and witty conversationalist, and he began to tell me much about life on board his ship, the H.M.S. Seafarer. I enquired how long he tended to be away from his wife and children on duty at sea. He explained that this could vary from a few weeks to several months. "However," he said, "My next assignment is to the Mediterranean to escort an 'important personage' on a state visit to Italy. We are likely to be anchored in Naples for some weeks, and I am very happy that Mrs Fitzjames and the children will be able to join me."

"Oh, Italy!" I breathed, "How wonderful. There is so much of interest to see there!"

"Yes, indeed, Miss Varens. If you like ancient history and art, beautiful architecture, sunshine and flowers, it is rich in all these."

I found no difficulty in conversing with everyone that evening, with one exception, Mr Rochester. He seemed to be ignoring me. I endeavoured to catch his eye, but he always seemed to be looking in the other direction or was deep in conversation with someone else.

At length the company decided to retire to be ready for Christmas Day.

Jane turned to me and whispered, "Edward likes to have a nightcap in his study. Come to me in my boudoir in ten minutes and tell me your exciting news."

CHAPTER 2

I stood on tiptoe at the window, hung with elaborate but rather dusty velvet curtains, looking down at the busy Paris street below. The cacophony of sound reached me in waves, street cries, loud conversations, raucous laughter; the rattle of wheels, creaking carriages and carts, snorting horses and the cracking of whips. It was morning and the sunlight formed squares of pale gold on the patterned carpet and the sofas and chairs in the dim room behind me.

A carriage stopped at the pavement in front of the house. The carriage door opened and a lady emerged, dressed fashionably, with golden hair piled high and a dainty hat perched on top. I felt a wave of relief. "Maman" I gasped. But the lady walked to the other side of the road and the carriage moved on. No, it wasn't Maman. A tear formed in the corner of my eye. "Where is Maman? *Where* is she?" I had been waiting there for two hours since my mother had hugged me frantically and left, declaring that she would be back soon. I began to whimper.

(The following conversations were all in French, of course, but I am giving an appropriate English translation.)

A harsh voice behind me exclaimed, "Looks like she's gone, Francois."

"Left the brat behind then."

.   "Gone off with that fancy Italian she's been seeing, I expect."

"What are we supposed to do?"

"She's owes six weeks' rent, you know. She's left a note, here it is, no money though."

There was a rustle of paper as the woman behind me in the shadows read it and then exclaimed, "Says she's written to the child's father and asked him to come and take her. Poor little blighter!"

"We'll leave her for a few days and see what happens." A heavy hand was laid on my shoulder. "You can go into the attic for the present, but don't expect any luxury from now on. We can't afford to give you much."

I started to weep bitterly with my hands over my face. "Maman! Maman! Where are you?"

"Stop that row, or I'll give you a taste of this!" The man held a large stick.

Soon I was sitting on a narrow bed in a dark room with one small window, looking out onto a tiled roof and the door firmly locked. On a table beside me was a mug of water and lump of stale bread. The bed had a rough blanket and a grubby pillow. I sat huddled in a corner, too frightened to move, sucking my thumb for comfort.

The day advanced. No sun reached the window but the sky became a pearly blue shot with pink as the sun set. The light began to fade.

Then the door opened and the woman's bulky figure appeared. She carried a tray. "'Ere's yer supper, child, and I brought you up this."

She set the tray down. It contained a plate of scraps of meat and some potatoes and another mug of water. But I only had eyes for what the woman held under her arm. It was my rag doll, Frou Frou. I grabbed the doll and hugged her close to me with both arms.

"There," said the woman, not unkindly "Eat up yer supper. We'll 'ave to see what to do with you tomorrer. Perhaps you can 'elp me out a bit in the 'ouse until your Pa comes."

But I only stared at her blankly, not really taking in what she was saying.

"Eat up yer food then." The woman went out shutting and locking the door again.

But I had Frou Frou now, and I could talk to her, and I believed Frou Frou could answer.

I looked at the unappetising food on the table and made an attempt to eat some of it. It didn't taste very nice. The meat was fatty and gristly and almost cold as were the potatoes. I drank a little water. Then I returned to the bed and my little friend.

"Never mind, Frou Frou," I whispered in the doll's ear. "We'll look after each other. Let's play. We'll listen carefully and see how much we can hear from outside and what the noises are. I can hear a cart's wheels. Can you?" Frou Frou nodded her head as I shook her slightly. "What can you hear?"

A blackbird sat on the roof and began to sing with sweet high notes. "What do you think that is Frou Frou? Is it a blackbird?" Frou Frou nodded again as I jerked her.

In this way the evening passed slowly and night fell. No one thought to bring me a candle but the moon cast its radiance on the window and the room wasn't completely dark.

At last, with Frou Frou cradled in my arms, I closed my eyes and slept.

I was awakened by the room door being flung open and the woman stood there.

"Come on child, get up," she said. "You can come down to the kitchen and 'ave some breakfast, and then you can give me 'elp with the washing."

I obediently left the bed, still clutching my doll.

"Leave it behind, child. It won't come to any 'arm. It'll still be there when you get back."

"Frou Frou," I whispered to the doll. "I've got to leave you now. Be a good doll and I'll see you later."

I followed the woman down the uncarpeted stairs, passing the rooms that Maman and I had occupied and down another flight of stairs to the dark basement.

We were standing in a large kitchen lit by a high window through which could be seen the legs and feet of passers by. An iron stove held a cheerfully flaming fire and there was a big wooden table covered with dirty crockery and saucepans.

"'Ere, 'ave yer porridge, child."

I took the bowl which had been thrust towards me.

The porridge was hot, but there was none of the milk, cream, or sugar with which I had been used to eat it. However, I was very hungry and managed to swallow most of the sticky, grey substance.

"Right," said the woman with the air of someone about to embark on a special task. She indicated a tall copper with the lid thrown back which sat on a stone shelf with a fire laid beneath, ready to be ignited, and a pile of dirty linen which looked like sheets and towels, lying in a basket beside the copper. "I want you to put all these into the copper with this." She handed me a long wooden pole with a hook on the end.

For a little girl of my age which was about four and a half and less than three feet tall, such a task was completely beyond me. The copper on its stone shelf was probably about three feet above my head. However, I took the long-handled tool she had given me and plunged it into the pile in front of me. I managed to hook a sheet, but it took all my strength to lift it upwards towards the top of the copper, and it was impossible to push it over the lip into its interior.

The woman watched me struggling with arms folded. At length, when even she could see that the task was impracticable, she produced a wooden stool for me to stand on which raised me off the ground by about two feet and told me to try again. However, the effort to lift the heavy mass of material was still too much for my little frame. I managed to get the first sheet into the copper, but was then told to push it down into the water, another Herculean task for me.

"Now the next one," she urged, without pity.

Again, I struggled, but I could feel my strength failing, and I sank down on the stool, exhausted.

"I cannot do any more!" I exclaimed and began to cry.

"Wot's this, wot's this.?" It was the man's gruff tones He stood in the doorway, dirty, dishevelled, and bleary-eyed, having just got up. "You can't do it, eh? You lazy little brat. Do yer expect to live 'ere rent free and do nothing to earn yer keep?"

But I was beyond reason or protest or even threats. I crouched on the stool weeping bitterly

"She's too small to reach the top of the copper," explained the woman. "Let me find 'er something else to do that she can manage."

"I'll learn yer to say yer can't do what we ask." The man seized a stick that stood in the corner and raised it threateningly. But the woman stayed his arm. "Best not, Francois! The father might come, and he'll see the bruises if yer beats 'er. We could be in trouble."

She turned to me and her voice was less demanding. "Could yer manage to sweep the 'all and stairs, child?"

I sniffed, "Spec. so," I muttered through my tears.

Fortunately, this task was not beyond me and I was given much sweeping to do. I swept not only the hall and stairs but the large kitchen and several other rooms. Scant food was provided. My diet consisted of a little stew, bread, porridge, and water. The days passed with this treatment and I began to feel ill. I was constantly tired and hungry. After about two weeks, I felt I had no strength left. I was sore and aching all over my body. I awoke each morning to another day of drudgery and fear of the violence with which I was frequently threatened by Francois.

One day, as I swept the stairs outside the kitchen, I overheard the conversation between my tormentors.

"It's no good," said the man to his wife. "E's not coming. I'm going to 'ave a word with Madame Blanche." I knew that Madame Blanche was a near neighbour who lived in a house which seemed to be full of young women. I had often seen them walking down the street when I was shaking the front door mat. I assumed they must be her daughters. Quite often I had noticed men, quite smartly attired, who rang her door bell and were admitted.

One day Madame Blanche appeared in the hall and was obsequiously ushered into what had been our rooms, by the woman. Our visitor was dressed all in black with glittering jet jewellery around her plump neck and on each of her podgy fingers. I was pushed forward and found her black beady eyes were studying me from head to foot. At length she turned to the woman with a patronising smile.

"Sorry, dear. I'm not interested at the moment. She's too young, too small, and rather weak. Perhaps in three or four years I might have a use for her."

And so, matters continued for another week. The man and his wife started to argue, and I could hear them in my attic room as I desperately clutched Frou Frou to my breast.

"Right," said Francois. "She's going out of this 'ouse onto the street!"

"Oh, you is 'ard Francois. I'll find some sewing for 'er to do; there's a lot of darning and stitching needed."

But they continued to argue and quarrel with each other.

And then, one evening I heard another voice from below. A cultured English accent speaking. French. A strong resonant voice, which sounded familiar to me.

"Madame....? This letter has reached me. I am Edward Rochester. I believe you have a young child here who has been left to my care by her mother, Céline Varens?"

There was a further murmur of voices. Francois and his wife were speaking softly in very polite tones.

"Where is she?" It was Mr Rochester's voice. "Up here, is it?"

Then, I heard heavy feet on the stairs. The door opened, and there he was; burly and powerful with his jet black hair and dark eyes.

"What have they done to you!" he exclaimed, seeing my wan face and shabby, dirty appearance. "The villainous couple! You are coming with me."

Firm arms lifted me and Frou Frou from the bed, and I relaxed thankfully against his broad chest. "Oh, Monsieur, please take me away. I am so tired. I want my Maman."

"Unfortunately, your mother has gone, my dear. But I will look after you." He spoke to me so kindly and softly, and I knew I was safe.

There was a further exchange with the man and woman downstairs. They were demanding money for the unpaid rent and also for my keep since Maman had left. Mr Rochester turned on them angrily and flung a few coins down on a table. "That will cover Céline's rent, but I'm not paying anything further. I can see that your treatment has reduced the child to illness and exhaustion. Do you expect to be paid for that? Out of my way!"

He rushed me through the street door and down into a waiting carriage.

*****

All these dark memories had stayed with me over the years. Sometimes I awoke in the night and remembered that unlit attic and the tiny window with the moon shining on the roof and experienced again those terrible feelings of fear and despair at my desperate position.

Fortunately, children do not look too far ahead. It is what is happening in the present that affects them. I did not therefore think that my terrible situation would continue and luckily for me it didn't. My saviour appeared; my gallant knight. But the impression left behind had always given me a sense of insecurity, as if I was walking across a shining floor of ice and at any moment the surface might break, and I might disappear into black and freezing water. I had little to hold on to. Nothing was certain in my life. I was dependant upon the goodwill of others, who had no obligation towards me. There was always the fear that, for inexplicable reasons, they might turn their backs and disown me.

One recurring nightmare was that I was seeking for those kind faces and loving voices, walking down a corridor not unlike the Thornfield grim vaulted passage, with many doors. At each door I would pause and turn the handle and find an empty cheerless room like my attic. I would begin to run down the passage and then feel myself to be pursued and experienced a nameless dread that my pursuer would reach me before I could find the safety of my loved ones. I would then awake in an agony of terror.

*****

After the happy evening I had just experienced, these thoughts had receded, and my mind was relatively untroubled. I walked down the corridor at Southlands and tapped on Tante Jane's door.

"Come in," she called.

Her boudoir was plain but comfortable, with a sofa and two chairs, a table, a small writing desk, many books, and in the corner, I noticed an easel and a few pieces of artist's equipment. I wondered if Tante Jane still did her painting or was she too busy with all the cares of managing a house and looking after her little sons and of course, Mr Rochester.

"Did you enjoy the evening Adèle?" she asked with a kindly smile, patting the vacant place beside her on the sofa.

I sank down with a happy sigh. "Oh yes, dear Tante. They are all so friendly and jolly and I love to be with the children."

"I must say that you seemed to get on very well with my cousins and their families. I have had several complimentary comments about you. My cousin Diana was suggesting that you might like to visit them at Portsmouth in a month or so. Captain Fitzjames is based there. She said they have very comfortable lodgings."

"Oh Tante, how nice of her. I would love to. But don't they have a permanent home somewhere?"

"Not at present. Captain Fitzjames' naval duties make it difficult. However, Diana was telling me that he has applied for a position in the Admiralty. If he is successful then they will seek a permanent home near London."

"London! Oh, I would like to visit London myself. I've never been there, but I've heard so much about it – the wonderful shopping emporiums, the theatres, the concert halls, the art galleries, the Royal Palaces. Oh, it would be lovely to go there!"

"Yes," said Jane, with a smile. "I sometimes think I would enjoy a visit there with Edward. Not that he is very keen on crowded places, but he does love music, and the arts, and the theatre. So, perhaps later on we can think about it. However, for the present, I have two angelic little darlings, who can be little demons if they choose and another I am expecting in April."

"Oh, Tante, that is delightful news!" I turned towards Jane giving her a kiss and a warm embrace.

"And now that I've told you my news," said Jane brightly, "What about yours?"

I leaned forward with hands tightly clasped. "It was something that happened at Madame Grevier's. I became very friendly with the Italian teacher, Signora Garilani. As you know, Madame Grevier aims that we all finish the two years being able to speak at least two languages, apart from our own," I laughed. "Rather a tall order for some, but I think I have what they call 'a good ear' and I managed to learn German and Italian. Of course, I already speak French and English as my mother tongue."

"Well done, my love," interjected Jane.

"So, I spent quite a lot of time with the Signora, who was a charming, vivacious lady. We became fairly close and one day I told her something of my past history."

"I see," said Jane thoughtfully, "Although perhaps it is not wise to reveal too much about yourself to strangers. You never know how things get passed on to others."

"Yes, Tante, I think you are right, so all I told her was that I was an orphan whose mother had been an opera singer and that when she died I had been looked after by a kind friend of hers, Mr Rochester, who had made me his ward."

"That was all you told her?"

"Initially, yes. However, one day she asked me my mother's name. The signora is very interested in Opera herself and has a fine contralto voice. I told her my mother was Céline Varens. The name meant nothing to the signora, and she didn't pursue the matter. However, one day when I went to her for my Italian lesson, she produced an Italian newspaper which she reads regularly and pointed to a paragraph on the back page with great excitement. By now, I had sufficient Italian to be able to read it, but even if I hadn't, a name on the page would have startled me. It was my mother's name, Céline Varens. The paragraph was an announcement of the marriage of Signora Céline Varens to Count Victorio Valdini at the church of the Blessed Virgin in Sorrento on a date in May last year."

I threw myself back on the sofa. "I was absolutely overwhelmed, Tante. I nearly fainted. Signora Garilani had to revive me with smelling salts."

"Oh, my dear child," Jane took my hand. "But how could it be?"

"It could only be because my mother didn't die after all. I remember those horrible people in the house where she left me saying that she'd gone off with someone, I think they said an Italian. But afterwards, Mr Rochester and Madame Frederic, with whom he temporarily left me, had both told me that Maman had died of a fever."

There was a pause while we both considered the situation. At last Tante said to me softly, "So what would you like us to do about it, Adèle?"

I hesitated and then I hurried on, "Well, something has already been done, Tante. Signora Garilani suggested that she might send a letter, care of the newspaper, asking for it to be passed on to the Contessa Valdini. In the letter, she said she would remind the Contessa of my existence as her daughter and ask if she wished to contact me."

"And you agreed to this, Adèle?"

"Well, yes, Tante. Did I do wrong?"

Jane took my hand gently. "I think it would have been better if you had referred the matter to Mr Rochester first. He is your guardian and furthermore he had a relationship with Céline Varens which did not end very happily. He may have strong views on the subject, for several reasons. Do not forget that she showed herself to be a very careless mother to you by leaving you with those dreadful people and not providing anything for your upkeep. Would you have any objection if I tell Edward about it now?"

"No, Tante, I think he should be told. But, Tante, do you think Mr Rochester would care one way or another about anything concerning me?" I sighed, sadly.

"Adèle! What a thing to say. Why do you think this?"

I sighed again, "Mr Rochester is so cold towards me. You, Tante are always very kind. You have been like a mother to me. But Mr Rochester...although he took care of me when I was a destitute little child and I agree that, under his guardianship I have wanted for nothing, he has never shown me the love I longed to receive from him as a parent and guardian. He is always so indifferent, always finding fault and pointing things out sarcastically." Here I began to cry and leaned against the back of the sofa weeping.

Jane took me tenderly in her arms and smoothed my hair. "Shall I tell you something, my love? After I had left you this afternoon and returned downstairs to greet Mary and Diana and their families, Mr Rochester took me to one side and said how pleased he was with you and especially your little speech of gratitude and affection towards us. He said he felt you had much improved in the last two years."

"Did he really, Tante?" I began to dry my eyes and blow my nose. But then I had a sudden recollection. "But why then did he ignore me all the evening and not look at me or address one word to me?"

Jane sighed, and then gave a little laugh. "He is a perverse creature, my Edward. He has done the same thing to me in the past you know. I think he likes to test people he cares about. He doesn't rush to praise them straight away. Perhaps, after an interval of two years, he feels he needs to see more of you and get to know the new grown up Adèle, before he shows you his true heart."

"Well Tante, I hope you are right."

"Anyway dear, you haven't finished the story. Did Signora Garilani receive any reply to her letter?"

"Not directly from the Contessa, my mother, no. She received an acknowledgement from the newspaper and their assurance that her letter had been passed on. That was last July, but nothing further has been heard."

"Do you really want to contact your mother, after all these years, when she treated you so badly?"

"I understand what you say, Tante, but do we know all the circumstances which prompted her to leave me? I am prepared to forgive her a great deal and love her as my mother if I can. I also have another reason for wanting to see her."

"Yes, dear, what is that?"

"I want to find out the identity of my true father."

There was a pause and then Jane said quietly, "Do you have any thoughts yourself, dear, as to who it might be?"

I hesitated. "Well, yes, Tante, the obvious person is Mr Rochester and if it were so, I should be very happy." Again, I hesitated, not knowing how to proceed and thinking that it might be a painful subject, as far as Tante was concerned. "I do hope this conversation is not upsetting to you, Tante."

Jane smiled at me in an understanding way, "As a matter of fact, my dear, I have thought for some time that you could be Edward's daughter. As for the subject being painful to me, it is not in the least. Edward told me most of the circumstances concerning his relationship with your mother long ago, shortly after we met and it had all happened some years before that."

Jane gave me a sad look. "I have since felt nothing but sympathy for him and his state of mind at that time. I did not of course know then about his marriage to Bertha which had proved to be a disaster because of her insanity and that he had no option but to have her secretly confined at Thornfield. That is something I discovered to my cost later." She paused and looked away for a moment. "Never mind, it is all in the past, and he has paid a terrible price. I have well and truly forgiven him." She gave me a quick brave smile and resumed. "But he told me that he had been wandering all over Europe, unhappy because of the unfair treatment of his father and brother. He was attracted to your mother, Céline, because of her beauty, and she became his mistress on whom he lavished every luxury that money could buy. He still went off on his travels and on one occasion, when he returned, she presented him with a newly born baby, yourself, my dear and told him you were his child. His words to me were that for all he knew, the baby could have been his daughter, except that he could see no likeness to himself in you. Then, six months later, he discovered that Céline was being unfaithful to him with a young viscount. He overheard them discussing him in an insulting way and laughing at him, particularly at his appearance. He burst in on them and flung Céline out of the apartment. Then, as was the custom, he fought a duel with the viscount and wounded him, but not fatally

"Oh, Tante," I gasped, "I had no idea that my mother had behaved so badly. Why did he then rescue me and take care of me?"

"Because, in spite of his perversity, Edward is a good man. He heard that Céline had run away to Italy with another lover, a singer, and had deserted you, and he felt a sense of responsibility towards you, although he always now maintains that he is not your father. He seems to be prejudiced against you, because of Céline's behaviour and because you resemble her in appearance, he imagines you have all her unfortunate faults as well.

"Tante, I do feel strongly that I am his child. I know I do not resemble him physically, but I feel a kind of empathy with him and that I have certain characteristics that I have inherited from him."

"Characteristics?" Tante looked at me curiously.

"Yes, determination, loyalty, an ability to love deeply and truly, fortitude, intelligence - well, he has said I am not bright, but I think he was labouring under considerable prejudice when he said it, as you have confirmed this evening. I was bright enough to learn two new languages and get good marks in a range of subjects at Madame Grevier's: history, geography, mathematics, and to take an interest in the sciences. My work was highly commended by one of the professors. Also, my love of music, singing, and drama. Music, as you know is one of his interests…."

Jane gave a little laugh, "I had no idea that you had such a range of interests and abilities. You have certainly developed greatly since that little girl of eight I knew long ago. Well done for all your academic achievements, my love."

I looked into her sea green eyes which were glowing with pleasure. "Don't forget, dearest Tante, that I have you to thank for much of this. I had you to inspire me when I was young and silly. I must confess I often put on my coquettishness in company because I thought it would please others, especially Mr Rochester. That flirtatious style I had copied from my mother, Céline, but as I now know, he particularly disliked."

"I suppose he felt that it was inappropriate for a young child. You seemed to be aping an adult then. But now, my dear, your manner is charming. You have a very pretty French accent, and I am sure that no one could find fault with your personality." Jane looked at me with an encouraging smile, "And I think, if you continue to show yourself to be the sensible young lady you seem to be now, after two years at Madame Grevier's school, and continue to demonstrate your warm regard for us both, Edward will eventually come around to accepting you as his daughter, and one to be proud of."

"Thank you Tante, I am very pleased to hear this from you. And I do hope you are right. But. I think that now I talk and behave as I feel, and I am not influenced by the need to put on an act or airs and graces to please or impress anyone. I hope I am now always sincere."

There was a faint tap on the door and Jane rose. "That was Mrs Tompkins letting me know that Mr Rochester is upstairs and preparing for bed. I must go, dear and you also. You must be exhausted after your journey and ready for a good night's sleep. Tomorrow will be a busy day for all of us."

I put my hand on Jane's arm. "Just one thing more, Tante. When and if I get a reply to my letter, which Signora Garilani will forward to me, can I discuss it with you and Mr Rochester to see what I should do about it?"

"Of course, my child. Mr Rochester will certainly need to be consulted. Goodnight my love."

We kissed and parted at the door, wishing each other a Merry Christmas as we went to our rooms.

Just before I sought my bed, I lifted the heavy curtain and looked out of the window. It was a frosty night with a full moon, the sky studded with a myriad of stars. I could see the lawn stretching away down the hill, like smooth silver, with a few dark patches of trees and shrubs, and at the bottom, the dim outline of the river, lined with trees and bushes but with an occasional glistening sparkle as the water caught the light. 'It will be a lovely view in daylight,' I thought to myself and gave a contented sigh to be here in this happy loving home. I was just about to lower the curtain when my sigh turned to a gasp. Creeping down across the grass, keeping to the concealing foliage as much as it could, I saw a dark figure. I thought it was a man, tallish and slim, but the shape was hidden beneath a cloak and the head covered by a hat of some sort. I stood rigid with alarm as the shape reached the bottom of the hill and then disappeared amongst the bushes.

What should I do? Should I tell someone? It could have been a burglar running away with his ill-gotten gains. On the other hand, perhaps it was a servant from the house creeping away illicitly to have a jolly evening at a public house. I glanced at the clock on the mantelpiece. It was past midnight. No public houses or places of entertainment would be open.

I opened my door and looked out into the dim corridor. A single oil lamp was burning at the far end. All was very quiet. There was a movement in the corridor, and I saw a familiar figure coming towards me. It was Jack Whitaker.

"Jack!" I whispered as audibly as I could.

He came towards me. "Miss Adèle! You're up late miss. Is everything all right?"

I moved closer to him; my hand touched his sleeve. "I, I…saw someone out on the lawn. Creeping away from the house. He looked very furtive. I thought it might be a burglar!"

Jack paused for a few seconds and then said soothingly, "It must have been one of the stable lads, miss. One of the 'orses isn't too well. I expect he was going home to the village after tending to it. Nothing to worry about."

"I suppose he was trying not to disturb anyone. Was that why he was creeping?"

"Yes, I expect so, miss. Now you just go to bed and get a good night's sleep. Don't forget it's Christmas Day, and we're all going to 'ave a wonderful time."

He shepherded me towards my room and opened the door, standing to one side to let me pass through.

"Thank you, Jack," I said as I slipped into my bed chamber. "Merry Christmas!"

He touched his chestnut curls. "And the same to you, miss, Merry Christmas!"

Chapter 3

The next few days passed in a whirl of excitement and merriment. The children were all up very early the following morning and descended on the pile of presents under the Christmas tree in the hall. From my room, I could hear them as I bathed and dressed, their excited cries and squeals echoing up the stairs, as each package revealed some longed-for treasure.

When I came down for breakfast, I found the hall full of happy children all trying out their new toys. There were rocking horses, miniature carts and carriages, dolls with bright blue eyes and beautiful flaxen curls, a whole zoo of stuffed animals, sets of toy soldiers, and lots and lots of picture and storybooks, all scattered over the floor in careless abandon.

"Now children" said Jane, her small figure clad in a gown of dark green tartan trimmed with white lace, "it is time for breakfast. Go with Mrs Tompkins to the breakfast room, and all your toys and books will be put up in the nursery for you to play with afterwards."

The adult guests began to appear in the hall and Christmas Day had begun.

After breakfast, Mr Rochester led his male visitors to the stables to see his horses, while a brisk walk around the gardens and grounds was taken by the ladies.

Jane had been very busy in the six months since they had been in residence at Southlands designing the garden and this was now laid out with walks and flowerbeds, seats and a summerhouse. A walled area enclosed a kitchen garden and hot houses. The ladies were all very interested to see and admire and much of the conversation centred on plants and horticulture.

At half past ten, the whole party attended Morning Service at the Parish Church and then it was time for a delicious Christmas luncheon with adults and children all sitting around the large oval table in the dining room, enjoying the traditional Christmas fare of roast goose with all its accompaniments and an enormous Christmas pudding which was spectacularly flamed with brandy before being served.

Everyone was in a jolly, happy mood. The children were quite well behaved, although there were a few attempts to disappear under the table for a little mischief, but this was quickly put to a stop by their watchful parents, and on the whole, their eating habits and manners passed muster. After luncheon, while everyone else relaxed in the drawing room or went for a stroll outside in the grounds, the children were sent upstairs to play with their new toys but allowed down again for a special Christmas tea in the hall.

And then it was supper time, with the adults in their evening finery and the children in bed and hopefully asleep after a happy busy day.

As everyone began to assemble in the drawing room, Mary Wharton sought me out. "I couldn't help noticing, Miss Varens that, when you sang the carol yesterday, you have a very sweet soprano voice. Would you sing for us this evening?"

My heart gave a lurch. I felt very apprehensive. It is one thing to join in when others are singing a carol, but quite another to be asked to perform in front of people who, although very friendly, might well notice my mistakes, particularly that one highly critical person, Mr Rochester.

I know I flushed and waved my hands disparagingly. "Oh, I don't think so, Mrs Wharton, I...."

But Jane intervened. "Please Adèle," she said softly, taking my hand. "We would all love to hear you."

"But...but I have no music with me!"

Still holding my hand, Jane led me to the piano. She opened the piano seat and pulled out a large bundle of music. "Some of these are well known songs." She leafed through them.

"What about this one? 'Where o'er you walk' by Handel? Surely you know this one and this by Schubert, 'The Trout'?

"Well, yes I do know those, but...but...."

"But me no buts, dear. Look, I'll play through the Handel. As you see there are lyrics on the score. You can hum it with me and then say when you are ready to sing."

Perhaps it was fortunate that the particular song chosen was one of my favourites.

"Sit down, everyone!" called Jane to the company, some of whom were standing talking beside the fireplace, "Adèle is going to sing for us"

There was a general rush of movement throughout the room as everyone found a seat near the piano. Soon they were all settled in hushed expectancy.

Suddenly I felt a different sort of thrill, not of fear or making a fool of myself, but a sense of power, exultation. I stood beside Jane at the piano half turned to my audience. As I looked across the room, I noticed the tall figure of Jack Whitaker. He was standing by the door, half hidden by a potted plant, but I felt his bright eyes upon me. I straightened my back determinedly.

Jane struck a chord and went through the first few bars of the song. I touched her shoulder and whispered, "I'm ready, Tante."

And then I began to sing. My voice rang out around the room, softly at first, but then gathering volume as I felt the beauty of the song take hold of me. My eyes accidentally met Jack's again and somehow, it felt as if a vibrant current had passed between us, and I found myself singing to him.

When the last few notes had died away, there was a short pause and then a veritable thunder of clapping and cries of pleasure. "Bravo, bravo, encore, encore!"

I stepped forward and bowed to my audience. "Thank you, thank you, you are very kind."

Mr Rochester was enthusiastically joining in the calls for an encore and banging a small table with his one hand.

I turned towards him and gave him an especially low bow and then a deep curtsy.

He laughed and bowed back. "Well done, Adèle, well done!"

The pleasure of those few precious words ran through me like fire. In a voice trembling with emotion I announced, "I will now sing 'The Trout'.

Jane played the first few bars and then I began, singing in German. At the finish, there was more very hearty enthusiastic applause, and one of the gentlemen, Captain Fitzjames, plucked a Christmas rose from a nearby vase and offered it to me ceremoniously.

"Well," said Jane, her green eyes alight with pleasure, "That was remarkable, Adèle."

I sank down on a sofa overwhelmed by my feelings.

*****

The rest of Christmas passed in a happy haze of good company, good food, conversation, laughter, and amusements of various kinds devised by our hosts.

One particularly memorable event was a reading by Jane, who had a lovely speaking voice, of "A Christmas Carol" by Mr Charles Dickens. The children were allowed to come into the drawing room and listen, and we were all by degrees suitably scared at the ghostly apparitions and equally saddened by Bob Cratchit and poor little Tiny Tim's final words, "God Bless us, every one." This was our last evening together and it was a lovely end to our Christmas celebrations. One which will probably stay with me forever.

Before she departed for home with her husband and children, Mary Wharton had a quiet word with me.

"Adèle, I just thought I would ask you if you would be interested in singing in a performance of The Messiah. Mr Wharton is organising the event at our church in late January."

"Well, that would be lovely, but I don't know the piece well, I'm afraid."

"I realised that might be the case, but we have an excellent choirmaster attached to the church, and I am sure he could coach you. Of course, you would need to come and stay with us for a short while beforehand. We would love to have you, my dear. As you know we live in Woldenshire and the city of Wolden with its cathedral is not far away. I am sure you would like the area."

"Oh, I'm sure I would. It is very kind of you to invite me. I will speak to Mr and Mrs Rochester."

The next day they all departed with many an expression of pleasure at our lovely Christmas. There were enthusiastic waves from the children, which we returned as vigorously, until the last carriage and little waving handkerchiefs were out of sight. Then we all stood together on the gravel in the pale December sunshine feeling, perhaps, just a little bereft.

Then the two little boys, Fairfax and Johnny ran inside to play with their new toys in the nursery. Mr Rochester made a few gruff comments about looking at his ailing horse in the stables and strode off in that direction and Jane took my arm and proposed a short walk around the garden.

As we strolled along the garden paths, I told Jane about the invitation I had received from Mrs Wharton.

Tante Jane was very pleased. "Do you think you would like to accept, Adèle?"

"Yes, I think I would. Of course, Handel's Messiah would be an enormous challenge for me, don't you think, Tante?"

She squeezed my arm affectionately. "Only you can decide if you would be able to meet it, dear. But it is quite a small church, as I remember, with a congregation of not more than fifty people, so it wouldn't be so very overwhelming would it? And, nothing ventured, nothing achieved."

"Tante," I began slowly, not knowing quite how to approach the subject. "Have you and Mr Rochester considered my future at all? How do you think I should live? I mean, we know I am from a dubious background…the daughter of an opera dancer, which is how Mr Rochester describes me…. So should I be thinking about earning my own living? Or do you suppose anyone will want to marry such a person as me?"

"A great many, I should imagine," said Jane drily. "But, as with all young ladies, we will have to be sure that your suitors are of good character and will make you happy."

44

"You say 'we', Tante, but am I to have no choice in the matter?"

"Of course, my dear. The young man should be one you love and who loves you in return. But I regret to say that in this world there are many fortune hunters who...."

"Fortune hunters, Tante! But I have no fortune, so they are hardly likely to be interested in me. The man I could love will be someone who loves me for myself."

With regard to fortune, my dear. Mr Rochester plans to settle a sum of money on you, well invested, which will give you an income, not enormous, but adequate for your needs as a young lady. Sufficient to allow you to live independently, if you choose, but I rather hope that you will want to continue to live with us here at Southlands, for a while longer at least. You will be very welcome to do so."

"Oh, Tante it is so lovely of you to say so. I would like to live here with you for some time, but..." I paused, unsure how to frame my words. "Maybe it is my unfortunate mother coming out in me, or even a characteristic from my paternal side, but I think after a while I may begin to feel the need for adventure. To seek out new experiences and to try my talents, such as they are, in the wider world."

Tante's green eyes searched my face anxiously. "I'm not sure what you mean, child."

I laughed, "I am not quite sure myself, Tante. But what I often think is that young ladies like myself, what are our lives to be? Is a good marriage and bearing children the only option?"

"Let us sit down here, dear," said Tante sinking down onto a bench which commanded a view of the, as yet, empty flowerbeds, waiting for flowers and shrubs to bring them to life.

"Surely I need hardly remind you of my own situation at your age. A teacher and ex pupil at Lowood who advertised in the paper for a situation and ended up working as a governess at Thornfield. I had no choice dear, I had to earn my living decently or starve. But you, with an independent income, can live as an independent lady and we certainly hope that a happy marriage will eventually follow."

"Yes, dear Tante, but is that the only choice I have?"

"What alternatives are there, my dear?"

I looked away from her across the garden to the dark trees beyond. "It seems I may have a talent for singing. Is there no way I could make use of that in the world? I mean professionally?"

"Well, I would not have thought that you could do so respectably. The invitation from Mary makes me think that, if you were successful there, you might find you receive invitations from other ladies asking you to sing at private social gatherings or in church performances, but not as a paid professional singer, earning your living."

"What about the theatre, concert halls, and so on?"

"Oh, my dear! Are you thinking of Music Halls, frequented mainly by gentlemen who go to ogle the women on the stage? Surely you would be emulating your mother, Céline. Can you really mean that?"

"Oh no, Tante, of course not," I said hastily. "But is there no middle way which would be acceptable to society and myself as a young lady?"

"I really don't think so, dear."

"And then, I said, after a silence. "I would dearly love to travel and visit other countries; meet all sorts of different people."

"Well, I suppose that may be possible, with a chaperone of course, not myself I'm afraid, but possibly you may meet with a respectable older lady of similar mind." Jane's tone became brisk. "Now, can we change the subject, Adèle?"

I felt that she was slightly disapproving of me and turned towards her anxiously. "Dear, Tante, you are not cross with me, are you? I feel I can talk to you and explain my thoughts more freely than with others."

"I understand, dear. But we will leave it there, for the present. However, there is something in which I would like your help shortly."

"Yes?" I said, eager to make amends.

"I need to visit Ferndean when the weather is suitable. At Southlands, we need some pictures for the walls, and I remember that quite a number of paintings and ornaments, which had not been damaged by that terrible fire at Thornfield, were transferred to Ferndean. There were some family portraits I believe. It is your guardian's fiftieth birthday in February and there is one particular portrait I would like him to have as a gift from me. It may need cleaning and reframing and if we are able to retrieve it now. I will have time to arrange it. Would you accompany me there and help me to sort it out?"

"Of course, Tante, I would be delighted to help you."

"I will let you know which day I want to go there." Jane rose from the seat. "But, Adèle keep this a secret between us. I want to give Edward a birthday surprise."

*****

A few evenings later, as we finished dinner, Mr Rochester said to me, "Adèle, I would like to talk to you. Would you come to my study in about half an hour?"

Jane and I had risen at the end of the meal to go into the drawing room, while Mr Rochester enjoyed his port at the dining table.

"Yes, of course, sir," I said, giving him a little curtsy as I passed.

My heart began to thud. All sorts of possibilities crowded into my mind, fighting for my attention Was it something to do with my conversation with Jane recently in the garden about wanting to be a professional singer? Surely not. I felt sure that she would keep my confidences strictly to herself. Perhaps he wanted to tell me about my finances and discuss my future? Quite possibly; or even, perhaps Signora Garilani had received a reply from my mother Céline and had contacted him? Although I would have thought she would have forwarded it to me. However, she was a bit of a stickler for etiquette, and I was still under my guardian's care, so she may have sent it to him. Would he be angry with me for acting without his consent?

I looked across at Tante Jane sitting quietly on the sofa.

"What do you think Mr Rochester wants to talk to me about, Tante?"

She looked up with a bright smile. "Don't be anxious my love, I'm sure it's nothing nasty."

At the appointed time, I stood in front of the closed study door with my heart racing and knocked timidly.

At that moment, Jack Whitfield passed me from the dining room bearing the tray on which reposed the decanter of port and a glass. "Everything all right, miss?" he remarked cheerily. "I should knock a bit louder, otherwise he may not 'ear you." He gave me a wink.

Although I should have been annoyed with Jack for this rather familiar intervention, somehow his manner contained a warmth and humour which made me feel more confident. I knocked again and heard from within Mr Rochester's growl, "Come!"

He was sitting at his desk, his back to the curtained window, facing the door. The room was dimly lit by a branch of three candles on the desk which threw dark shadows across his face and heightened the effect of his black patch and single gleaming eye. He looked at me, unsmilingly.

However, his greeting was genial enough, "Hello my dear, come and sit down." He indicated a small armchair to one side of the desk. "I believe I should ask your pardon, Adèle. Mrs Rochester said you were a little upset because I appeared to ignore you over the past few days when our guests were here.

I felt a mixture of relief and guilt at these conciliatory words. Had I really made so much of so little? He was my own dear guardian all the time.

"Oh guardian, I think I was being too sensitive. Of course, you were occupied with your guests and had a great deal to do to entertain them."

"No, I will not be excused by you, my child. I know I have an unfortunate manner at times, and these injuries of mine don't help." He held up his maimed arm.

"Believe me, sir, I do understand, and I am only happy and grateful to be here with you and Tante Jane."

"But don't imagine," said he, "That I have not been observing you. I wanted to tell you that I was impressed by your little speech to me on your first evening and very pleased that you fitted in so well with the rest of the company, several of who have expressed favourable opinions about your personality and character. I have also received an excellent report from Madame Grevier about your progress over the past two years in which she says..." There was a short pause as he studied the paper in front of him.

I was pleased to notice how much the sight of his one eye had improved and that he could read more easily, with the help of an eyeglass attached to a ribbon around his neck.

He began to read, "Ah, yes here it is, that you have been hard working and studious and have made excellent progress in all the subjects you undertook, particularly in music, singing, and the languages of German and Italian. Also, that you have been helpful and have deported yourself like a lady at all times."

A tide of relief and pleasure flooded over me.

He leaned back in his chair, "Well done, my dear!"

"Oh, Mr Rochester!" On an impulse I sprang to my feet, ran around the desk, and before he could protest, I had planted a kiss on his sallow, lined cheek.

He put his arm around my shoulders and gave me an affectionate pat.

"Now, go and sit down again," he said with mock severity. "I have something else to say to you."

I returned to my seat and looked at him expectantly.

"I believe you were asking Mrs Rochester if we had given any consideration to your future?" He gave me an enquiring look from under his dark bushy brows.

I nodded, but my heart had begun to flutter a little.

Mr Rochester picked up another piece of paper from the desk before him. "You are not, of course, my daughter, nor any relation, but I do feel it is my duty to look after you and have done so since you were a tiny child."

I looked down at my hands clasped in my lap. I couldn't help a sinking sensation at the words, 'you are not of course my daughter, or any relation'. But then I remembered my conversation with Tante about his prejudice due to my mother's behaviour, and I looked up again at him brightly, trying not to show my disappointment.

"I have therefore decided to set a capital sum aside and to arrange for you to receive the interest of this which will be invested, as an allowance. The sum is £3,000, so, at current rates of interest, this should produce an income which will more than cover all your needs, whether you continue to live with us here at Southlands, or if later on you decide to have an establishment of your own. Mrs Rochester tells me that you would eventually like to be independent and travel and see the world?"

I looked down at my hands again, "Yes, sir, that was one of my thoughts"

"Well, I expect that would be possible if a suitable chaperone can be found. This allowance is made entirely at my discretion. If you conduct yourself in the way you are doing now, it will continue, but if I become dissatisfied with your behaviour, then I may have to think again."

There was a short silence and I felt a sudden coolness had seeped into the study.

"When you reach the age of five and twenty, subject to what I have just said, the capital sum will be yours, to which, again at my discretion, I may add a further sum. Upon your marriage to a suitable young man, of whom I and my wife approve, even if you haven't reached twenty-five by then, again at my discretion, the £3,000 plus a further sum may be given to you personally as a wedding present. However, your husband must be able to support you, and if I am in any doubt about your choice and suspect him to be a fortune hunter, I may withdraw the money and income to see how the marriage progresses. The sum to be restored if I decide all is well.

I looked him firmly in the face as I said, "I am very grateful for your kindness, guardian, and, although, as you say, I am not your daughter or any relation, I will continue to look upon you as my protector and adviser, and I hope you will never be disappointed in my behaviour in any way."

"There is also the matter of your mother, Céline. Mrs Rochester has told me about the announcement in the Italian paper concerning her marriage to Count Valdini and that the tutor at Madame Grevier's contacted the newspaper. I gather that you have heard nothing further?"

"No, sir, I have not."

"Of course, it may not be the same Céline Varens. We will have to wait and see."

"Why did you tell me she was dead, sir? It was a shock to discover that she may be alive." I suppose my tone was a little reproachful.

"You were only a small child then, and I felt it was for the best that you believed she was dead rather than thinking that she had abandoned you. I am afraid that my opinion of her had sunk to a very low level at the time."

"I expect it is very painful for you to recall her."

He ignored this remark and continued, "Nevertheless, if it does turn out to be your mother, Céline, I will do my best to advise and help you."

"Thank you, dear guardian, I hope I am not going to be a burden on you, bearing in mind that I am no relation, as you said previously."

I rose from my chair and walked to the door. I think my expression must have been a little sad because he was there before me to open it and he put his good arm around my shoulders and kissed my forehead. "Goodnight, little Adèle" he said softly.

"Goodnight, my dear guardian!" I said, all sadness vanishing as I returned his kiss gladly.

CHAPTER 4

About a week later, it was a clear and sunny morning. The lawn in front of the Morning Room windows was white with frost, and the sky was an unbroken pale blue. Tante Jane and I took breakfast alone together, Mr Rochester having ridden out early to Fremingham, where he had business. He was not expected back until the early afternoon.

"As it is so fine," said Jane, bright and crisp herself as the morning, "I thought we would walk down to Ferndean. There is a path which crosses the lawn and goes through the trees to the drive."

"Are you sure, Tante?" I asked, looking at her rather anxiously. She was now about five months gone with child, and her figure had swelled a little. The dress she wore helped to conceal the change, but it was evident.

"Oh, I am as fit as a fiddle!" she laughingly exclaimed. "It would take more than an easy walk to affect me. Dr. Brightside advises gentle daily exercise. We shall only walk one way. I will ask Jack to collect us at Ferndean at about twelve noon. We are likely to have a few things to bring back here in any case. Put on your sensible walking boots and a warm cloak, dear."

She rang the bell at the side of the fireplace and Jack appeared.

"Yes, madam?"

"Jack, Miss Adèle and I are taking a walk down to Ferndean this morning. There are a few things I want to collect from the house. I would like you to drive the carriage down there and meet us at about twelve noon to transport the items and ourselves back here."

Neither of us was quite prepared for Jack's reaction to this instruction. He started and stared at Jane and then at me with a look of almost horror on his mobile features.

He gulped "I do not think that is a very good idea, madam!"

"I beg your pardon, Jack, what do you mean?"

"Well, it's...it's quite a long walk, madam, and Ferndean is a very cold, dank place."

"Thank you, Jack," said Jane, with a touch of asperity, "I used to live there. I know what the house is like and, as to the distance, why, I've done many a walk four or five times longer than that."

"But...."

"No," said Jane firmly, "No buts. Please do as I say Jack. We will see you, with the carriage at Ferndean at twelve noon."

Jack cast me a quick look, then touched his curls to Jane, "Very well, madam, but please wrap up well. It's a very cold morning out and very muddy around Ferndean, owing to the autumn rains."

So it was that, clad in brogues, fur lined bonnets and cloaks with muffs to keep our hands warm, Jane and I set off for Ferndean.

The walk down past the garden to the linking pathway was very pleasant. The sun warmed our faces, and the crisp cold frosty air was exhilarating. The grass sparkled in the sunshine.

"He's very protective is Jack, isn't he? A nice lad, I don't know what we would do without him. He looks after us all so well."

"Yes Tante," I said in an absent tone. "Tante, I've been meaning to ask Mr Rochester. How is the sick horse?"

"Oh, I believe he has recovered. It was horse influenza."

"The stable lads seem to have looked after him well, even until late into the night. I saw one of them returning home to the village on Christmas Eve."

Jane looked at me in surprise. "Returning to the village at night? What time was this?"

"About half past twelve."

"Oh no, it couldn't have been either of the stable boys. They both sleep in a room above the stables and neither of them come from our village. I believe their parents live in Fremingham. In any case, I'm sure there was no necessity for them to stay up late with the sick horse. I gather that once settled down at about nine o' clock, the horse, White Star, was peacefully asleep in his stable." Jane stopped for a minute to stare at me. "What did you actually see, my dear?"

"I looked out of my window and there was the silhouette of a man, wearing a cloak and a large-brimmed hat, stealing down from the house towards the river."

"What made you think it was a stable lad?"

"I…I wasn't sure what to do, I thought it might be an intruder, a burglar. I felt I ought to tell someone. I looked out into the corridor and saw Jack. I told him what I had seen, and he said it was probably a stable lad returning home after tending to the horse."

"How strange, surely he knows that our lads don't come from the village?"

We walked on silently and took the path which crossed the lawn and led through the trees

At length Jane said, "A little mystery, I will ask Edward about it. I'm sure there is a simple explanation."

We were now amongst the trees. The ground was covered in dense ivy, and there were large holly bushes, some of which bore scarlet berries. The woods were silent with only the occasional squawk of a pheasant to break the peace.

Soon afterwards, we reached the drive leading to Ferndean from which the new carriage way to Southlands branched off.

"I remember coming here for the first time when I returned to Mr Rochester after an absence of a year," said Jane reminiscently. "I had gone to Thornfield to seek him out and had seen the dismal ruin of the place after the fire. I heard all about it from the landlord of the inn. He told me the terrible tale of how Bertha Rochester, having started the fire, met her end leaping from the battlements to escape my Edward who was trying to rescue her, the poor, mad creature. I also learned that he had been badly hurt in the fire trying to rescue the others. You can imagine my feelings, dear, as I trod this path then, not knowing what I should find at Ferndean.

You weren't at Thornfield when the fire broke out, were you Adèle?"

"No, Tante, Mr Rochester had sent both Mrs Fairfax, the housekeeper, and myself away. Oh, it must have been so distressing and terrifying for you, Tante, but, what a wonderful ending to the story. After all you had both suffered in your separation, you were reunited, and married, I gather, very quickly after that. It was so romantic!"

We were both silent for a while, thinking our own thoughts, as we walked along. The trees were now much closer together. The path sloped downwards towards the river, and the ground was becoming muddier at each step. No sun's rays seemed to penetrate the thicket of branches overhead and the atmosphere was becoming very damp and chill. Our breath steamed on the icy air.

After some time, we rounded a bend in the drive and there in front of us, across a wide clearing of unkempt grass, once no doubt a well-tended lawn, was Ferndean.

I remember having stayed there briefly as a child when Tante Jane had found me at that rather strict school to which I have been sent. She had whisked me away, and for a few weeks, I had lived here with both of them. They were such a happy couple, and I was so relieved to be with them that, although I was conscious that Ferndean was a rather dark, gloomy place, I don't remember feeling at all unhappy or scared or any other emotion but contentment.

Now, however, it seemed as if the dark old house was crouching like a sick animal. The mossy latticed windows reflected no light and were blank like the eyes of the blind. The walls were stained with mould and moss and ivy crept up them snakelike across the old stones, partially obscuring some of the windows and lying thick on the tiles of the roof.

"Oh dear," said Jane. "Poor old house. I remember that when I was expecting Fairfax, we decided we needed to move to somewhere healthier and brighter, which was when Mr Rochester took a lease on Fremingham Grange, near the town. As you know, we have lived there for the past ten years until our new and very dear house, Southlands, was built on the Ferndean estate owned by Mr Rochester."

"Yes, I remember," I murmured, as we walked across the mossy gravel surrounding the lawn to the house.

We were now standing at the front door set deep in the ivy-covered porch. Jane grasped a bell pull concealed amongst the foliage and gave it a vigorous tug; We heard the bell echoing inside the house and waited. There was no response. This time, I tried, giving it an even firmer pull. Once again, we heard the echoes die away.

Jane grasped the door's massive ringed handle. It turned reluctantly, and she pushed the ancient door open. Its hinges gave a protesting groan, and we were staring into the dark interior.

I must admit, I felt no inclination to step over the threshold. There was a musty smell of damp which pervaded everything, and I experienced a shiver of apprehension.

We were now in the hallway with stairs rising in front of us and a dark corridor leading to the ground floor rooms and kitchen quarters. A few pieces of heavy, ancient-looking furniture stood forlornly around the walls.

Jane ran her finger over a table and examined the dark stain of accumulated dust on her glove. "I don't understand this!" she exclaimed. "There are supposed to be a couple acting as caretakers here, the Burtons. Where are they? Mrs Burton!" she called, moving towards the staircase so that her voice could carry upwards, "Mrs Burton, Tom Burton, are you there?"

We listened, but no sound broke the silence, except for a little scuffling noise as a mouse ran across the end of the corridor.

"The place is deserted!" cried Jane. "It doesn't look as if anyone has been here for weeks or months."

"Perhaps it would be better to leave," I suggested hopefully. I was beginning to shiver in the cold, partly from the chill, but also from the menacing atmosphere of the house. There was a creeping sensation running up my spine. I sensed something wasn't right about this place.

But Jane was undeterred. She marched forward down the corridor which eventually led to the kitchen. "The items I want, including a particular portrait, are in the cellar. It is off the kitchen"

'Oh no!' I thought. 'Not the cellar of this gloomy, forbidding house! If the downstairs is like this, what will we find in the cellar?'

We had reached the main kitchen, which had a scullery and laundry room leading from it. On the big deal table in the centre were several plates bearing the remains of food going green and mouldy. Mice scampered away at our approach.

Jane took no notice. "Here it is," she said triumphantly.

In a dark alcove was the cellar door with the key in the lock.

Jane unlocked and opened the door. We were looking down a flight of stairs descending into darkness.

On a shelf beside the door were several candles in their candleholders, some burnt down and others only half used. Jane handed me one of these and she selected another. We lit the candles with a Lucifer also on the shelf, and Jane began to walk down the stairs cautiously, holding on to the banister rail with one hand. I followed her reluctantly.

The two flames threw a dancing light on the contents in the area. Furniture, boxes, ornaments were all strewn and piled around in a jumble, but Jane seemed to know exactly what she was looking for. "Here it is." Her voice was full of excitement.

A picture lent with its face against the wall. Putting her candle down, she picked the painting up with both hands, turned it around, and began to study it intently.

I moved quickly down the last few steps into the cellar and was just going to join her when there was a crash above our heads. The cellar door had been violently shut, and we heard the sound of the key turning in the lock.

We stood transfixed, staring upwards. I was shaking with shock and horror, glancing over my shoulder at the candlelight casting enormous and fearsome shadows on the walls. Then there was another shock.

It was a laugh. It started as a low and dry chuckle, repeated and then it swelled into a raucous peal which transmitted to its listeners a terrible feeling of viciousness and evil.

I heard a sound behind me and turned. In the uncertain light I could see that Jane had gone deathly pale. She had dropped the picture on a pile of sacking

"It is her. It is her. It can't be, but it is her!"

She put her hand to her head, staggered backwards and sank down onto an old velvet sofa. Then she collapsed completely, and her head rolled backwards in a dead faint.

"Tante, Tante!" I screamed. I flew towards her and took her inert body in my arms, but she was past hearing or feeling anything.

I leapt up and rushed back up the staircase. When I reached the door, I tried the handle but we were locked in. I battered on the door calling as loudly as I could.

"Help! Help us! HELP!" I screeched. I called for several minutes, and then there was a sound outside and a familiar voice.

"Miss Adèle, is that you?" It was Jack.

With a great wave of relief, I called out, "Jack, Jack, we're here in the cellar locked in. Tante Jane has fainted. We heard something. She's had an awful shock. Please get us out. Please."

"Just a moment. Where's the key?"

"I don't know. When we came down here, it was in the door. But somebody slammed the door and locked it…and then there was this horrible laugh, really horrible, and Tante fainted, as I said. Oh!" I began to sob. I was very near to fainting myself.

"Calm down, miss, calm down. I'll have a quick look for the key, but if I can't find it, I'll break the lock. Just stay calm. I'll get you out, don't worry."

There was a short silence and then, "Sorry – No sign of the key, but I've found something to use as a battering ram. Stand back, miss. Stand back. Go back down the stairs."

There followed a series of heavy blows on the door. Fortunately, the doorframe was fairly rotten and it began to give way. At last, after a few more violent assaults, the door burst open, and Jack was standing in the doorway looking down at us.

He rushed down the stairs to Jane who still lay unconscious on the couch. "I'll carry her up to the hall, miss. You follow me. Keep close."

He picked up my little Tante as if she was a featherweight and ran up the stairs with her. I had no need to be told to follow closely and quickly. In the hall he laid her gently on an armchair by the front door.

"I'm just going to bring the coach nearer!" He exclaimed. From the door, I watched him sprint across the gravel towards the drive and disappear amongst the trees. I couldn't help wondering why he had arrived so early. It was an hour to noon, which was the time we had requested to be collected. Why hadn't he brought the carriage to the front door? Almost as if he was hiding his presence.

The carriage, driven by Jack with its two horses appeared, and he placed it close to the entrance. Then he leapt down and came into the house. He lifted Jane and carried her to the vehicle, depositing her carefully inside, where I quickly joined her.

As I did so, I suddenly remembered the picture which Jane had been so keen to collect. But I dismissed it from my mind. This was no time to worry about a painting. We knew where it was, and Jack could be sent to collect it later. My main concern was for Tante and the baby. Was she going to be all right?

What would Mr Rochester say about our escapade? The thought of his anger and possible sorrow, if something went wrong for Jane and the baby, filled me with deep anxiety. I also felt guilty. I should have reasoned with her and insisted that we forget the expedition until much later on.

When we reached Southlands, Jack told me to wait with Jane while he aroused the household.

After a few minutes, the Housekeeper, Mrs Tompkins, appeared at the front door and looked inside the carriage at Jane. "What's 'appened t' mistress Miss Adèle?"
"She's had a bit of a shock, Mrs Tompkins and will need your help and nursing."

Jack appeared again. "I've sent one of the stable lads to get the doctor," he said quickly. "And now, Mrs Tompkins, I'm going to carry the mistress upstairs to her room. Will you come with me and alert the other women that their help may be needed when the doctor comes?"

Mrs Tompkins and I followed Jack carrying Jane up the stairs to the large main bedroom. Jack laid Jane down on the four-poster bed, and Mrs Tompkins removed her shoes and cloak, covering her with a quilt.

Jane was beginning to regain consciousness and to stir. Her eyelids fluttered. We all looked at her anxiously. "What? Where?" She raised her hand to her brow.

The Housekeeper rushed to a drawer and produced a small blue glass bottle of smelling salts, which she applied to Jane's nose.

Colour flooded back into her white cheeks and her eyes opened fully. She saw me beside her and reached for my hand. "Oh dear, oh Adèle. What happened? What am I doing here?"

Jack looked at me and put his finger to his lips shaking his head. I understood what he meant. It was best not to remind her yet of what had occurred.

"You've just had a little shock, dearest. Nothing more than that," I said soothingly, hoping Jane wouldn't remember too quickly the events of the morning and that terrifying laugh we had both heard.

"We've sent for the doctor, ma'am, just to be on the safe side," said Mrs Tompkins, giving Jane a little curtsey. "I think it best if you leave 'er to me now, Miss Adèle," she added.

Turning to Jack, she exclaimed, "And you can go too, Jack! Nothing further for you 'ere now."

"All right, Mrs T., all right! You're in charge," he responded humorously touching his forelock and giving me a wink as he left the room.

"When t' doctor comes I'll ask you to be present, miss," said Mrs Tompkins softly, "because you know what 'appened and I don't."

"Of course," I said quietly. "I'll just go up to my room and get rid of my outdoor things, and then I'll be back to be with her or do anything else you require."

"Ee I don't know what t' master's going ter say!"

Once in my room, I had time to sort out my whirling and confused thoughts.

First of all, I wondered why that laugh, blood curdling though it was, had such a disastrous effect on Tante Jane, whom I would have considered a very strong person with steady nerves. I remembered her saying in her distress, "It is her." Who was the 'her' she referred to? Then I began to wonder about Jack Whitaker and his role in this. I remembered the horrified expression on his face when Jane had announced we were going to Ferndean. Surely, quite out of proportion to the proposed expedition; a short walk on a frosty fine day to a house where we had both lived previously, although not for some time. Was there something or somebody at Ferndean he didn't want us to disturb?

But the most suspicious fact was that he had obviously driven up and hidden the carriage out of sight of the house. He must then have approached on foot shortly after we got there, since when I called for help from the cellar, possibly ten to fifteen minutes later, he was there outside; an hour before we had asked him to collect us. But he appeared not to have encountered the sinister individual who had locked us in the cellar and given that frightful laugh.

Could it have been Jack himself – perhaps playing a joke on us for his own amusement? But from my short acquaintance with him, I had come to regard Jack as an honest, sincere person who wanted to help us all. Could he be capable of doing anything so harmful and stupid? True his coach driving was, at times, a little wild and his sense of fun kept bubbling up in his winks and comic expression. But that to me was endearing. Humour can brighten a situation as long as it isn't misplaced, as it had just done to lighten our feelings, in his exchange with the Housekeeper.

My thoughts were interrupted by a knock on the door. It was Daisy with a message from Mrs Tompkins that Dr

Brightside had arrived, and I hastened with her along the corridor to Jane's bedchamber.

The dark blue velvet curtains had been drawn around the bed and Jane was hidden from view as the doctor carried out a necessary examination. I sat down beside Mrs Tompkins on a small sofa and heard the muffled conversation on the other side of the drapery. It was mainly the doctor saying "Hmm?" and "Ha" with a few soft replies from Jane which we couldn't decipher. After about ten minutes, the doctor emerged from the curtained bed. He was a man of medium height, corpulent, and in his fifties with grey hair and a short well-trimmed beard. His manner was a little pompous but kindly.

"Well ladies," he said as he removed his stethoscope and pushed it into his black bag. "I am pleased to report that everything appears to be normal. I could hear the baby's heartbeat and all is in place. Mrs Rochester needs to rest completely for the next few days in bed, after which, subject to a second visit from me, I think she will be able to get up, but still take things easily for a while. She must avoid overstraining herself either physically or emotionally. I believe one of you ladies was with her when she fainted. Could you tell me what happened?" He looked at each of us in turn.

"Miss Adèle was with her, sir," said Mrs Tompkins, indicating me with her hand.

"Yes, doctor," I said "We took a walk down from here to Ferndean which lies about a mile away in the woods. Mrs Rochester wanted to remove a few items stored there for this house. She asked our coachman, Jack Whitaker, to collect us by coach at twelve noon."

"So, what was it that startled her?"

"The house seemed deserted. We couldn't find the caretakers. Mrs Rochester knew the things she wanted were, in the cellar. So, we lit candles and went down there."

"Hmm, a little unwise in her condition."

I ignored this comment, and continued. "We found one of the things Mrs Rochester wanted very easily, but then." I paused, feeling that horrible chill I had experienced in the cellar and tried to collect myself. "But then, the door of the cellar was shut with a bang and we heard the key turn."

"Oh my lorks!" exclaimed Daisy, her hands to her face.

"I see, very frightening for you both!"

"Yes, Doctor, it was terrifying. But then we heard a horrible laugh, and Mrs Rochester staggered and collapsed onto a sofa."

"And then you called for help?"

"Of course, sir and very fortunately Jack Whitaker, our coachman, had arrived early and heard my cries. He couldn't find the key, but he broke the door down and rescued us."

"So," said the doctor thoughtfully, "It was the laugh that shocked her?"

"It was both, sir. The thought that some malevolent person wanted to frighten us and possibly harm us and the sound of the laugh which was evil."

"Did the laugh sound male or female?"

"Difficult to tell, sir. It could have been either."

At this point, there was the clatter of horse's hooves on the gravel.

"Ooh!" said Mrs Tompkins, rising hastily and looking at the clock over the fireplace. "It's one of the clock. It must be t' master back!"

67

"Don't worry, my dear," said the doctor soothingly. "I'll go and meet him downstairs. The great thing is that Mrs Rochester is unharmed and the baby is safe."

I too felt some trepidation. But all I could do was wait, hoping that the doctor would make it all right.

We heard Mr Rochester's booming voice in the hall and the doctor's quieter tones. Then the door to Mr Rochester's study was opened and they both went inside.

We stood together on the landing waiting, and finally they came out. The doctor sounded cheerful and bid Mr Rochester a good day, announcing that he would call again in about a week. Mr Rochester's responses were inaudible but sounded rather curt and growling to me. Then, we heard him mounting the stairs rapidly. When he reached the top, he glared at us both.

"Where is my wife?" he said abruptly.

"In 'er room, sir, resting" said the Housekeeper shakily.

"Right. Both of you stay there until I call you. Where is Jack Whitaker? I want to see him. Mrs Tompkins, send Daisy to fetch him. I want to hear his side of the story."

At that moment, Jack appeared at the foot of the stairs and looked upward at Mr Rochester, questioningly.

"There you are, Whitaker. Good. I shall want a full report from you shortly."

Jack climbed the stairs to join us. "Of course, sir." He said, apparently imperturbable, but there was no humour in his expression this time.

Mr Rochester strode off to his wife's room, and the three of us stood on the landing talking in whispers.

"Jack," I said softly. "You'll be pleased to know that Tante Jane is all right, and the baby's safe. She's got to rest for a few days and take things easy but she is not harmed."

"That's very good news, miss."

"Jack, nobody has thanked you for rescuing us and bringing Mrs Rochester back home so promptly, but please accept my thanks for your swift and brave actions."

"Well, that's kind of you, Miss. I appreciate your thanks."

The door to Tante Jane's room opened again, and Mr Rochester came out, his dark brow furrowed and his one eye gleaming. His mouth was stern and set. "She's asleep," he said by way of explanation. "I couldn't speak to her and did not want to disturb her. Come downstairs all of you to my study, and tell me precisely what happened."

We all trooped down to the study behind the master. At the door of his study, he said, "I'll see you each in turn. "You first Adèle. You others can wait outside."

Mr Rochester and I went into his study together.

I told my story, explaining that Tante had asked me to help her retrieve things from Ferndean. I tried to stress that I had expressed my concern about her making the expedition on foot and that Jack had also attempted to dissuade her, but that she was adamant. I told him that when we reached Ferndean it was empty, and I recounted our visit to the cellar. I then told him about the door being slammed and locked and then described in some detail the sound of the laugh we had heard which had caused Tante Jane to react so badly and about her words, "It is her. It is her. It can't be, but it is her." and then about her fainting.

At my description of the laugh, Mr Rochester seemed to pale. He put his head in his hand for a minute like someone who had received a blow. Then he looked up at me fiercely.

"And could you not have tried harder to persuade her? It seems to me that you have been extremely irresponsible, miss. Just like your mother. I will check your story with Mrs Rochester as soon as she wakes up."

Stung by his attitude towards me, I felt anger. "You will check my story, sir? Do you think I am a liar? As I have said, I tried to make her see common sense about the expedition as did Jack, but in any case, it wasn't the walk to Ferndean, not even the cold and damp of the empty house, that upset her so badly. It was the fact that someone, we did not know who, locked the cellar door on us and then gave the frightful laugh I have described, which Mrs Rochester seemed to recognise."

"What cock and bull nonsense is this? The product of an over-vivid imagination, by the sound of it. Probably it was a gust of wind which shut the door, and the sound could have been a raucous bird on the roof - a crow or a magpie."

"Do you think I am stupid and can't believe the evidence of my own ears and observations? There was no wind this morning. Everything was still, and I may not be fully conversant with the cries of all birds, but I do know the sound of a magpie from a human laugh, sir!"

I think my anger and vigorous defence rather startled him, but he glowered at me from under his bushy brows, his eye sending off sparks of fury. However, he remained silent.

I turned to go but then stopped and looked round at him. "Another thing, sir. The doctor advised us not to overstrain Mrs Rochester and to keep her free of emotions. It would be as well if you do not try to arouse Tante's memory of the event. I do not think it will do her any good. Wait until she mentions it to you herself."

With that I swept out of the room straight past Jack and Mrs Tompkins waiting outside and rushed up to my bedroom where my anger gave way to bitter tears.

CHAPTER 5

I stayed in my room, fretting and weeping, for some time. But then there was a tap on the door.

It was Mrs Tompkins. "Luncheon is ready downstairs in the dining room, miss."

"Thank you, but I am not hungry."

"Shall I bring you something up, miss?"

"No thank you, Mrs Tompkins. I have a headache. I will just rest here."

Finally, at about three o'clock, I could not tolerate being in the house any longer. I needed to feel the cool breeze on my face. I put on my bonnet, donned my boots and fur cloak and crept out by a side door, which gave onto the garden.

It was intensely cold outside. The sky was heavy with dark, threatening clouds. I wandered about in the garden, hardly seeing anything because of my raging thoughts. I felt deeply hurt by Mr Rochester's distrust, but at the same time, and I was too proud to admit it, something in me longed to be back on good terms with him again.

I opened a little wicket gate which led onto the grassy open expanse, leading down to the river. Here, I wandered along the riverbank. The water was flowing freely, fed by the rains of last month. It chattered and foamed over and around stones and slid smoothly over rapids. Further along, there was a calm area of deep water, surrounded by bull rushes. I paused there to look down into the dark depths with a heavy heart.

"Don't do it!" exclaimed a familiar voice at my elbow. Simultaneously, a heavy cloak was thrown about my now shivering shoulders. Small white flakes were beginning to flutter down, as the sky darkened even further.

Strong arms held the cloak around me, and in my distress and weariness, I turned and leant against a broad chest. The cloak held the aroma of Mr Rochester's cigars, but it was Jack who enfolded me

"Oh, Jack," I murmured into his velvet waistcoat.

"It's all right, miss," he said cheerily. His arms tightened. "Mr Rochester knows you was telling the truth. You was both just a bit upset, that's all. He's sent me to find you. He wants to apologise."

I lifted my head and found my face close to his. Then, we both had the same irresistible impulse. Our lips met in a kiss, which seemed to last forever. I had the sensation of floating free, lifted by an unaccountable emotion, in which there were elements of delight, desire, and surrender, so intense, that I felt it must be sinful, and I struggled against it, like a swimmer caught in a strong current.

We both sprang apart.

Jack was the first to speak. "Oh, miss, forgive me. You're miles above me. I'm sorry. I couldn't 'elp meself!"

"Neither could I, dear Jack. As to being far above you, I am not. Not at all, if you knew my background."

"I know all about you I need to know," he said fervently. "But there's a lot about me you don't know. Can't tell you at the moment. Someday I will."

"We had better go back to the house," I said, with an attempt at briskness I was far from feeling.

We struggled back up the hill together against a driving wind, full of whirling snowflakes and at last we reached the house, wet through. We entered by the front door, stamping our feet and shaking ourselves to remove the snow from our shoes and outer garments.

Mr Rochester was sitting beside a roaring log fire and a loaded tea table. He rose as we crossed the hall. "Come to the fire, both of you and get warm."

Jack stayed by the blaze for a few minutes and then he said, "I'll take your boots and cloaks to the kitchen to dry, miss." So saying, he disappeared down the corridor to the servant's quarters

"Sit down, my dear." Mr Rochester waved his hand to a seat. "First of all, I must apologise for my behaviour towards you. I now see how unreasonable I was. Nobody could have known what would happen this morning. You both had a very nasty and frightening experience, and I appreciate your warning about not mentioning it to Mrs Rochester. It will, as you said, do her no good to remember at the moment. It has not done me much good either," he finished ruefully. "However, I think I now have an idea of what lies behind it and even of who could have been the culprit."

"Oh, dear guardian, I do accept your apology, and I do understand what you must have been feeling. How is Tante Jane? Has she spoken about this morning?"

"She seems better. But I know there is something bothering her. Not that she has said anything yet. However, as soon as she is feeling stronger, I am going to tell her something of my suspicions in the hope that it will ease her mind."

"Am I going to be allowed to know your suspicions, sir?"

"Nothing is certain yet. But I think we are getting to a point of clarification. We will know more in a few weeks, and then, all will be revealed."

"It all sounds very mysterious and intriguing."

I began to pour out tea for my guardian and myself. The sight of a plate of Mary's delicious scones reminded me that I had had no luncheon; to say nothing of the recent amazing incident in the snow with Jack, and I realised I was extremely hungry. I helped Mr Rochester and myself liberally to the delicacies before us.

Another thought flashed into my mind. "Guardian, there was something I was going to ask you, at least I think Mrs Rochester said she would ask you, but as she is not well…,"

"Yes, my dear?"

I then told him about the dark figure I had seen on Christmas Eve and how Jack had said it was one of the stable lads, but that Tante Jane said it couldn't have been.

"Don't worry about that, Adèle. I think I know what happened. It was…a friend of Jack's who is helping him with a particular task on which he is engaged for me. But, as I have said, all will be made clear eventually."

So, I was none the wiser, but if it did not bother my guardian, I would not let it trouble me.

*****

The next morning came a letter addressed to Mr Rochester from Mary Wharton, repeating her invitation for me to visit them in Lower Poppleton, near Wolden and take part in their church's performance of Handel's 'Messiah'.

Mr Rochester handed me her letter at breakfast with the words, "You have my full permission to go, if you wish. It will be an interesting change for you, a lovely area."

74

However, I demurred a little. "I could not think of leaving Tante, if she needs me, sir. I certainly do not want to miss the happy event in April".

He rustled the newspaper he was reading. "Thoughtful of you, my dear, but that event is quite a long way off and there are plenty of us to look after Mrs Rochester. I was thinking of inviting Mrs Fairfax to stay for a while. She would be a soothing presence."

"And not have skittish ideas like me, I suppose," I said, with a rueful little laugh.

"Nonsense, Adèle, we will all miss you. But it will only be for a few weeks, and I know singing with this choir is something you would enjoy and would make use of your undoubted talent." He adjusted his eyeglass and returned to his newspaper.

This last speech rather took me by surprise. Mr Rochester was showing rather more understanding and appreciation of me than I would have thought possible.

I spoke to Tante about it that morning.

She was sitting up in bed, looking quite bright, if a little pale, with a book propped in front of her. "It would be good for you, dearest," she said. "You will only be gone for a short while and it will give you a chance to try out your abilities and see where it takes you."

So, I wrote back to Mary Wharton, my letter enclosed with a reply from Mr Rochester, and it was arranged that I would travel to Wolden by train on a date later that month, where I would be met by Mr Wharton.

The weather in January was proving to be difficult. We had several heavy snowfalls and strong winds, which encouraged drifting. Looking out on a white world through the windows of Southlands, it was hard to imagine spring with all its warmth and delicate greenery.

However, by the time the agreed date had arrived, a thaw had set in, and I entertained no further doubts about the feasibility of the train journey to Wolden. In any case, it was vastly safer and more convenient than a stagecoach would have been, a few years ago.

Jack conveyed me to the station. In the intervening period, since that stupendous kiss on the riverbank, we had tended to keep out of each other's way. If we did meet in corridors or on the stairs, we would smile briefly and pass on, me with a fluttering heart and he with his usual airy, nonchalant ease. In fact, I began to think I had dreamt what had happened between us. Was it all part of my vivid imagination?

He drove me at his usual rather reckless speed, drew up on the forecourt at Fremingham station and offered me his hand. This time I took it and descended from the carriage, feeling like a princess. I seemed to experience an electric thrill at his touch, but, again, was that just my fancy? I was conscious of looking my best in a pale blue bonnet trimmed with pastel yellow flowers and matching cloak with white muff and boots, my golden ringlets swept over one shoulder.

"I'll come to the platform and see you off, miss." His voice was unusually gruff.

I had five minutes to wait for the train. I noticed Jack was wearing a daffodil in his buttonhole. "That is early," I said, touching the flower.

He removed it and handed it to me with a little bow. "For you, miss, it smells as sweet as you are."

"Oh, Jack," I said in a rush of emotion, "I will miss you."

He looked away down the track.

The train steamed in and enveloped us with its smoke. Jack opened a compartment door and handed me in. Then he put my suitcase on the rack above my head and jumped down to the platform, closing the door.

"Goodbye, dear Jack!" I cried, feeling a tear coursing down my cheek.

"Goodbye, my…miss," he called, and I thought I saw a look of sadness pass across his usually bright face. But then he gave me a cheery wave.

The whistle blew and I was speeding away from him.

*****

The journey to Wolden took about an hour, and I was met on the platform by both the Whartons: Mary, with her dark hair and earnest, but pleasant manner, and Stephen with his brown-rimmed glasses and studious demeanour. They both greeted me warmly, and soon we were bowling along in their pony and trap through the busy streets of Wolden, the towering cathedral above us dwarfing its surroundings.

Soon we were out into the Woldenshire countryside, which was gently rolling with the moors in the distance. We passed through several small villages, all attractive and well kept, with their little mellow golden stone houses and village greens.

Lower Poppleton was very similar to the other villages. St. Mary's church was quite a small building with a square bell tower, perched on the side of a hill and the vicarage lay just below, a sturdy stone house with a walled garden in which there was just a hint of spring. The points of daffodils were thrusting up through the soil and a little cluster of snowdrops gleamed by the front door.

Inside, the house was plain but comfortable and I was greeted excitedly by James and David, their two small sons.

Over supper that evening, Stephen Wharton said, "Tomorrow I thought we would show you a few places of historic interest in the town. Wolden cathedral is a magnificent building and we have a complete Romano-medieval town wall, extending for over two miles, from which the city can be viewed.

"Stephen, dear," exclaimed Mary, casting her eyes up to the ceiling, "We must not overwhelm Adèle with too much history. I expect she will be a little tired after her journey."

"Oh, please Mrs Wharton!" I exclaimed. "I shall be fascinated to see all that Wolden has to offer, and I am very interested in both history and architecture."

Stephen Wharton's eyes brightened at these words.

The next day, I accompanied the Whartons into Wolden, by the same conveyance, leaving their two little sons at work in the study with their tutor.

The weather was quite pleasant for January. The dampness of early rain was beginning to disappear and the sun was shining though the clouds.

We left the trap on the edge of the city and Mr Wharton guided us up the well-worn steps which led to what had once been the city's defences; a wall which almost encircled the town with breaks for the four entry gates: north, south, east, and west.

The prospect from this high point took in the whole area. On one side I could see a vista of jumbled medieval rooftops, broken by the occasional taller building or tower and, of course, the massive bulk of the cathedral, with its four towers and decorated west front. On the other side were green and rolling fields with low-growing trees and hedges and a river meandering through. Cows and sheep grazed on the more distant pastures. Here was all peace and orderliness, and I could not help but reflect on the beauty of England.

After walking at least a mile along the walls, Mrs Wharton stopped and looked at her husband. Mr Wharton had been explaining to me how Wolden had been founded by the Romans and about the battles with the Danes. He was going on to tell me about the building of the cathedral and about the histories of other notable buildings we could see from this eminence, when Mary Wharton intervened.

"Stephen, dear, I am sure the Romans, Danes, and Bishops will excuse us if we have a little break now." Turning to me, she added, "There is a delightful coffee house in West Gate Street called Bingles, and I am sure you would like just a glance at some of the shopping emporiums in Wolden."

"Of course, of course," said Stephen Wharton hastily. "I did not wish to bore our visitor with too much history."

I protested that I certainly was not bored. I was very interested, but that some refreshment would be most welcome.

We retraced our steps and were soon seated in Bingles, watching the busy life of the city pass by. Later, after some dalliance in one or two fashion emporiums, when I suspected it was Mr Wharton who might be bored, we had lunch in a comfortable old hotel. Then we wended our way to the cathedral.

Here, of course, Mr Wharton was in his element and able to expand on the architecture of the building, both outside and inside, at some length. We marvelled at the magnificently towering nave, which Mr Wharton informed me was 'Decorated Gothic', whereas the quire was 'Perpendicular Gothic' and the north and south transepts 'Early English'. I was invited to admire the extremely fine west window, the great east window, and the truly beautiful rose window of heart-shaped design, which he informed me, was very similar to the one at York Minster.

Looking upwards at all this magnificence, I wondered what it would be like to sing here. Overwhelming, I decided. I imagined my voice and other voices rising and expanding in this vast and ancient place.

On Sunday, The Reverend Stephen Wharton led the service and gave the sermon, attended by his family and myself. After the final blessing, a small, dark-haired, bespectacled man, with a fussy, nervous manner, came forward and was introduced to me by Mrs Wharton as Mr Cedric Pinto, their choirmaster.

"Delighted, I am sure," he said. He had a pronounced Welsh accent and peered at me through his thick glasses.

"This is the young lady I mentioned to you, Mr Pinto," said Mary. "She has recently come from school in Switzerland and we heard her sing at Christmas. We all agreed that she has a very fine soprano voice."

At these words, I interjected hastily, "I sang in a drawing room, Mr Pinto. No doubt my voice sounded well there. I have no idea what it would be like in this church." I looked around at the ancient grey stone interior doubtfully.

Mr Pinto gave an expressive shrug, his hands extended, and his mouth down-turned. "Well, we can only listen, Miss Varens and judge accordingly. I understand you are staying with the vicar and his family for a while?"

"We are hoping you can find Miss Varens a part in 'The Messiah', which you are putting on soon," said Mary Wharton eagerly.

"Well, as to that, I can make no promises," said Mr Pinto. "It will depend on how Miss Varens comes over." He turned to me. "Can you read music, Miss Varens?"

I nodded. I was feeling rather deflated by this conversation. Mr Pinto was less than enthusiastic.

He rubbed his hands together. "Good, good, that will be a big help. Some of my choir cannot read at all, let alone music. And have you had any singing training?"

"Yes, sir, I had a singing master in Geneva who told me I had a good soprano voice and should make use of it."

"Perhaps then," said the little choirmaster, taking a small diary from his waistcoat pocket with a quick flourish, "We could make an appointment for you to come down to the church one day next week for an audition?"

Audition! The sound of this word threw me into a panic. What had I let myself in for?

"Do you have any preference for day and time, Miss Varens?"

"Er…well, perhaps…." I looked at Mary, unsure if she and Mr Wharton had any particular plans for me.

"I think Tuesday would be a good day," Mary said. "We were thinking of taking Miss Varens on an expedition to Haydon Abbey tomorrow."

"Ah, yes, a fine old ruin!" exclaimed Mr Pinto. "Good, we will make it Tuesday then. At what time?" His pencil was poised above his diary awaiting my response.

"About…eleven o'clock?" I suggested tentatively, thinking that my voice would probably be at its best at that late morning hour. I felt I was slipping down a steep, slippery slope and heartily wished I had never agreed to the idea of singing in his oratorio. Suppose he rejected me?

The expedition to Haydon would have been a very pleasant and interesting one. But all the time, I was thinking about the dreaded audition the following day.

Tuesday dawned. I hardly ate any breakfast; I was so nervous.

Mary looked at me anxiously. "I hope you are not unwell, Adèle. Please do have something. Try a little toast and honey and a cup of tea."

I nearly choked on the toast, but was grateful for the soothing effect of the tea.

"Would you like me to accompany you to the church, dear?"

I think she was feeling a little concerned and perhaps a trifle guilty, since the whole thing was at her instigation and the idea of an audition was affecting me so badly.

"Yes, Mrs Wharton, I think I would appreciate your support this morning," I said gratefully.

The little choirmaster was sitting at the church organ playing softly when we arrived. We sat in a pew for a few minutes listening to the music.

Then, he turned and saw us, jumping to his feet and pushing back his spectacles. "Oh, ladies, I do apologise, I did not realise you were there."

He seemed in a nervous flurry. As bad as me, I thought.

"Did you bring any music with you, Miss Varens?"

I had thought that this would be necessary, and before leaving Southlands, I had sorted out a few pieces from the collection in the piano stool, most of which I knew well. I handed him a song by Purcell

"Dido and Aeneas," he muttered. I will play the first few bars, Miss Varens, then give a signal for you to start singing.".

I looked around the church. Mary Wharton was sitting in the front pew and an old woman, probably a cleaner, was shuffling about at the back with a mop. Another elderly lady was sitting in a pew near the door. This was my audience; nothing to worry about.

82

At Mr Pinto's raised hand, I began to sing, gaining strength and confidence and finally expression, as the song developed.

When I had finished, Mr Pinto jumped up and passed me some sheet music with a trembling hand. "This is an extract from 'The Messiah' for a soprano. Could you sing it for me, as before, at my signal?"

I quickly scanned the music and the words and then, at his command, started to sing. It was quite a short passage, but it contained some very high notes. However, I had no problem with these.

When I had finished, there was a silence for a few minutes. Mr Pinto seemed to be staring into space.

I joined Mrs Wharton in her pew.

"It was lovely, wonderful, Adèle," she whispered.

A dynamic energy suddenly took hold of Mr Pinto. His glasses flashed as he turned towards us. "You are an angel from Heaven, Miss Varens!" he exclaimed, jumping up and rushing towards me. He seized both my hands. "My only worry is that the rest of my choir will be able to match you!"

CHAPTER 6

When, a few evenings later, I met the other members of the choir, I could see to what Cedric Pinto was referring. They were a mixture of the genteel residents of Lower Poppleton and the somewhat rougher hewn individuals from the surrounding farming community.

There were about ten young boy choristers and twenty adults, some of whom were taking solo and leading roles. Possibly a few would have difficulty in following the music score, due to lack of education, but they all had one thing in common; tremendous enthusiasm for what they were doing. Yes, occasionally a voice might be off-key or too loud in relation to others, but, given an understanding audience, it was to be hoped that this would be accepted because, after all, we were amateurs.

Mr Pinto seemed to be regarding me as an expert, and he frequently consulted my taste and judgment in the arrangement of the choir with regard to the acoustics of the church. I did my best to help him in a commonsense way, but obviously I totally lacked experience. However, I found my previous training in Geneva was quite useful in advising the other singers on such matters as breathing and phrasing and that, on the whole, as the days went by, there was an improvement in our performance.

I found I related well to the rest of the choir and we were soon on friendly terms. I became 'Miss Adèle' to them all. There was one young girl, a farmer's daughter, Annie Thomas, with a good, clear soprano voice, to whom I became quite close. Unfortunately, she was slightly crippled in one foot and had to walk with the aid of a stick. But she was a sweet-natured, merry little soul, and I could see that her evenings with the choir were a great release for her.

As the date of the performance came nearer and nearer, I had more or less mastered my role. We frequently found at the end of a rehearsal that we had acquired a small audience of people who had crept in to listen. This was rather daunting, but I suppose in a quiet village like Lower Poppleton, such an event as a performance of 'The Messiah' would be regarded with great excitement.

Cedric Pinto was full of enthusiasm and energy. The day before the performance, Mr Pinto told me that he had spoken to the Director of Music at Wolden Cathedral about the event, and the Director had said he would like to come and hear it, which Mr Pinto said was a very unusual response from this eminent being.

On the evening of the performance, the Wharton family were all on the cusp of expectation and anticipation. There was to be a party in the church hall afterwards for the choir and their audience with wine and refreshments, organised by Mary Wharton and other ladies in the village

I decided to wear a simple high-necked gown of white silk, with a single pink satin rose at my throat. My hair was dressed high in a coil on top of my head with a few ringlets falling at the back.

"You look absolutely beautiful, my dear!" exclaimed Mary Wharton, as I came down the stairs to accompany the family to the church.

The boys were both jumping up and down with excitement, as we walked along in the sharp winter air.

Arriving at the church, we were surprised to find an unusually large throng of people. Several carriages were standing outside; some recognisable as those of the local gentry, and the church itself was full to overflowing. Most of the gentry had found seats. But quite a number of the ordinary working people and farming families were standing at the back respectfully, having given up their seats to their 'betters'. A row at the front had been reserved for the vicar and his family.

I was greeted by Mr Pinto and ushered into the vestry, where the rest of the choir were assembled. On the stroke of half past six o'clock, led by Mr Pinto, we all trooped into the church and took our places. The choirmaster was to conduct, while a colleague of his played the organ. There was an expectant hush as Mr Pinto raised his hand and the music began.

I felt I was about to swoon. Fortunately, there was a passage of choral singing, during which I was able to collect my wits. But then we reached the part where I was to sing solo. I stepped forward, my mind in a whirl. My throat was dry. I had forgotten the words! Mr Pinto nodded at me and raised his hand.

I heard a voice soaring. It was mine! And then, all terrified feelings vanished. I was singing joyously, experiencing again what I had felt in the Southlands drawing room, exultation. The words were beautiful and the music sublime. I was transported upwards, floating on a cloud outside the little church, amongst the moon and stars. Then I was back on my feet into reality, and the whole choir were singing again.

The performance continued, and I gathered strength from each solo passage and each combined choral effort until, finally, the oratorio reached its finish.

The applause was tremendous. The clapping and stamping of feet went on for some minutes. Mr Pinto bowed low several times and then, in turn, he led each solo performer forward to receive their acclaim. He took my hand, and I stepped forward to receive a storm of applause and voices calling, "Encore, encore" and "Bravo," I, too, bowed low.

A bouquet was presented to each solo singer. In my case, I received a lovely spray of spring flowers from little James Wharton.

Then we were all ushered out of the church and into the church hall. This quickly filled, but I noticed that few of the lowly villagers attended. The reception was mainly comprised of the choir, some middle-class villagers and the wealthy families living in the neighbourhood.

However, I did see the Thomas family standing with Annie, on the fringe of the crowd, and I purposely went over and spoke to them. She and I had sung a duet halfway through the oratorio, which I thought had sounded very well, and I complimented her on her performance.

"Oh, Miss Adèle," she said fervently. "I couldn't 'ave done 'en but for you and t' 'elp you gave me. She were so kind and good to me," she added, turning to her parents.

"She be our reglar little noightingale at 'ome, miss," said Farmer Thomas, a burly red-faced man with a loud, jolly voice. "She sings to all t' animals, cows, sheep, lambs, even t' pigs!"

We all laughed at this.

"Faither, what a thing t' say!" exclaimed his laughing, but slightly embarrassed daughter.

Yes," said a merry-faced younger version of his father, obviously her brother, "And the piglets all squeal back."

"Now, Frank," admonished, Annie, "That's quite enough from you,"

Mrs Thomas, a kindly-looking little woman interjected, "We don't live fer from Lower Poppleton, miss, we 'opes as 'ow you might come and 'ave a sup of tay with us soon."

"That is very kind of you, Mrs Thomas," I said. "I certainly will. Mr Wharton can drive me out to your farm. Perhaps next week?"

At that point, Mr Pinto appeared at my elbow. Ignoring the Thomases, he said, "May I introduce Mr James Boulding, the Director of Music at Wolden cathedral?"

The Thomases faded into the crowd.

A smooth plump hand grasped mine, and I was looking at a rotund, well-dressed gentleman of about forty, with sleek, rather oily-looking dark hair and long dark eyes, which gazed appraisingly at me from behind a pince-nez.

Thin lips stretched into a smile, which did not reach his eyes. His voice was as smooth as his hair, "Miss Varens, this is an honour. I was totally entranced by your singing tonight. You are of course a professional?"

I lowered my eyes, modestly, "No, sir, I am a complete amateur and have never sung in public before, except at Christmas in front of members of my family"

Mr Boulding turned to the choirmaster. "But this is amazing, Mr Pinto. This young lady must have a natural talent. Are there singers in your family, Miss Varens?"

"I believe my mother, who is French, was a singer in Paris."

"Miss Varens, your fame has gone before you. Mr Pinto had informed me that there was someone of unusual talent here and that I should come to this performance of 'The Messiah' and hear you. Fortunately, I was available this evening. I deeply enjoyed your quite delightful and inspiring performance."

I curtseyed. "I am much obliged to you, sir, for your commendation."

Inwardly, I was wondering how I could escape from this over-complimentary and smarmy man.

"However," he continued, "I will not beat about the bush, Miss Varens. As Director of Music at Wolden, I am about to organise a concert in the cathedral shortly." Here he studied his fingernails. "I have complete discretion in the arranging of all the musical events at the cathedral and having heard you sing, I should like to invite you along to the cathedral for an audition in connection with my concert. Could I interest you in taking part, Miss Varens?"

"Well, possibly, sir, but it would depend on the date. I am only staying with the Whartons for a week or so longer."

"Could there be an extension of your visit, Miss Varens? The concert will be in mid February."

I remembered that Mr Rochester's special birthday was in February, but I was not sure of the date. "I would have to consult my guardian and his wife, Mr and Mrs Rochester. In any case, Mr Boulding, I may not be found suitable for your concert if I fail your audition."

"Oh, Miss Varens, I think you will pass with flying colours. It is only a formality. But, nevertheless, if we can agree on a date when you might visit Wolden cathedral, hopefully next week, we can make further arrangements after that.".

He whipped out a small pocket diary and leafed through the pages. "How about next Wednesday morning at eleven o' clock?"

"I would need to ask Mr Wharton, sir. I know he frequently drives into Wolden in the middle of the week and I could come with him."

"Perfect, perfect," purred Mr Boulding.

"Excuse me then, sir, I will speak to him."

I crossed the hall to where Stephen Wharton was standing, talking to an elderly couple.

"Ah, here is our little songbird!" he exclaimed.

I laughed and then explained my errand.

We both looked across at Mr Boulding, who was eating a sandwich and chatting to another gentleman. But I felt those narrow dark eyes were watching us closely.

"Well, you have definitely arrived, my dear. Mr Boulding is a well-known figure in Wolden and is noted for his taste and knowledge of music Yes, of course I can drive you into Wolden next Wednesday. I am attending a meeting at the cathedral myself."

So, it was agreed. But I could not help a feeling of disquiet. Mr Boulding was not someone I liked. There was something altogether too unctuous and, at the same time, predatory about him. However, I told myself, it was just a song or two in his concert. I did not need to have any closer contact with him than that.

*****

The following Wednesday was a dry, clear day and Mr Wharton and I bowled along to Wolden through the intervening villages, chatting in a relaxed way. He drove the open trap to a large old inn on the edge of the city, near the station and we both walked up to the cathedral from there. Mr Wharton went to his meeting in the Dean's office and I entered the portals of the cathedral.

James Boulding must have been watching for me because he appeared almost immediately from the dark depths of the cathedral, rather like a hungry spider waiting for its prey. I shivered slightly. The antipathy I felt towards him was very strong. Even the scent wafting from the handkerchief he produced to polish his pince-nez, filled me with revulsion.

"You echo the beauty of the morning, Miss Varens," he exclaimed. "Come with me."
He began to lead me up the nave and turned off down a dim passageway. "Did you bring any music with you?"

Following behind him apprehensively, I replied, "Yes, sir, a few pieces with which I am familiar."

We had now entered a small area, enclosed on three sides, containing the massive tomb of a past bishop and a piano. A delicately carved stone archway gave access from the main cathedral.

Mr Boulding leafed through the scores I had given him, humming slightly to himself. "Yes, yes, these would all be acceptable. Do you know this one by Schubert?" He handed me another score. The title was 'Ave Maria'.

"I have heard it sung, sir, but have never done so myself."

"I think it would suit your voice admirably. Let us try first the pieces that you know and then, perhaps, you can sing the one I have suggested.

He chose the song by Handel, which I had sung in the Southlands drawing room, 'Where O'er You Walk' and started to play, giving me a wave of his hand when I should begin. There then followed several of the other songs and, finally Mr Boulding's choice. But, not having sung this one before, I was conscious that I had made a few mistakes.

During the session, I had become aware of whispering behind me. People, who, hearing my voice echoing around the ancient walls, had walked through the cathedral to the archway and were all standing listening. I was slightly taken aback, however, when, having finished singing, I turned around and saw an audience of about twenty persons.

Mr Boulding jumped up angrily and waved them away with his small plump hands.

"Ladies and gentlemen, this is a private audition! Thank you, thank you, good people, but please go away about your business."

They drifted away, reluctantly.

He turned to me, with an apologetic smile. "You see how your beautiful voice attracts, Miss Varens?" Then, almost in the same breath, "That went very well, as I had thought it would. You will need to practice the last piece a little more for perfection, but otherwise, excellent." He closed the piano. "Could we now discuss your participation in my concert?"

My heart sank a little. I felt trapped into a commitment I would prefer not to have made. "I will have to write to my guardian and his wife and see if this would be convenient, sir, and also consult the Reverend and Mrs Wharton. I will let you know.

He nodded. "Of course, of course, Miss Varens, but now let me escort you to the Dean's residence. On hearing about the audition, he has invited you and the Reverend Wharton to lunch."

He came towards me and offered me his arm. I gingerly placed my hand upon the smooth material of his sleeve, to have it gripped as in a vice. I was whisked along out of the cathedral and down the street to another equally ancient building, The Deanery, close by.

We walked up a short flight of steps to the heavy, carved front door, where, thankfully, my arm was released.

"Mr James Boulding and Miss Adèle Varens, lunching with the Reverend and Mrs Grimmond," he announced to a small maid, neatly dressed in grey with crisp white cap and apron.

The maid ushered us through a dark hall to an equally gloomy room in which a number of people were standing or sitting, talking and holding small glasses of sherry.

Stephen Wharton came towards us immediately. "Good day to you, Mr Boulding. Have you and Miss Varens finished your session?"

"Yes, indeed, Mr Wharton. I think we can safely say that the morning has been a most satisfactory one and that Miss Varens will be an excellent choice for my concert in February."

They both looked at me for confirmation.

"The only problem is," I began slowly, thinking how I could avoid making it too definite, "it is Mr Rochester's special birthday in February and I will have to be there. Also, Mrs Rochester is not very well at present and may have need of me."

Luckily, I sensed that Mr Wharton had caught a hint of my reluctance. "It will probably be best if Miss Varens consults her guardian and his wife, Mr Boulding, before making any commitment."

Mr Boulding's smooth smiling countenance did not change, but I sensed a touch of impatience and annoyance at these possible obstacles to his plans. "Yes, Miss Varens has already indicated as much to me," he said coldly. Then with a change of mood, "Let me introduce you to the Dean and his wife, Miss Varens." He led me across the room to a bald, stooping, elderly man, with a heavily wrinkled face and white beard. The Dean greeted me kindly, if a little vaguely and then waved his hand towards his wife, equally elderly, with grey hair, drawn back into a severe bun and a long, unsmiling face.

I cannot say that I particularly enjoyed the luncheon at The Deanery. Most of the other guests were ecclesiastical and their conversations dealt with church matters, of which I had no knowledge. I sat quietly between Mr Wharton and Mr Boulding, opposite the Dean's wife, Mrs Grimmond, who looked down her long nose at me, as she made a few desultory remarks about the weather and enquired about the state of the roads between Wolden and Lower Poppleton. She then became involved in a long conversation with her neighbour about a charity event he was organising and took no further notice of me.

At the end of the meal, everyone was departing, and cloaks, hats, and bonnets were being donned in the dismal hall. I was putting on my own bonnet and cloak, when Mr Wharton whispered to me, "Miss Varens, do you think you could amuse yourself in Wolden until half past three o'clock? I still have business to discuss with the Dean."

The idea of freedom for at least two hours to explore the quaint little streets and shops of Wolden thrilled me, and I concurred happily. Mrs Wharton had given me some commissions to carry out for her, matching silks for a new altar cloth she was embroidering, and I relished this task. We arranged to meet at the hostelry where the trap had been left, at an agreed time.

Unfortunately, Mr Boulding had overheard our conversation. "My dear Miss Varens, you cannot possibly wander around the city streets alone and unescorted. Have you seen our old walls? I should be honoured to give you a guided tour and…."

"Oh, excuse me, Mr Boulding," I said firmly. "I have already been on a tour of the old walls with Mr Wharton and his family, and Mrs Wharton has asked me to undertake various commissions for her in the Wolden shops. My time is likely to be fully employed on this task."

But Mr Boulding was not easily put off. "Perhaps, when you have finished your shopping, you would like to take tea with me at Bingles in West Street?"

"That is very kind of you, Mr Boulding, but I do not know how long my errands will take, so I will have to decline."

Mr Boulding gave me a sharp look from those dark narrow eyes and bowed slightly. "Very well, Miss Varens. I am sorry I cannot be of more assistance to you."

Then he turned away and began to talk to someone else.

CHAPTER 7

Freedom at last! Before me lay the city with its ancient buildings, waiting to be explored. I located the little haberdashery shop where Mrs Wharton had said I would find her silks and successfully matched and bought what she had requested. Then, for the next half hour, I had a delightful wander, looking at all sorts of curiosities, both in the shop windows and in the architecture around me.

I came down the main thoroughfare of North Street, turned into West Street and was standing on tiptoe examining an interesting plaque on an old wall, when a tall hurrying figure in

a tweed many-caped coat and cap almost collided with me, as he came round the corner.

Looking into a pair of startled brown eyes, I realised that it was Jack Whitaker.

"Oh my Goodness. Oh my! If it isn't little Miss Adèle!" he exclaimed.

"Jack! What on earth are you doing here?"

"I've had business here at the County Court." He indicated vigorously with his arm the direction from whence he had come.

I gazed at him in alarm. "The County Court, you are not in any trouble are you, Jack?"

He laughed. "Not at all, Miss Adèle. I've been giving evidence at a hearing there."

I looked puzzled. "I don't understand."

"No, of course you don't, but you soon will." He took out a heavy silver watch on a chain from his waistcoat pocket and consulted it. "I'm catching a train back to London, but I've got half an hour or so to spare and I'm rather hungry. Why don't you come and have some refreshment with me, and I'll tell you a bit about things?"

Mystified, I allowed him to guide me to a coffee house nearby, which I noticed was Bingles, where I had had coffee with the Whartons. We opened the weighty oak door. Inside, heavy Tudor beams lined the ceiling and little latticed windows looked out on the busy street.

Jack selected a table for two beside one of the windows and threw off his heavy coat and cap. Underneath he was wearing a smart brown tweed suit with crisp white linen. I also noticed he had a pair of expensive-looking leather gloves. His appearance was that of a gentleman, and there was little trace of the Southlands footman or coachman, except for his Cockney twang, but even that was greatly refined.

A waiter came to our table and Jack ordered a pot of Indian tea for me, I declined anything else, and a pasty and a glass of ale for himself. His manner bore no hint of the demeanour of a servant.

Then he turned his attention on me. "You look as beautiful as ever, Miss Adèle," he said with a warm smile. "And so, how did the concert go?"

"Very well indeed, Jack. I was extremely nervous. At first, I thought I had forgotten the words I had to sing, but then I began, and suddenly, I wasn't nervous any more. A great many people attended the performance. The church was full to overflowing."

"I'm not a bit surprised. I expect they'd heard about you. Things get around you know, especially in a small village."

"It wasn't just village people, Jack. It was a great many of the gentry as well."

"They'd obviously cottoned on to a good thing. Beauty and a lovely voice; they couldn't go wrong."

I returned his smile. "And what about you, Jack? You don't look like a coachman or footman any more."

He laughed. "That's because I'm not. I have finished my employment with Mr and Mrs Rochester." He looked at me keenly.

"You mean you will not be there at Southlands when I return?" I think my crestfallen expression must have been evident, because he reached out his hand and patted mine as it lay on the table.

The tea, ale, and pasty arrived at that moment, and there was a pause in our conversation while I poured out my tea, and he drank his ale and took a large bite from his pasty.

Then he continued, "I'm afraid not, but I'm going to return soon and explain to everyone what has been going on. I hope you will be there, Miss Adèle." His gaze held mine, and in it I read something which made my heart flutter. I could also feel the colour rising in my cheeks.

"But, but why can't you tell me now?"

"I would love to, my... dear Miss Adèle, but everything is not completed yet, and I want to tell the full story to the whole Southlands household. I think they deserve to hear it."

"Oh, it sounds so exciting." I clapped my hands together and then had a sudden thought, "Will you be able to explain about what happened at Ferndean to Mrs Rochester and myself and about the person who locked us in the cellar and that horrible laugh?"

"Yes, all of it."

"But will you be getting another job in service?"

"No, my dear. The job at Southlands was with Mr Rochester's agreement and was what we call a 'cover'."

"A 'cover'? What is that? And who or what is 'we'?"

He took another large bite from his pasty and a gulp of ale. "No, I'm not telling you any more for the present." He gave me a mischievous look.

"But when are you coming back to Southlands? I must be sure of being there."

"Probably next Friday. When do you plan to return yourself, Miss Adèle?"

"It would have been next week, probably Wednesday, but," I sighed, "I seem to have got myself involved in performing in a concert in Wolden Cathedral in two weeks time. Quite honestly though, Jack, I rather want to get myself out of it."

"Ah, there you are, my dear Miss Varens."

We both looked up, in surprise. James Boulding was standing at our table staring down at us, his dark eyes snapping through his pince-nez, as he took in every detail.

"Oh, Mr Boulding, how you startled me." My heart was thudding, but I endeavoured to sound cool and collected.

"I could not help noticing you through the window, Miss Varens." His voice held more than a tinge of accusation.

I gave a little laugh. "You will never believe it, but as soon as I had finished my commissions for Mrs Wharton, I bumped into Mr Whitaker, who has come to Wolden on business." I indicated Jack with a wave of my hand.

Jack stood up and with complete self-possession, offered his hand to Mr Boulding.

"Jack Whitaker at your service, sir."

Mr Boulding took the proffered hand reluctantly and shook it briefly. "I take it you are an acquaintance of the lady, sir?" he said stiffly.

Jack looked at me with a smile. "I most certainly am, sir and of her guardian and his wife. I know the family well."

"My apologies for having interrupted your…little tête a tète," Mr Boulding said with a sneer.

"I would ask you to join us, Mr Boulding," I said, with what I hoped was a breezy manner, "but Mr Whitaker is just about to catch a train for London."

Jack took my cue and looked at his watch. "And I have less than ten minutes."

He summoned the waiter and paid the bill. Then he began to don his outer garments.

"I will walk with you to the station, Mr Whitaker," I said hurriedly, taking his arm.

I turned to Mr Boulding. "Thank you for the audition, Mr Boulding, and I enjoyed the luncheon, but I have a few things to discuss with Mr Whitaker, and I must therefore bid you Goodbye."

I held out my hand and Mr Boulding grasped it. "Do not forget the concert, Miss Varens. I am counting on you to be available."

"That, sir, will depend on my family commitments. I will let you know."

Jack and I hurried out of Bingles into the street.

"Phew!" said Jack, as we walked quickly along. "What a self-important character he is."

"I'm afraid I do not like him, Jack. There is something scheming and repellent about him. I don't want to take part in his beastly concert, and now that I know you are likely to be returning to Southlands next week with your explanation to everyone, I am certainly not going to miss that. I will tell him I cannot manage it after all."

"What sort of fee has he offered you?"

"Fee, what do you mean? Why, nothing, of course. I am not a professional singer, am I?"

"You are better than many a professional singer I've heard, including at Covent Garden."

"You sound as if you know a lot about these things, Jack"

"Yes, well, I do, but that is another side to me you may find out, one day. Anyway, Miss Adèle, there is a going rate for this type of concert." He named a figure in guineas.

I looked at him in surprise. "I suppose it may be a charity concert, in a good cause."

"Even so, he will have been given a budget to pay those taking part. No doubt a percentage of the ticket sales goes to a charity, but the singers can expect some remuneration for their trouble."

We had now reached the station, and Jack had about six minutes to catch his train.

"I will be contacting the Rochesters next week to let them know when to expect me. So, I hope to see you at Southlands."

"Of course, you will." We were standing close together by the ticket office. I raised my head and looked into his eyes. "I wish..." My voice trailed away tearfully.

He put out his hand and took mine. "What do you wish, my dear?"

"I wish you didn't have to leave me," I whispered.

He raised my hand to his lips. "Au revoir, my darl...dear."

"Au revoir, dearest Jack," I said, fervently.

I watched as his tall figure strode through the barrier to the platform. He looked back once, waved and was gone.

CHAPTER 8

Stephen Wharton was waiting for me at the inn and we were soon driving back along the lanes, chatting amicably, as before.

As soon as we reached the vicarage at Lower Poppleton, I went to my room, and sitting down at a small writing desk, I wrote to Tante Jane:

"Dearest Tante,

Firstly, I do hope and pray that you are better and have put that disturbing experience at Ferndean behind you.

My performance at St. Mary's church, Lower Poppleton was a great success. So much so that I received an invitation from a Mr James Boulding, who is the Director of Music at Wolden Cathedral, to take part in a concert he is organising in two weeks. However, to be quite honest with you, Tante, I would much rather not. I long to return to Southlands to be with you, Mr Rochester, and the boys. I feel sure that you need me, and, in any case, I want to be there for Mr Rochester's special birthday celebration, although I am not sure of the exact date.

My time here has been very pleasant and instructive. Mr and Mrs Wharton have been very kind and have taken me to various historic sites, as well as a tour of the City of Wolden and the cathedral. Wolden is a most interesting place. I love wandering around its ancient cobbled streets.

I was in Wolden today. I had gone there for an audition with Mr Boulding for his concert, and who should I encounter in the city centre but Jack Whitaker. He tells me he has left Mr Rochester's service but will be returning to Southlands to explain various matters, including what happened at Ferdean. He said he had been working as our coachman and footman, with Mr Rochester's knowledge, as a 'cover'. I am most intrigued. It all sounds very mysterious. He said he would be letting you know when he can come, as I gather he is now living in London. So, this is another reason for my return and I plan to be back with you by next Wednesday.

Do please give my love to Mr Rochester and Fairfax and Johnny.

Yours affectionately,

Adèle"

That evening, while Mary and I were working on her altar cloth, she enquired, "How did your audition with Mr Boulding go, Adèle?"

"Oh, quite well, thank you, Mrs Wharton," I replied casually, threading a needle. "Mr Boulding said he was quite happy with my choice of song, and he also gave me another one to practise, 'Ave Maria' by Schubert."

"Ah, that is a beautiful piece, but requires a very good strong voice. I think you would do it admirably."

"I expect I would be satisfactory," I said, stitching away at a rose. "However, I feel quite strongly that I do not want to take part."

"Adèle!" exclaimed Mary Wharton in surprise. "Why ever not? It would be such a good opportunity for you to develop your undoubted singing talent."

"Possibly, Mrs Wharton, but there are other ties at Southlands which call me back, and I must confess that I have formed an aversion to Mr Boulding."

"Why, Adèle, has he upset you or affronted you in some way? He always seems such a polite man."

"Polite, but in a sort of insinuating way, as if he had some other motive for his attentions."

"Really, do you feel that Adèle? So, his politeness and attentions are not acceptable to you?"

"No, definitely not. There is something about his face, his eyes, his mouth which I do not like."

I must confess I was beginning to feel a bit ridiculous, over-fussy, and critical as I said these things.

There was a silence for a few minutes and then, to my relief, Mary Wharton said, "Do you know, Adèle, I think I know what you mean. I have felt this myself about him. It is as if I do not want to be near him or have much to do with him. Is that how you feel?"

"Yes, Mrs Wharton, that is it."

"I may as well tell you something else, which may have a bearing on our impressions. I have thought, for some time, that Mr Boulding is not a kind man. I think he is self-centred, self-congratulatory, and possibly quite cruel."

"Mrs Wharton, what on earth can you mean?" I was agog to hear more.

"Mr Boulding is fairly new to Wolden. He came here about five years ago. He had recently married a widow with two very young children, her husband having sadly died quite suddenly of a fever. She was a very pleasant woman, devoted to her two little children, a boy of four and a girl of five.

"Very unfortunately, Mrs Boulding developed the consumption and died last year, leaving her little ones motherless. Naturally we, that is Stephen and I, assumed that Mr Boulding would be a loving father to these little innocents. However, I regret to say that this was far from the case."

She sighed and dabbed her eyes, and then, picking up the embroidery she had dropped, she continued. "I met Mr Boulding a few months after his wife's sad death and enquired about his step-children. To my amazement, I found that he had sent them both away to separate schools where he said they would receive a 'good education'.

Horrified at this for such young children who had been deprived of their mother's love, I then asked him if he would visit them and look after them in the holidays. He told me he was 'far too busy', but that they would be looked after at these schools and that he probably would not be seeing them for some time. He said this quite casually, with apparently no regrets, as if it was what any sensible person might do."

"But how appallingly cruel and unkind to those little creatures!" I too felt tears welling up in my eyes. "How could he do such a thing?"

"Well, there is really nothing to stop him. He obviously felt that they were not his offspring and wanted to get rid of them as quickly as possible, no doubt with a view to seeking another wife. For I must tell you, Adèle, that he is on the lookout for someone at present."

"Well, it certainly won't be me!"

We both laughed and changed the subject.

A few days later I received a reply to my letter from Tante Jane:

My Dear Adèle.

How lovely to hear from you and to know the performance went so well. Mary has also written and given me a full account. I gather you carried all before you.

I was interested to hear about Mr Boulding's invitation to take part in his concert. It does seem to be a marvellous opportunity to promote your talent. but the fact that you seem so reluctant makes me think that there is some other factor holding you back.

As far as I am concerned. although it would be lovely to see you here next Wednesday. I would certainly not want to stand in your way. and I am sure that Mr Rochester feels the same. His birthday is on the fourteenth February. but it is entirely up to you, my love. If you would like to take part in the concert, then follow your own inclinations.

With regard to Jack Whitaker, I am as much in the dark as yourself. Mr Rochester told me he was leaving our employment and has in fact engaged a new coachman, William, and a new footman, Robert, both of whom are older men and quite pleasant and satisfactory, but I must confess I do miss Jack. He was such an engaging personality, with such a wonderful ability to cheer people up. So I, too, look forward to his 'explanation' with interest. He has advised us he will call next Friday.

Let me know what you decide to do, and we will await your return with happiness.

Much love,

Jane"

I felt that Tante Jane, with her quick perceptions had read between my lines that I was unhappy about Mr Boulding. Of course, after the further revelation from Mary Wharton about his character, I was even more averse to him and couldn't bear the thought of seeing him again. I quickly wrote back to Tante Jane, confirming I would see them next Wednesday.

It was with horror that the next day, after our four o'clock tea, Stephen Wharton's voice was heard in the hall, the sitting room door opened, and there, following him into the room, was Mr Boulding.

"Mrs Wharton and Miss Varens, how delightful to see you both," he gushed.

Outwardly cool, I extended my hand. "Good afternoon, sir."

"I met Mr Boulding in the village, where I understand he had some business and have invited him to dinner, Mary," said her husband eagerly.

"Oh," said Mrs Wharton, with no great enthusiasm, "Then, I had better have a word with cook."

Mr Boulding bowed, as she passed him. "I hope I am not inconveniencing you, Mrs Wharton?"

Mrs Wharton gave him a rather sickly smile. "Not too much, I suppose. I should be used to Stephen's sudden invitations to people. I expect we can manage."

Apparently undaunted by Mrs Wharton's lack lustre response, Mr Boulding turned his attention to me. "Well, Miss Varens, have you written to your guardian and ascertained the date of his birthday and whether Mrs Rochester has need of you?"

"Yes, I have, sir," I said coldly."

"And have you made a decision about my concert?"

"Yes, Mr Boulding, I have made my decision. I am afraid I shall be leaving Wolden next Wednesday, which will mean I am back at Southlands in time for Mr Rochester's birthday. There are also some other matters which have arisen which make it imperative for me to return."

"Other matters?"

"Yes, private family matters," I said with an emphasis on 'private'.

"And no chance that you will be able to return to Wolden a little later, in time for the concert?"

"No sir, I regret not. I have other plans."

"Well, this really is a blow," he said, almost angrily.

"Surely not a great one, sir. There must be plenty of suitable singers," and I could not help adding the comment, "Although, if they are professional, they may require a fee for their services, unlike myself."

There was a cold silence.

I suddenly realised that the Reverend Wharton had left the room, and Mr Boulding and I were alone.

"You seemed to be very intimate with that young man, when I saw you through the window at Bingles last week. Does your guardian know of your relationship?"

I stood up. "Intimate, sir! What can you mean? I explained that Jack Whitaker was closely connected to Mr Rochester's family. He was an employee but also a trusted friend to us all."

Mr Boulding gave a sneering smile. "A coachman and footman, I believe?"

I was completely taken aback by this thrust. This loathsome man had been making enquiries and spying on the Rochesters and myself.

"I do not think that any of this is your concern, sir. You seem to have been checking on matters that are none of your business. Excuse me, Mr Boulding. I must leave you."

With that, I marched furiously out of the room, shutting the door firmly.

I sought Mary Wharton in the kitchen, where she and the cook were studying the menu for that evening.

"Mrs Wharton," I said. "I have a headache. Would you mind if I had a light meal in my room?"

"Dearest Adèle, what is the matter?" said Mary Wharton, rushing towards me. "You look as white as a sheet.

Thank you, Mrs Brown," she called over her shoulder. "We will do as you suggest about the menu."

She took my arm, as she and I climbed the stairs to my room and there I gave her the gist of what Mr Boulding had said.

"I agree he has taken quite a liberty," said Mrs Wharton, "But, who is this Jack Whitaker person?"

"You probably remember him at Christmas, Mrs Wharton. He got the children to sing the carol around the Christmas tree. He has been working for Mr Rochester as coachman and footman, that is true, but I think he was just posing as that as a sort of disguise, with Mr Rochester's approval, in order to conduct some sort of enquiry. He obviously has another identity and is much more than a servant. He is planning to return to Southlands next Friday to explain to everyone what has been going on, which is one of the reasons I want to return."

"Are you in love with him?" asked Mary Wharton softly. "I think you are."

The directness of this question gave me a little shock, but it helped to focus my thoughts more clearly. "With Jack? I...I...don't know. I am a bit confused. I think he is the most exciting and attractive young man I have ever met, but I know almost nothing about him."

"Well, be careful, my love. It does all sound very mysterious and intriguing. I hope you or Jane will tell me all about it one day, but I also hope that you will not be hurt by giving your heart too easily to someone unsuitable."

I remained silent at this comment, not knowing what to say.

"Mrs Brown will bring you up something in your room as you requested," she said soothingly. "You certainly don't have to meet Mr Boulding again this evening if you don't want to."

"Thank you, Mrs Wharton, you are very kind and understanding. Could you let me know when Mr Boulding has gone, and I will come down later?"

"Of course, dear," she said, with a kindly smile, as she left me.

I rested on my bed, confused and upset. Would Mr Boulding take this further? Would he write to Mr Rochester saying he had seen Jack and myself together at Bingles, behaving 'intimately'?

Then, my other self took over. So, what if he does? I told myself, you have nothing on your conscience. Whatever your deeper feeling for Jack, he is just a friend at the moment and nothing else.

I felt my confidence beginning to rise.

CHAPTER 9

The following Wednesday, I duly caught the morning train and arrived at Fremingham to be met by the family carriage, driven by a middle-aged, grey haired man with a quiet deferential manner, who introduced himself as William. There was no wild driving from him, and my bonnet feathers remained intact.

I found Tante Jane looking much rested and in very good spirits. She seemed to have put the horror of our experience in the Ferndean cellar well and truly behind her.

She kissed me warmly. "I am delighted to have you back with me, my dear."

"And so are we," chorused little Fairfax and Johnny, who had been playing in a corner of her boudoir. They ran to me and each gave me a hug. "Come and see what we've made."

Each taking me by the hand, they led me to their play area, and I was able to admire a complex building with steps, little corridors and turrets, which had the appearance of a castle.

"And who lives in that castle?" I enquired merrily.

"A bad man who…" Fairfax paused to think.

"Kills people and eats them for breakfast," cried Johnny.

A strange feeling of chill stole over me at these words. However, I spent the rest of the morning playing with them and reading to them from a storybook.

The day after my return, Mr Rochester handed me an envelope that had arrived in the morning post. It bore a Swiss postmark. Inside was a letter from Signora Garilani enclosing another letter addressed to me. It was with some emotion that I realised that I was looking at a letter penned by my long-lost mother Céline.

I felt Mr Rochester's dark eye on me, and I got up hastily exclaiming, "Excuse me guardian, but I must read this in private first, and then I will discuss the contents with you later, if you so wish."

"Of course, Adèle," he said with a wave of his hand. "Please do as you think best."

I almost ran out of the breakfast room and quickly mounted the stairs to my bedroom.

There, I locked the door and, with trembling fingers, opened the letter. It was in French and dated two months previously, no doubt due to the round about route it had taken to reach me. I give the English translation:

"*Ma Chère Adèle,*

Signora Garilani's letter reached me some time ago, but I regret I have been heavily engaged in the business of getting married to the Conte de Valdini and have not had the necessary time to attend to the enquiry.

I am pleased to hear that you want to get in touch with me. I had thought that Mr Rochester might have erased all memory of me from your mind. It was unfortunate that I had to leave you as I did, but, in the circumstances, I had no alternative. I knew that Mr Rochester would take care of you, and I am pleased that I was right.

It would be nice to meet you again, after all these years. Guiseppi and I finished our relationship some time ago, and I met the conte about a year ago. He is a wealthy man, with a beautiful villa in Sorrento and a castle in the mountains to the north, which I have not so far seen. He also has a son of about your age.

Both father and son have expressed a desire to meet you, so I hope you will be able to visit us here soon. The conte is away at present on business but is due back shortly. I believe we are then going to Paris. I do so want to catch up on the latest fashions, and after that, I will let you know when it would be convenient to receive you.

Yours affectionately,
Céline, Contessa de Valdini"

My reactions to this somewhat cold and rather careless letter were very mixed. Céline could have been writing to a distant friend or acquaintance, rather than her own daughter, whom she had not seen for sixteen years. The lack of emotion hurt me deeply. If it was not for the other information about my birth and parentage that I hoped to gain from her, I would have torn the letter into a hundred pieces and tried to forget my mother as completely as if she were indeed dead. I also wondered why Count Valdini and his son were so interested in meeting me. Who was this man, Valdini, with his wealth, large villa, and castle? I remembered my feeling of foreboding at Johnny's words about the owner of their castle and shivered. What nonsense, I told myself. Plenty of respectable people own castles.

At dinner that evening, I suggested to Mr Rochester that I would show him my letter and see what he thought.

Accordingly, we met in his study later and I placed the missive in his hand.

He perused it twice, using his eyeglass, and then flung it down on the desk before him scornfully. "This letter says everything about Céline. She certainly has not changed for the better. She is vain, selfish, and unfeeling, with no sense of responsibility. In her empty-headed way, she has no doubt been attracted to this man Valdini because of his wealth, title, and luxurious way of living." He looked at me keenly. "What do you want me to do about this rather vague off hand invitation to visit them?"

"I was deeply disappointed in this letter, sir. It shows little feeling for me, as you say, but I would like to meet her again, and I cannot help being a little curious about the man she has married."

"In other words, you would like to visit her in Italy?"

I nodded.

"If that is what you wish, Adèle, so be it. But we know nothing about this man Valdini, and I feel we should find out more before you reply. I think I have a useful source for investigating such matters."

"Yes, sir, that seems a good idea, and I have no objection."

So, the matter was left for the present. Mr Rochester kept the letter and said he would let me know what, if anything, he had discovered. I did wonder about his 'source' for investigating someone living in another country, but he seemed very confident, so I left it in his hands.

The next morning was Friday, and at breakfast, Mr Rochester announced that he had received a communication from Jack Whitaker which said that he would be paying us a visit that afternoon to explain 'everything' to our whole household. My heart missed a beat at this news, and I am sure I flushed scarlet.

The whole household seemed to be in a state of excitement when they received the message via Robert, the new footman. Everyone seemed to be speculating about Jack. Word had got out that he was 'not what he had appeared to be, when he worked for Mr Rochester and that he was going to explain it all to us.' There was a great deal of speculation. One thought he might be a duke in disguise, another, a royal prince, and even the possibility of his being a bishop was discussed. All highly improbable, remembering Jack with his Cockney speech, even when modulated, his cheeky manner, and lively, free, and easy personality.

At about two o'clock, carriage wheels were heard on the gravel and there was a sharp rata-tat on the front door. Robert glided in a stately manner to the door and opened it. My whole being leapt as Jack appeared, his tall figure swathed in a dark cloak and a dark cap on his chestnut curls, both of which he quickly removed and handed to Robert. Beneath, he was dressed in the same tweed suit he had worn in Wolden.

We were all assembled, either sitting or standing in the hall. Jane and I were sitting near the fireplace. The staff were all standing stiffly around near the servants' entrance, except for Mrs Tompkins, whose seniority entitled her to a chair.

Mr Rochester came forward to greet the visitor. "Welcome back to Southlands, Mr Whitaker." His voice and courteous manner were those he would use to receive a person at his own level visiting the house and not an ex-servant. This caused much amazed whispering amongst the household. "Thank you, sir," said our visitor. "Glad to be

Not Forgetting Adèle CHAPTER 9

back and to see you all." He gave a sweeping bow to Jane and myself and raised his hand in greeting to the rest of the staff.

Then he positioned himself in front of us all and began. "Firstly, my dear good people, let me introduce myself properly. You know me as Jack Whitaker and that is my name, although some call me John." He reached into an inner pocket and produced a small card. "However, I am really Detective Jack Whitaker of Scotland Yard, London, and here is my warrant card." He passed it to Mrs Rochester, who studied it, and then it was passed around to everyone.

When I received the card, I read:

'Detective J.R. Whitaker,
Metropolitan Police Force,
Scotland Yard,
London.'

There were gasps all around and cries of surprise, particularly from the women.

Mrs Tompkins couldn't help herself. "But Jack, I'm sorry, I mean Detective Whitaker, what was you doing 'ere as a servant and doing all those things like cleaning boots an' all?"

There were a few hysterical little titters from the other women servants at this.

Jack threw back his head and laughed. "I seem to have fooled you completely, Mrs T. and the other ladies. But what I was doing was concealing my true identity in order to gain information for my criminal investigations."

There were murmurs of astonishment.

"Yes, you see, at Scotland Yard, it had come to our attention that there was a criminal gang of thieves working in this area, and a number of burglaries had taken place. A

117

quantity of valuable jewels and silver had been stolen, mainly from the big houses of the wealthy families around here. There had also been a couple of murders of unfortunate people who had got in their way.

A certain Justice of the Peace," here he nodded at Mr Rochester, "had requested that a Detective from Scotland Yard should come to the area and investigate. With the cooperation of Mr Rochester, it was decided that, by disguising myself as a servant, I would be able to work on the case, with nobody suspecting."

"Was you on your own doing this?" asked Mrs Tompkins, who seemed to have made herself the spokesperson for the other servants.

"No, I wasn't. I had a team of police officers with me. Some of these infiltrated themselves as servants into different households, including here." He indicated one of the stable lads. "May I introduce Police Sergeant Richard Holness?"

The young man so addressed grinned sheepishly at those around him.

"Dick!" said the other stable boy. "I thought there was something rum about you, but I never guessed."

"We found the burglaries were often committed on a particular day of the week, often a Saturday, or when there had been a big party or ball in a house, and the ladies had been wearing their jewellery and then stayed there overnight.

"Once the theft had taken place, in the early hours of the morning, the gang all met in a particular lonely house, where they were unlikely to be disturbed. I wonder if you can guess where this might have been?" He paused.

There was a short silence, but I instantly felt I knew. It all fitted.

"Ferndean!" I cried.

Jack turned to me and bowed. "Yes, Miss Adèle, so it was. A lonely, empty house, hidden in woodland. A perfect place for the gang to reconnoitre. Mr Rochester had mentioned to me that the house was empty. The caretakers, the Burtons, had given him notice at the end of October, and he had decided not to replace them." He looked at Mr Rochester, "Because, I believe, sir, you were planning to renovate the house with a view to letting it?"

"Yes, correct," grunted Mr Rochester.

"Oh", said Jane in surprise. "I hadn't realised you intended that, Edward."

"I am very sorry my love. It must have slipped my mind to tell you."

"Anyway," said Jack "They had discovered an ideal place for them to meet and disgorge their loot, as well as plan their next burglary."

"Detective Whitaker," I cried. "Was it Dick Holness I saw on Christmas Eve creeping down the garden towards Ferndean?"

"Yes, Miss Adèle, it would have been him that you saw. You see, Sergeant Holness was playing a double game. He was the stable lad at Southlands, but he had also managed to infiltrate himself as a member of the gang, so he was able to report back to me where they planned to operate next."

"But, Detective Whitaker," exclaimed Jane, "What about the terrifying experience of Miss Adèle and myself at Ferndean after Christmas?"

Jack Whitaker looked at Mr Rochester. "I think, sir, you might prefer that I give you the explanation of that in private to just yourself, Mrs Rochester, and Miss Adèle?"

"Yes, that would be preferable, Detective Whitaker. We can adjourn to my study."

"And perhaps Detective Whitaker would care for some refreshment?" interjected Jane.

"That would be most welcome madam," said Jack.

Jane nodded at Robert. "Will you arrange for tea and cakes to be served in Mr Rochester's study, and see that the fire is burning well on this cold day, Robert?"

"Certainly, madam," said Robert, sailing sedately towards the kitchen quarters.

"However, just one further announcement to everyone," said Jack looking around. "You will, I am sure, be pleased to know that most of the gang have been rounded up and are at present in the County jail, awaiting trial."

There were murmurs of relief from several of the women.

"But, unfortunately, the head of the gang, a man called Albert Eales, known as 'The Eel' in criminal circles, has escaped capture. I would describe him as a 'Master Criminal'. He often disguises himself in other identities and lives quite normally amongst respectable people, until his cover is blown. He is an extremely dangerous, but clever and intelligent man. He speaks several languages and appears to be quite cultured. At present, I suspect, he may have left the country, but if anyone of you hears anything unusual amongst your contacts in other households – and I do know that there is quite a network of gossip from one house to another – however trivial the piece of information may be, I should like to have it. You can write to me, Detective J.R. Whitaker, care of Scotland Yard, London, or, better still, send a telegram if you think it is urgent. There is a reward of £200 for Albert Eales' capture."

There were more cries of surprise and other rather exaggerated demonstrations of fear, plus hysterical giggles from the servants, as they filed out to their quarters.

We all settled in the study with tea and Mary's delicious pastries, and I made sure that I took Jack his cup and kept it replenished and that he had the pick of the cakes.

He turned to the Rochesters. "I am sure, sir, you will remember a woman in your employ called Grace Poole?"

There was a stunned silence as both of them remembered why Mrs Poole had been engaged. Jane paled a little and I noticed Mr Rochester had stretched out his good hand and was gripping hers firmly.

"After the fire at Thornfield, when the first Mrs Rochester unfortunately died, it was discovered that Grace Poole had been drinking heavily, which is how her...charge had managed to escape and start the fire."

"Yes, that is correct, and it had happened before, for the same reason, as my dear present wife can confirm, but fortunately, on that occasion, we were able to put the fire out. Following the fire and destruction of Thornfield and the death of my first wife, although I was not in a fit state to do anything about it myself, I gave orders to my man of business that Mrs Poole be discharged without a reference."

"Quite so, you could of course have made charges against her then, but you chose not to do so."

"As I say, I was not in a fit state both mentally or physically at that time."

"I understand, sir," said Jack with a sympathetic glance at them both. "However, Grace Poole was not a very desirable character. She had criminal tendencies and associated with the dregs of the underworld in the East End. When she was a young girl, she had an illegitimate son called Albert, who took her maiden name of Eales. She later married a man called Poole, a burglar and very bad character who is at present doing time in prison. Her son, Albert Eales continued on the criminal path, and as I have already explained, is the head of the gang of jewel thieves we have been investigating. Grace Poole is also deeply involved as one of them. She was arrested with the rest of the culprits and, under interrogation, she told me the following story.

"As I have said, Ferndean was their meeting place, and, shortly after Christmas she was at Ferndean one morning, when, to her surprise, she heard two female voices outside and then a lady calling the name of the caretakers, Burton. She was in the kitchen and she quickly hid in a tall broom cupboard there. She heard Mrs Rochester say she was going down into the cellar, and she waited until both she and Miss Adèle had gone down the stairs, and then she slammed and locked the door, intent on making her own escape. But she decided to scare them so badly that they would never want to come back to Ferndean again and probably tell others that the place was haunted.

"Poole had recognised Jane as the young lady governess at Thornfield who had very likely been familiar with the frequent deranged laugh of her charge, the first Mrs Rochester, and. being quite adept at imitation, she gave the laugh that you heard. In her spiteful and malicious way, she made the laugh as unpleasant and evil sounding as she could. Then, she crept quickly away into the woods."

I looked at Jane. She was still pale, but an expression of intense relief had flooded her face.

"Oh, Jack, I mean Detective Whitaker," exclaimed Jane. "So, it wasn't a reincarnation or a ghost. I cannot tell you how grateful I am to you for telling us all this."

She produced a handkerchief, dabbed her eyes and blew her nose. Then, she sank back against the protective arm of Mr Rochester.

"What do you think will happen to these criminals when they have been tried?" I asked.

"They will be punished in accordance with the due process of the law," said Jack in a matter-of-fact way. "If found guilty, it is very likely they will pay with their lives."

"I am sure we are all very grateful to you for using your valuable time to come here and give us this information," said Mr Rochester. "And I, for one, am pleased to know that most of the gang have been caught and are now behind bars. With people like you, Detective Whitaker, and the Police Force, we can all sleep peacefully in our beds."

Jack glanced at his timepiece. "Unfortunately, I have to go. My train is due in half an hour at Fremingham station. Sergeant Holness will travel back with me. I assume you will have no further need of his services, Mr Rochester?"

"Oh no, thank you, I can easily hire another stable lad, although I must say he did his job well. We will all see you out."

We followed Jack into the hall, where Robert was ready to help him on with his heavy cloak.

"There are one or two things I would like you to look into, Detective Whitaker," said Mr Rochester, handing him an envelope. "They are explained in this letter."

Jack nodded and stuffed it into his pocket.

I was desperate. I longed to have a private word with him, but there seemed to be no opportunity. Then I had a bright idea. As Robert helped Jack on with his cloak, and he donned his cap, I stepped behind him, out of sight of the Rochesters. His gloves were half hanging out of his cloak pocket and I quickly removed one and hid it behind my back. He took his leave and walked through the front door which Robert held open for him

"Oh dear," I said, pretending to pick up the glove from the floor, "He has left his glove." And, without giving the others time to say anything, I rushed towards the door and followed Jack down the steps.

"Jack! I, I mean, Detective Whitaker, you have left your glove behind."

He paused at the foot of the steps. "Quick thinking, Miss Adèle." He gave me an amused look as he pocketed the glove. "I wondered if we were going to be able to say a word to each other."

"Jack, I'm going to try to come up to London somehow. Can I write to you at Scotland Yard?"

"No, not there," he said hurriedly. "Take this." He handed me a piece of paper. "I've written an address. It's my family home, which I visit frequently. "Write there."

I glanced down at the paper. He had given me an address in Lambeth.

"I really have to go, my dear, but I too hope we can meet again in London."

He took my hand and pressed it to his lips. "Once again, and we always seem to be saying it, goodbye, Miss Adèle"

He leapt into the carriage to join Dick Holness and waved as the vehicle, driven by William, moved speedily away and was soon lost to sight down the drive

*****

About a week later, when I came down to breakfast, at which only Tante was present, her husband being busy with urgent matters elsewhere, I found her all beams and excitement with an open letter in her hand. "Adèle, Adèle, this is a letter from my cousin, Diana. Captain Fitzjames has been successful in his application for an Admiralty post!"

"Oh, but how wonderful for her, Tante and for the children."

"Yes, she says they are going to look for a convenient house in London, but, in the meantime, they have taken rooms in Tavistock Square, Bloomsbury."

Of course, my mind immediately flew to Jack.

If only I could visit her there.

My longing for him grew intense.

Jane was still reading the letter, and, as if in answer to my thoughts, she exclaimed "Diana is asking if you would care to visit them, once they are settled in."

I could hardly believe my ears. It would be perfect. I could see Jack and experience all the interest and excitements of London, how absolutely wonderful.

Aloud, I said, "Oh Tante, what a lovely opportunity. Does she say when this is likely to be?"

Jane turned the letter over. "Ah yes. She is talking about early March. How nice, just think, you will probably be able to visit the Great Exhibition at the Crystal Palace in Hyde Park."

When do you think your baby will be due, Tante?"

"Oh, don't worry about that, dear."

"But I do worry about it. I would like to be with you then."

"Well, Dr Brightside says it will probably be the first week in April. So early March would be all right, wouldn't it? But, really Adèle," Jane extended her hand and touched my arm. "You can't live your life in step with mine. You are an independent young lady."

"Even independent young ladies may feel they have responsibilities and duties to those they care about."

We looked at each other and then laughed at our solemn faces.

"I must say. It is very gratifying to find that you have grown up with such a strong sense of duty, my love, but life is for living, and I think you should take your opportunities when they present themselves. I have plenty of people here, including a loving husband, to care for me."

So, it was agreed that Jane would write back to Diana and confirm a suitable date in early March for my visit.

CHAPTER 10

"And what is all this?" queried Mr Rochester in a tone of mock severity to his wife, as he entered the breakfast room, on a sunny morning in mid-February. His usual place at the head of the table was surrounded by small, brightly coloured and beribboned packages and envelopes, all addressed to him. Another much larger parcel was leaning at the side of the table.

Mrs Rochester gave a little laugh. "Just wait there, Edward dear, we have a few surprises for you." So saying, she left the room.

Then the door burst open and in came Fairfax and Johnny, wearing their best blue suits with white collars, each holding the end of a banner, which bore the words 'HAPPY BIRTHDAY PAPA' in large rather shaky letters. Their mother walked behind carrying a dish on which was a large birthday cake, inscribed with 'Happy Birthday Edward' and I followed, bearing a tall vase full of spring flowers, whose fragrance pervaded the room.

The little boys propped their banner along the back of the sideboard, and before Mr Rochester could say anything else, his little sons rushed to him and smothered him with kisses, which he returned. Jane then went to him to give him a fond kiss, and I approached him, rather nervously, and gave him a quick peck on the cheek and my birthday wishes.

Mrs Tompkins then entered carrying a tray containing a selection of Mr Rochester's favourite dishes, such as devilled kidneys, kippers, eggs and bacon and so on. She gave a bobbing little curtsy and a quick "'appy Birthday, sir," before exiting the room.

"What a conspiratorial family you are!" he exclaimed. "I have not been aware of one hint of this."

"We hope it pleases you, Edward," said Jane.

"I am very touched, my dear."

"And now," said Jane, "We will have this lovely breakfast, and you will open all your presents and greeting cards."

"And what would you like to do today, papa?" said Fairfax, as he ate his breakfast.

"Perhaps you would like a drive to Hockly Hill, Edward? It is a beautiful day, and the views from there are very fine. We could take an al fresco luncheon."

"A capital idea, my love," said her husband, helping himself to the dishes on the sideboard. "No lessons today, boys; we shall all have a holiday and spend the time together."

There were squeals of delight from the children.

Once breakfast had been consumed, Mr Rochester started to open his birthday presents and greetings cards. A card each from Fairfax and Johnny, drawn by them, a new cravat, handkerchiefs, and a silver watch and chain from Jane, some embroidered book marks from me, and various other small gifts from members of the household. Finally, the only parcel left unopened was the one leaning against the table.

"And what about this one?" cried Fairfax. "I am longing to see what it is."

Jane produced a pair of scissors fro the sideboard drawer, and Mr Rochester cut the string around it and removed the brown paper wrapping. It was a painting.

"It has been stored in the cellar at Ferndean all this time. I had it cleaned and reframed, Edward," explained his wife.

Mr Rochester held the painting close to his face and studied it with his one good eye.

"Why, it is a portrait of my mother, Elizabeth, when she was very young, prior to her marriage to my father. She was Miss Elizabeth Henly then." He turned to Jane, "I thought it had been destroyed in the fire at Thornfield."

"No, fortunately John managed to rescue it, and it has been at Ferndean ever since. Lean it against the wall, Edward, so that we can all see it."

Mr Rochester did as he was bid, and we all looked at the portrait with interest. It was of a young and beautiful girl of about my own age with dark ringlets, which lay over one creamy shoulder. She wore a red dress, low cut, as was the fashion of the day. She was seated underneath an old tree and a smile played about her sensitive mouth. I could see that her eyes were hazel in colour.

"Do you recognise that tree, Edward?" asked Jane softly.

"Why, yes, it was the self-same horse chestnut which you and I used to sit beneath and which got blown down in that frightful storm." He continued to look at the painting. "I never knew her, of course," he said reflectively, "She died shortly after I was born."

"Does... does she remind you of anyone, Edward?" his wife enquired. She gave me a quick significant glance.

Before he could answer this, the door opened and in came Mrs Tompkins with her tray to clear away the breakfast things. She looked at the portrait and gave a gasp. "Oh, what a lovely portrait. Is it Miss Adèle, sir?"

"Miss Adèle!" exclaimed Mr Rochester. He looked again at the portrait, but said nothing else.

"Mrs Tompkins has noticed it, Edward. Do you really see no likeness?"

My guardian gave a "Hrmph" and then said "Of course not; nothing like, nothing like."

I studied the painting myself and had the strong sensation of looking into a mirror. Miss Henly's face was indeed very like mine, although her colouring was different. She was dark, whereas my hair was golden, but her eyes were hazel, like mine and of a similar shape. However, I knew that I could say nothing. Recognition had to come from Mr Rochester, and he was determined not to see it.

Jane gave a little sigh, but then continued brightly, "I thought we could have it in the drawing room."

"If you like, my dear, if you like." He appeared to dismiss the subject. "Now boys, let us all go and get ready for our outing. I think we should take the carriage for you, my love, and for Adèle and the boys. I will ride White Star."

The journey to Hockly Hill, with William driving the coach and Mr Rochester trotting along at our side on the fully recovered stallion, White Star, was a delight. The sun cast its golden radiance over the landscape, bringing out all the varied colours of tree, grass, and shrub.

The trees were still bare of leaves, but their graceful shapes were silhouetted against the delicate blue of the sky and fleecy white clouds, on this warm, early spring day. In the distance, we could see the misty purple outline of the moors. Now and then, we glimpsed the half-concealed presence of a cottage, amongst surrounding trees or hedges, giving the scene a feeling of homeliness.

We reached the foot of Hockly Hill and began to follow the lane which wound round and round until it reached the top. At the summit was a flat area of grass, where we all descended, and Jane, aided by William, began to organise a suitable place for our luncheon. The boys began to play hide and seek amongst the trees, until called by their mother, and we all sat down on various logs and tree trunks, which were dotted about, to enjoy our repast, which included freshly baked pasties, kept hot from the oven by thick cloths, home made bread, cheese, and apples.

Leaving William to clear the remains of our meal away, we all began to wander around looking at the views.

"You can just see Southlands from here," said Mr Rochester, applying a telescope to his good eye. He then began to point out other features of the landscape, spread before us like a contoured map, and we all squinted through the telescope, in turn.

Afterwards, Mr Rochester proposed a walk to a further vantage point, where other views could be seen. He and Jane set off arm in arm, while I followed and the boys gambolled around us playing hide and seek, like two little puppies. I think we all felt the delight and relaxation of this expedition on such a lovely day.

At last there were signs that the short afternoon was coming to a close and the sun began to sink into a vivid orange glow in the west, blending with the soft pastel shades of evening. Dramatically, dark purple clouds sailed like ships across this heavenly sea. We all gazed in rapture at the glory of the sunset and then retraced our steps to the carriage. Horses and carriage then bowled us home along verdant lanes, with hedgerows full of the twitters of nesting and mating birds.

When we reached Southlands, we were surprised to see a strange carriage sitting at the front door. As we entered, Mrs Tompkins approached and advised us that we had a visitor. My heart leaped. Could it be Jack returned with some new piece of information? But no…

"Mr James Boulding is in the library, sir."

"I do not recall the name," said Mr Rochester.

"This is his card, sir," said the housekeeper, handing it to him.

"It is someone I met in Wolden," I remarked indifferently.

Jane glanced at me curiously.

"I have no idea what he wants, but I think I will go up to my room. If I am needed, I will come down."

I made my escape as quickly as I could, my thoughts seething with unpleasant possibilities. Was it about the concert? I made up my mind that, whatever he said, I was not going to take part. I wanted nothing further to do with him.

Supposing, however, it was a proposal of marriage? Mary Wharton had said he was looking for a new wife. I flew to Madame Grevier's 'Little Book of Etiquette' and feverishly thumbed through the pages, until I found 'Marriage Proposals'.

There was a great deal about the preparation that the hopeful suitor should make. That is, speak first to the young lady's parents and establish his suitability in terms of prospects and position, clearing the air of any objections they may have. The proposal should take place at a private interview between the suitor and the young lady, and it seemed that she had three options:

If the answer was to be a firm 'Yes', then I was advised to seek no further and the writer wished her every happiness.

If the young lady was not sure, she should request more time to get to know the gentleman and perhaps an interval should be proposed by her, after which she may be able to give her answer.

If the answer is a firm 'No', then one should be definite, but polite, using such phrases as: 'While I am sensible of the honour you do me, sir, I regret that the answer must be no. Then, if she wishes she could give a reason, such as: 'Because I do not feel we are well suited,' or 'Because my parents object to your proposal and I must follow their wishes,' or 'Because my heart is already engaged elsewhere'.

If he queries this, make it clear that you have a right to make a choice and do not wish to discuss it further. If he is a gentleman, he will not pursue it but should respect your decision.

If he persists, then, the advice was to 'LEAVE THE ROOM'.

There was a tap on my door. It was Daisy, the housemaid. "If you please, miss, Mrs Rochester asks you to join them for tea in the library."

My head was buzzing with Madame Grevier's advice as I tripped down to the library.

Tante Jane and my guardian were sitting drinking tea and making desultory conversation with Mr Boulding. As I entered, he was expounding some detailed theory of his own about a particular piece of music, to which his audience listened in glum silence. He looked as plump, well fed, and oily as ever.

His moist dark eyes slid away to me. "Ah, Miss Varens, how delightful to see you. I trust you are well?"

My manner and answer were cool and indifferent, as I briefly gave him my hand.

Mr Rochester stood up. "I hope you will excuse me, Mr Boulding, but I have some urgent letters to write." He bowed to his guest.

"Of course, of course, my dear sir." Mr Boulding also rose to his feet, giving a slight bow, as Mr Rochester departed.

Jane then told him briefly about our family excursion to Hockly Hill and extolled the lovely weather, beautiful views, and spectacular sunset, to which he replied politely, but without great interest.

Then, after ensuring that I had received a cup of tea and that Mr Boulding's cup had been replenished, she also rose, making some excuse about checking with Mary in the kitchen and left us.

It was obvious to me that this evacuation had been planned, and I sat on the sofa, sipping my tea with a sinking feeling, in anticipation of what would come next.

Mr Boulding got up and walked towards me, standing in front of me. "May I sit here, Miss Varens? I have something particular to say to you?" Without waiting for my assent, he sat down heavily on the sofa next to me. I moved along as far as I could, so that I was pressing up against the padded arm at the extreme end.

Mr Boulding assumed an expansive pose, with one arm laid nonchalantly along the back of the sofa, nearly touching my shoulder and I had the strong desire to shrink away even further.

"Miss Varens, I was most disappointed that you were unable to take part in my concert at the cathedral."

"Yes, sir, it was a pity, but I considered my duty lay here at Southlands."

"Very commendable, of course; however, the concert was a success, and we raised quite a large sum for our various charities."

"I am pleased to hear it, sir."

He leaned forward towards me. "Miss Varens, did you know that I am a widower?"

"Yes, Mrs Wharton mentioned the fact to me." I said this as indifferently as I could. I did not want to give him the impression that it interested me.

"I am in need of a wife to share my life and be a stepmother to my late wife's two little children."

"I hope you find someone suitable, Mr Boulding." And then I added wickedly, "I suppose you could always employ a nursery maid for the children."

"A nursery maid is not what I want!" he said with a touch of irritation. "I need a wife, Miss Varens. From the first moment that I saw you, I felt a strong attraction. Your beauty, your charm, and your wonderful voice have thrilled me. Will you be my wife?"

He was now on one knee before me, his hand seeking mine. I could smell the sickly perfume of his hair pomade.

I jumped up. I forgot all Madame Grevier's suggested wording about 'being sensible of the honour he did me'. In my panic, I reverted to my mother tongue. "Non!" I said loudly. "Non...nous ne sommes pas compatible. No, please excuse me." And, with that, I rushed out of the library.

I raced up the stairs to my room in a kind of frenzy and turned the key in the lock. But then I stayed there with my ear to the door panel, listening.

At first, I heard nothing, and then Mr Boulding's voice, followed by Mr Rochester's. The study door opened and closed. After about ten minutes, I heard Tante Jane's voice. The front door opened and then, to my relief, I heard carriage wheels on the gravel. He was gone.

I flung myself into a chair and tried to recover my composure.

There was a tap on the door. "Adèle, dear are you there? Can I have a word with you?" called Tante.

"Has he gone?"

"Mr Boulding? Yes, he has."

I opened the door. Jane took one look at my distressed countenance and took me in her arms. "What is it, Adèle? Did that man say something to upset you?"

"No, dearest Tante, but I cannot abide him, and he asked me to be his wife."

"Yes, we knew he intended to do so because he discussed the matter beforehand with Edward and myself. He said you knew him well and seemed very confident that you would accept him."

"Did he, Tante? I cannot think why. The last time we met, I discovered that he had been spying on me, and I told him my affairs were none of his business. However, he is so conceited, what in France we call 'suffisant', that it seems to have made no impression on him."

Jane laughed. "He was a little put out when he told Mr Rochester afterwards that your answer was a rejection, but he seems to think that you may come around to accepting him in the end."

I jumped up from my chair. "What on earth made him think that? I do hope that you and Mr Rochester have not encouraged him in this belief?"

"No, certainly not Adèle. I was not at all surprised at your answer to him, and I think Edward felt the same. Neither of us liked him. That suave overblown manner, that mean mouth, and those calculating eyes!"

"Oh, Tante," I gave her a hug. "You felt it too? I suppose he was just saving his face by saying that I would come around, and he is so conceited, he obviously thinks he is irresistible." We laughed.

"That is better," said Jane, studying my face. "You look much more cheerful now. Edward would like to see you in his study, when you are ready. Apparently, Mr Boulding said something else he wants to ask you about."

"I will come straight away," I said, and we went downstairs together.

I found Mr Rochester standing at the window of his study looking out at the misty evening.

"I understand you refused Mr Boulding's offer of marriage, Adèle?"

"Yes, guardian. I said 'no' in no uncertain terms. I do not like him. I find him rather repulsive, as a matter of fact."

"I am not surprised. He struck me as a self-opinionated bore. I am pleased you refused him. But he said something else, which I want to query with you."

"Yes?"

Mr Rochester took a seat at his desk, and I sat down on the chair beside it.

"He said that ...these are his words, he 'caught you having tea and flirting in an intimate way' with a man whom you introduced to him as Jack Whitaker, 'a family friend', but whom he later discovered was our coachman and footman and that he, I quote, 'was concerned for your safety', so he followed you both to the station and saw you take leave of Jack Whitaker in a 'very affectionate way', with Mr Whitaker kissing your hand. Is this true Adèle?"

CHAPTER 11

There was a fairly long silence, while I recovered from my surprise and considered my answer. I could feel my indignation rising at the thought that Mr Boulding, disappointed in my rejection of his proposal, should have had the spite to tell tales about me to my guardian. However, I did not blame Mr Rochester, because I knew that he had my best interests at heart.

I cleared my throat, "In essence, yes, but my meeting with Mr Whitaker was entirely accidental. It was not prearranged in any way. He was hurrying down from the County Court in Wolden, where he had been giving evidence, as we now know from his explanation to us all, as a Police Detective, presumably in conjunction with the case he had recently been working on in our area. I had about two hours before Mr Wharton was free to take me back to Lower Poppleton, and I was just exploring the town on my own. Jack, I mean, Mr Whitaker, had about thirty minutes to wait before he caught his train back to London and we bumped into each other on a corner in West Street. He invited me into a coffee house called Bingles, which was close by, for some refreshment and I saw no reason to refuse."

Mr Rochester nodded, a slight smile playing about his stern features, and I relaxed back into my chair and went on with my explanation. "Our conversation was initially about the fact that he had now left your employ, but that he was going to return to Southlands shortly, to tell us all what had been going on. He gave me little information about this, saying that he would wait until he had the full story to tell." I paused to recollect for a moment and then continued, "Then, I think we talked about my performance in 'The Messiah', and then I mentioned that I had received an invitation to take part in a concert in the cathedral in February, and I said there were various reasons why I wasn't keen to accept. One of these being, of course, that I wanted to be at Southlands to hear his explanation. And then it was that Mr Boulding butted in. He had seen us from the street, as we were sitting at a window table.

Mr Rochester nodded. He too leant back in his chair with his arms folded, as he listened to me.

"I introduced Mr Whitaker and later said that he was well known to myself and my family, which is surely true. I then made it clear that Mr Whitaker was in a hurry to catch his train for London. Jack, Mr Whitaker, took his departure, and I went with him, explaining to Mr Boulding that we had several things to discuss, on the way to the station."

"Hmm, all this sounds quite harmless to me. What happened then?"

"We walked down to the station. He gave me some indication of when he would be visiting Southlands and I said I would make sure I was there. We said Goodbye and …then…he kissed my hand." I closed my eyes and waited anxiously for Mr Rochester's reaction.

"Oh, did he?"

His tone was still quite mild and I hurried on, "Yes, because he could see I was upset by the fact that he had left your employment, sir, and would no longer be at Southlands in a permanent capacity." I leaned forward earnestly. "I assure you, sir, that at the present time there is nothing between Mr Whitaker and myself, other than friendship."

"But if, say, Robert or William had met you accidentally in another town, would you have accepted an invitation to have refreshments with them, or be upset if they told you they were leaving my employment? Not forgetting that, at that stage, you did not know that Mr Whitaker was anything other than a servant."

"I see your point, sir, but, in the first place, Robert and William are definitely servants and would have not considered it their place to issue such an invitation to me, whereas Jack knew he was not in that category, even if I was unaware of it. And, as to feeling upset, well…I must confess I do have a very high regard for Jack. I think his prompt and caring actions in rescuing Tante and myself in the incident at Ferndean, shows him to be an infinitely superior individual."

"I agree with you about the latter, my dear. However, the impression I am receiving from you is that, although there is nothing much between you except friendship at the present time, you would like it to be more."

"I admire and respect him, sir, particularly now that I know more about him from his visit to Southlands. I think he must be a very brave and capable young man."

"Was there anything else which occurred between you earlier which might make you think he has similar feelings about you, Adèle?"

Oh dear, I was going to have to confess that kiss in the snow. I knew my honest nature would not let me tell an untruth.

"I think he likes and respects me," I began tentatively, "but well, yes, we did kiss each other in the snow by the river." I rushed on. "It was when I was feeling upset by your anger with me over the Ferndean business. I felt you were very unfair and I went out in the freezing cold. I believe you sent him out after me, did you not, sir? He brought your very thick cloak and wrapped it around me. I turned 'round towards him and…we kissed…It sort of happened naturally, a kind of impulse by both of us. But then," I went on hurriedly, "We moved apart quickly, and he begged my pardon and said I was far above him, and I said I was not - thinking about my rather dubious background. And then we walked back through the snow together."

"Well, what you have told me sounds like the seeds of something, which may or may not develop into more, my dear. But do beware. You are a very young twenty-year-old, unversed in the ways of the world, and particularly men. My advice is, do not be too eager and forward. Let the next move come from him and then, if you spend any time together, do it in a circumspect way and try to find out as much as you can about him, before you take any sort of plunge and lose your precious little heart."

This speech was so kindly and understanding that it made me glow with pleasure. Mr Rochester was at last talking to me like a father and not as the sardonic master of Southlands, who had recently reminded me that I was not his daughter or any relation. Perhaps he was having a change of heart towards me. And I was pleased to note that his strictures and advice did not centre on wealth and position, but were about true feelings.

"However," he continued, "Jack Whitaker is a Scotland Yard Detective and can probably make a career in that profession, if he chooses, but I have no idea what he earns and whether he could support a wife, particularly one used to a good standard of luxury, like yourself." He gave a little chuckle. "Could he keep you in feathers, do you think?"

I laughed too, remembering my bent feather when I arrived at Christmas. Our whole conversation seemed to lighten.

"Not if he drives me the way he did when he collected me from the station, sir!" I answered merrily. "But, I agree there is a lot I do not know about Jack, I mean…Mr Whitaker. From what he has hinted, he has a considerable background other than being a Police Officer, some of which sounds at variance with his present job. But I would like to get to know him better, as you say, in a controlled way, as a friend. I am hoping that we can meet when I go and stay with Captain and Mrs Fitzjames in London."

"Yes, that would be a good opportunity. I will write to Captain Fitzjames and his wife and say that I approve of Mr Whitaker, should he come to call on you."

"Oh, thank you, guardian. You have relieved me greatly. You have been so understanding."

"Well, I have had some experience of being in love myself, and I do not think like a conventional Victorian guardian, that is, putting all the emphasis on money and status in society. It is what a man's character is, as much as what he does for a living, which is important."

That conversation will always stay in my heart as the moment when Mr Rochester and I became friends, and I thought of it as the start of a conversion in him, from thinking of me as the silly little child of the despised Céline, to a person who might, in time, be well regarded, perhaps even as his true daughter. But, of course, we had a long way to go yet.

*****

The weeks sped by, and the date in early March, given by Diana arrived. It had been agreed that I would go up to London by train. Mr Rochester was concerned that I should not travel alone, and he had enlisted the services of my old companion, Mrs Fairfax, who was to accompany me. Mrs Fairfax had been the housekeeper at Thornfield when Tante

Jane, then Jane Eyre, had come to be my governess, many years ago, and she had the care of me until Jane took over. She was now a lady in her upper sixties but quite spry and active. She had relations in London, and after she had stayed a night with the Fitzjames family, she would go on to them for a few weeks

I was used to Mrs Fairfax and felt at ease with her. Unfortunately, however, I had forgotten how trite and tedious her conversation could be. She had always taken the extremely conventional view of everything and had little understanding of anyone who did not completely conform to what she considered as normal. She irritated me by the way she disparaged the Rochesters' marriage, referring to the fact that Mr Rochester was so much older than Jane, and wasn't it a terrible tragedy about the fire at Thornfield and Mr Rochester's injuries? As if Mr Rochester was a miserable old cripple and a burden on his young wife.

I was quick to point out that, in my view, the Rochesters were an extremely well suited and happy couple, who loved each other dearly. "He may be twenty years his wife's senior," I said, crisply, "But surely it is better to have a shorter span of married bliss than, say, forty years of unhappiness, as is sometimes the case." I went on to remind her that Mr Rochester's sight had much improved and commented on how well he had adapted to his injuries. I also praised their loving relationship with their two little sons and how delighted I was that Jane was expecting another in April.

Faced with my partisan and vigorous defence, Mrs Fairfax fell rather silent, no doubt in a bit of a huff, and I do no think either of us was sorry when our journey came to an end at Kings Cross Station.

We took a cab to Tavistock Square, where the Fitzjames had taken rooms. Like all squares in that part of

London, substantial terraced houses surrounded on four sides by a pleasant well-kept garden, where in the warmth of a London spring, pale pink and white cherry trees bloomed.

Captain Henry Fitzjames and his wife, Diana, greeted us warmly, as did their two children, Harriet, a pretty little six-year-old with dark curls, like her mother and four-year-old Harry.

My room was at the rear of the house and looked into a small walled garden. In the majority of these houses, this is where the washing is hung out, but the Fitzjames had made some attempt to have a few flowers and shrubs and a place to sit in a sunny corner.

The excitement of the large city was all around me. It was like being part of a great machine, which never ceased, day or night. Echoes of this reached us faintly, but here in Tavistock Square, all was quiet, with only the occasional vehicle, or passer-by.

Mrs Fairfax stayed for only one night and then left after breakfast to visit her relatives in Fulham, which she could reach by omnibus. I kissed her before she left and said I was sorry if I had sounded indignant with her yesterday on our journey.

She looked at me with a smile. "On the contrary, my dear, it is nice to find a young person so appreciative and grateful for all the advantages they have been given. It does you credit. You mustn't mind an old woman's opinion; I have seen so much more of life than you. However, I think you are right about Mr and Mrs Rochester. They do seem to be a very happy couple with a lovely family and I wish them all the good fortune in the world."

Captain Fitzjames joined us for breakfast, and when Mrs Fairfax had departed, he said, "We thought you might like to go to the theatre this evening. There is a very good

show on at Covent Garden at present, called 'The Magic
Forest'. It has had quite a long run so far, all over the
Christmas period, and I gather people are still flocking to see
it. I can get tickets for tonight through a contact of mine.
Would you like to go, Miss Varens?"

I felt thrilled. "I would love to. What a good start to
my visit and, please, Captain Fitzjames call me Miss Adèle.
Miss Varens sounds so formal."

"Thank you, Miss Adèle, I will. I thought we could
have supper somewhere afterwards."

"That would be lovely."

He got up and kissed his wife. "Duty calls, my love.
I'll be back at the usual time and we'll all have an enjoyable
night out. "Oh, by the way," he put his hand into his jacket
pocket and produced a folded piece of paper. "Here is a
playbill for 'The Magic Forest' which will interest you both."
He handed the poster to Diana.

We called "Goodbye" as he left the room.

Diana opened the playbill and spread it out on the
table and I went around and looked over her shoulder. The
colours were bright yellow and misty blue. There were
various figures of animals, such as cats, mice, and frogs
dotted over the page. A mysterious long fingered hand with
sharp-looking fingernails held a slim stick or wand, the end
of which seemed to sparkle against the surrounding misty
blue. The words, 'The Magic Forest' were emblazoned in
lengthy spidery black letters. But then, I gave a little gasp of
surprise. The names of the principle actors were listed, and
the name of the producer and director and to my
astonishment, I read 'J.D. WHITAKER'.

"What is it, Adèle?" asked Diana, her dark eyes
looking at me curiously.

"J.D. Whitaker!"

"Yes, he's a well-known entrepreneur in the theatre. Captain Fitzjames tells me he has been around for years. He is famous for his exciting and highly creative productions. Usually they are fantasies like this one. He seems to specialise in the mysterious and the magical. They say the special effects on the stage in this production are almost unbelievable. He nearly always has music too and poems and songs. Have you heard of him?"

'Whitaker,' I thought to myself. 'It is probably just a coincidence. Jack is J.R., so it cannot be him. In any case, this must be a much older man. After all the name Whitaker is fairly common.'

Intrigued by my silence, Diana asked, "Are you all right, Adèle?"

I laughed. "Perfectly, it was just the name. It is the same as…someone I know, that's all. But it certainly is not him." And then I added, "It sounds really exciting and interesting. I'm looking forward to it very much, Mrs Fitzjames."

"Oh, please call me Diana, as I call you Adèle," said my hostess. "Incidentally, I am pleased to say that Henry's new job at the Admiralty has introduced us to a really good social life. Loads of people have left cards. He works with a really nice group of young men, who are always organising something and inviting us to their parties, picnics and social gatherings."

She gave me a rather saucy look. "If you are looking for a husband, Adèle, you will be spoilt for choice."

I laughed. "Not really, at the moment, Diana."

"So you say, so you say," she said darkly. "But some of these young gallants are really handsome and well connected. You could be tempted."

*****

The evening, as promised, was very enjoyable and exciting, initially.

I wore my cream lace over amethyst satin and an amethyst necklace and earrings. I also had a cloak in white fur and there were white flowers in my hair. Diana wore a very becoming dress of plum satin, with a dainty ruby pendant and earrings.

Captain Fitzjames and two of his young male colleagues from the Admiralty accompanied us, all attired for the evening.

Immediately, I entered the foyer of the theatre, with all its rich velvet trappings, the atmosphere of excitement and anticipation took hold of me. Our party was only one of several hundred, who were all milling about in their gorgeous evening satins and silks, enhanced by the glitter of jewels.

Captain Fitzjames shepherded us efficiently to the auditorium and we were soon sitting in our places at the front of the dress circle. I was between Diana and a young man called Jonathan Baxter, with blond hair and side whiskers. He was very charming and attentive, ready to provide any service I required.

I was soon looking at the programme which Mr Baxter had obtained for me. I saw there was a description of the history of J.D. Whitaker, which I did not have time to read then, but promised myself I would peruse later. In the meantime, I looked around at the sumptuous setting. The decoration of the proscenium arch in scarlet and gold, the scarlet velvet curtains, with their gold trimmings, the golden figures on the front of the circle and the boxes, which, if not in perfect taste, created an atmosphere of lavish luxury.

Then I looked at the audience. They were young and not so young with quite a number of children, even although this was an evening performance. Diana had said her children were a little too young for the theatre as yet, but these were probably being allowed to stay up late as a special treat. The noise of so many voices, all chattering away to each other was deafening, but, at last, there was a hush as the orchestra started up, and the lighting was dimmed. All eyes were concentrated on the stage.

Then, the curtain rose slowly to reveal a dark and misty forest, in the middle of which stood the commanding figure of a sorcerer, with his long purple and silver robes and tall pointed hat.

The story was quite a simple one, designed to be amusing, rather than horrific. The sorcerer, rushed off his feet, needs an assistant, as he wants to go on holiday. He picks a likely looking fairy and gives her basic instructions about certain spells which needed to be done regularly. The assistant tries these out, while he is away, successfully, but then becomes ambitious and finds his Book of Spells. She endeavours to turn an ugly fairy into a pretty one but turns her into a rabbit. Her experiments on others are equally disastrous and all these unfortunate creatures are demanding to be changed back, as they were. Finally, she manages to turn her lover into a lion, and he roars around the stage, threatening everyone. The sorcerer returns and sees the devastation his assistant has created. He snatches the wand and everyone is returned to his or her original shape. The fairy assistant is admonished severely, but in the end, she is forgiven and marries her lover in a grand finalé and everyone lives happily ever after. It was a childish piece, but done in such a humorous way, and the special effects of the spells were so well managed that everyone was delighted with it.

There were also some comic and some soulful songs, in which I took a particular interest.

During the first interval, Mr Baxter asked me if I would like some refreshment, perhaps an ice cream. I was feeling very warm in the overheated atmosphere and agreed thankfully. I fanned myself and looked around with my opera glass at the many faces on either side of the curving dress circle and at the tiers of boxes. Then, I was rather startled to see another pair of opera glasses, some distance away, which appeared to be trained on me.

As soon as the individual concerned realised I had seen him, he put down his glasses and turned away to his companion, but not before I had recognised him. It was Jack Whitaker.

I raised my hand to wave excitedly, but he turned right around, with his back to me, to talk to the lady sitting next to him. From this distance I could not see detail clearly, but she was dark haired and her face looked young and beautiful. She wore a black dress and over her hair, a sparkly black mantilla. There was a glittering necklace around her throat.

A shaft of jealousy pierced me. Something I had never experienced before, and I felt the delight of the evening beginning to evaporate. Why had he ignored me? Who was Jack's beautiful companion? Perhaps she was a sister? Or could she be just a chance acquaintance? But somehow, I did not think so.

CHAPTER 12

For the rest of that evening, I struggled to appear normal and cheerful, but I felt as if a great weight was pressing down on me, and I fear I lost my usual vivacity. Diana kept enquiring if I felt unwell. To which I replied that I was perfectly well, but that I had a slight headache.

The supper afterwards, at an expensive restaurant, which sparkled with crystal chandeliers, immaculate white table linen, gleaming cutlery and attentive, deferential waiters, would have been enjoyable, but I was like the ghost at the feast. Eventually, I whispered to Diana that my headache was worse and that I would like to leave. Jonathan Baxter, overhearing this, quickly offered to escort me home by hansom.

He was so kind and attentive. As we parted in Tavistock Square at the Fitzjames' front door, I expressed my concern that I had spoiled his evening.

"Far from spoiling my evening," he said gallantly, "You have enhanced it. I hope I may call on you again in a few days, perhaps, when you are feeling better?"

What else could I reply? "Yes, of course, Mr Baxter. I will let you know when I have recovered." Knowing full well that I was unlikely to do so – unless of course, things went completely wrong between Jack and myself.

Several days passed, during which I worried and fretted about the incident at the theatre and its meaning. I also studied the details about J.D. Whitaker in 'The Magic Forest' programme, thinking that there might be a clue. I wondered if there could be a connection with Jack. It said that J.D.

Whitaker had been a theatrical director and producer for twenty years, with many successful productions to his credit. His origins lay in the sphere of the circus, and he was a member of the famous Whitakers Circus family. It was here that he had learned many of the arts of illusion, and the theatrical effects which we enjoyed in his productions. What could I make of this? Nothing very definite; could Jack be related to this circus family? Not that it helped me at all in understanding why he had snubbed me at the theatre.

In the meantime, Diana had arranged all sorts of other entertainments for my pleasure. Unfortunately, The Great Exhibition was not due to open until May, but there were visits to museums and galleries to study great paintings, attendance at concerts, where I heard wonderful music, and to the opera, in which I could feel particularly fascinated, in view of my own abilities in that direction.

Before I left Southlands, I had written to Jack at the address in Lambeth he had given me, but I had received no word from him. However, just as I was beginning to despair of ever seeing him again, Diana and I were in the drawing room one afternoon, when Ellen, the housemaid, brought in a card on a salver.

Diana picked it up. "Oh, how nice, Adèle, it is Mr Whitaker. Show him up, Ellen."

Mr Whitaker! Did she mean Jack, or this other theatrical Whitaker? Or was it someone else?

I was breathless with tension and anticipation. The door opened and...in walked Jack. He was smartly and fashionably dressed and quite at his ease. To my surprise, he greeted my hostess like an old friend.

Seeing my puzzled expression, Diana laughed. "Mr Whitaker, I really must explain the situation to Miss Varens." She turned to me. "You see, dear, Henry and I know Mr

Whitaker. When he was in his normal job as a detective at Scotland Yard, we had reason to consult him on a certain matter and Henry and Mr Whitaker then discovered that they both belonged to the same gentleman's athletic club near Piccadilly and they are now firm friends." She nodded and smiled at Jack, adding, "I believe they see each other at their club frequently, and he often visits us here."

At Diana's invitation Jack seated himself in an armchair and took up the story. "When I realised that they knew Mr and Mrs Rochester and were going to spend Christmas at Southlands, I had to warn Captain and Mrs Fitzjames about my little subterfuge in advance, so that they could act as if they had never seen me before. Otherwise, they might have given the game away. I also let Mr Rochester know of the situation."

"I am totally amazed," I said, my thoughts in complete confusion. I supposed that no harm had been done by this little deception, but it just added to an already extraordinary state of affairs.

"I believe you have now explained everything to the folk at Southlands, have you not, Mr Whitaker," enquired Diana.

"Yes, Mrs Fitzjames, I have, and as Miss Varens knows, I managed to clear up the mystery surrounding an unpleasant incident at Ferndean, which had upset both Mrs Rochester and Miss Varens greatly."

"Yes, I heard about that."

"Can I now hope that you are who you say you are, Mr Whitaker, and that you do not have some other surprising disguise up your sleeve?" I think my tone was verging on the indignant as well as the sarcastic.

No doubt, in order to pour a little oil on the waters, Diana interjected quickly. "I have had a letter from Mr

Rochester saying that you might be calling, Mr Whitaker, and," she gave me a significant look, "that he has no objection and thinks that Miss Varens would be pleased to see you."

I felt Jack's quizzical gaze on me and looked away hastily, a blush suffusing my cheek.

"You are always very welcome here, Mr Whitaker," said Diana, getting up. "But I have a few words to say to Cyril, our footman, so I will leave you both alone to...talk over old times."

When Diana had left us, for a few seconds, I felt bereft of speech and remained silent.

Jack continued to look at me in a meaningful way. "To answer your question. Yes, I am who I say I am at the moment, but my job quite often requires me to dissemble. However," He gave me a merry smile, "if I feel a new disguise coming on, I will be sure to let you know."

My cool manner melted away at this, and I laughed. "Thank you, sir, but you must admit that you are a very mysterious sort of person."

"I freely admit that I may seem so to others, but I promise you that from now on, I will always try to be open with you, unless of course the situation demands complete secrecy, even from you."

Changing the subject," he continued, "did you enjoy the play at Covent Garden last Tuesday?"

I felt pleased that he had raised this, which was uppermost in my mind. 'Let us hope he means what he says.' I thought. "Very much, Mr Whitaker, I noticed you were there as well, sitting further along the Dress Circle from me, and I was just about to wave to you when, although I thought you had seen me, you turned away without acknowledging me." I could not help slight indignation creeping into my voice, as I said this.

"Yes, I am sorry if I offended you. I feel I must explain, Miss Adèle."

"Very well,"

"I was with a woman, an informant, from whom I hoped to gain some useful knowledge, to help me with an investigation I am making at present."

"A woman, surely you mean a lady? She was young and beautiful and very well dressed."

"No, I say 'woman' advisedly. She is no lady. She comes from the underworld of Naples. She is as hard as that brass fender, and although youthful in appearance, she is years older than her actual age in experience. She moves in circles where the most heinous crimes have been committed. She herself would think nothing of cutting the throat of anyone who crossed her. She is as dangerous as a viper."

I felt myself pale at this description, and my hand flew to my throat in horror. "But Jack, Mr Whitaker, why are you associating with her?"

"Because, as I have said, she has information that I need. I took her to the theatre, the best show in town and then, afterwards, to supper at the best restaurant to 'soften her up'. When I saw you, my first concern was that I did not want her to know of our connection, or anything about you. She can be extremely treacherous. As it is, I am perturbed about what she tells me and very concerned for your safety."

"My safety, what on earth can you possibly mean?"

Jack moved to a seat on the sofa next to me. "Mr Rochester has told me of your correspondence with the Contessa Valdini, who is your mother, Céline Varens. I believe you thought she was dead until you heard of her recent marriage to Count Valdini. I understand she has invited you to visit her in Italy to meet her and her new husband?"

"Yes, that is correct."

"Mr Rochester has asked me to find out more about Valdini, before you venture to Italy."

"I knew he was going to check on him further," I interjected softly. So now I knew who was the 'source' of information my guardian had in mind.

"Well, this woman, my companion of three evenings ago, was an associate of Valdini's. In fact, she was his mistress, one of many. He is the sort of man who has a number of women in his life, both in Italy and other places. This person, her name is Marietta, by the way, considered herself to be his principal lover and confidante. The marriage to your mother has put her nose severely out of joint. She is furious and very jealous and is swearing that she will get her own back on him." He paused and looked earnestly at me, his velvet brown eyes full of concern. "When such a woman vows revenge, she is probably contemplating something extremely unpleasant."

"But how am I involved in this?"

"I am afraid, my dear Miss Adèle, the danger is with Valdini. My investigations show that he is a very bad character indeed. He has married a succession of wealthy wives over the past few years, all of whom have died in mysterious circumstances and their fortunes appropriated by him. Whether or not he really is a count, we do not know, he certainly styles himself as such. Marietta tells me there is word in the underworld that if you visit your mother, it is likely that you will be kidnapped and held for ransom, or even forcibly married off to his son and that Mr Rochester will be subject to heavy demands for money to ensure your safety. He is using your mother, his newly married wife,

155

Céline, as bait to tempt you to Italy." He paused and took my hand.

I sat, shocked and horrified by these revelations.

"There is also another aspect to Valdini which I am trying to ascertain as well. I strongly suspect that Albert Eales and Valdini could be one and the same person. Eales, who is the master criminal in the United Kingdom underworld; the leader of the gang which perpetrated all those jewel thefts and murders. As I told everyone at Southlands, when I made my explanation, Albert Eales, 'The Eel', is a master of disguise and language and could easily be passing himself off as Count Valdini.

"But what evidence is there?"

"A great deal of circumstantial evidence, Miss Adèle. Dates when Eales was out of the country which coincide with Valdini's activities. For example, the period of his courtship and marriage to your mother, and of course, evidence from Marietta, who has been involved with him in this disguise and others. His appearance is not dissimilar to Eales, give or take a moustache and different hairstyle, together with an Italian accent, which could easily be assumed. Once we have Valdini in custody, Marietta can absolutely verify whether or not he is Eales."

"Do you have any sort of plan to thwart and arrest Valdini?"

"I have, but it depends on a number of things, including you."

"Me?" I was feeling breathless not only with the horror of these disclosures but also with a sensation of something like excitement.

"Miss Adèle," He looked out of the window, "It is a pleasant day, would you care to take a stroll with me, so that we may discuss this further?"

I looked into his face in the hope that his eyes would communicate more than just my usefulness as a witness in his plan, and I felt satisfied that they did. "I would like that very much, Mr Whitaker." I rose from the sofa. "I will go and inform Mrs Fitzjames that we are taking a walk in the sunshine and collect my parasol."

I found Diana hovering at the back of the passage leading to the kitchen quarters.

"He has suggested a walk," I whispered.

"A nice idea on such a lovely day. Invite him to dinner. We dine at half past five." She handed me my bonnet and parasol from the hallstand.

"Yes, I will, but he may be too busy with his police duties."

"Well, if not this evening, then tomorrow. I leave it to your judgment."

I put on my bonnet in front of the hall mirror and returned to Jack, and we passed out through the front door. I raised my parasol and took his proffered arm. I had the delightful feeling of being with the man I admired and whom, I sensed admired me. This was the first time we had walked together as equals, our relationship approved by friends and family. It carried with it a sense of belonging, which I had rarely experienced before.

"Let us take a turn about the square garden," he suggested.

The sun shone down on us, and the spring flowers in the centre of the garden glowed like jewels. Scent from the cherry tree blossoms wafted towards us on a slight breeze.

We walked slowly, not conversing. I was savouring the moment. The world had suddenly become a delightful place for me. I wondered if he felt the same. I stole a look at his handsome profile, so dear to me.

He turned his head and gave me a smile, full of tenderness and warmth. "What were your thoughts when you knew what I really am?" he said lightly.

"Astonishment, of course, Mr Whitaker, but also admiration. You played your part very well as a footman and coachman, except, of course, for your rather violent driving at times." I laughed as I said this. "It must have been difficult for you to assume such a lowly position, but you carried it off extremely well and got on excellently with everyone at Southlands, from Master and Mistress down to all the servants."

"Not really so difficult, Miss Adèle. I am a Cockney, born and bred, not a gentleman, and I have lived with very ordinary working class people most of my life in Lambeth, which is where I first saw the light of day. We Cockneys are a warm-hearted friendly lot, and we get on with most levels of society. We don't tolerate snobbishness, though. But Mr and Mrs Rochester are not snobs. They appreciate people for what they are, not what class they come from."

"Strangely enough, Mr Rochester said very much the same to me, the last time we spoke."

"He is a very good man and a true gentleman."

"I have the impression that you enjoy your job as a police detective."

"Yes, I do. My previous background has given me many contacts, which are very useful when it comes to investigating crime. I feel I know quite a lot about how the criminal mind works. However, it is a tough job with long hours. I am often in danger from one villain or another and have had some near squeaks. It is really a job for a single man, not a married one. There is little chance of family life, and wife and family could be in a constant state of anxiety."

"I suppose it would depend on the character of the wife."

"My married colleagues are all agreed that it is no life for their wives, and some are seeking to leave the police force for a safer way of earning a living."

"I suppose that would apply equally to a wife married to a soldier or sailor, liable to meet their deaths in war, or in the case of a sailor, by drowning at sea. Take Mrs Fitzjames, for example. Captain Fitzjames has to leave his family for long periods to go to sea with all the dangers associated with that."

"Yes, I appreciate what you say, but the soldier is part of an organised army and wars do not occur all the time. As to Captain Fitzjames, you will notice he has sought to find a post in the Admiralty, rather than stay on active service, mainly because of his wife and family."

"Would you want to be like him then, Mr Whitaker, taking a position in an office, organising other people to do things, rather than engaged yourself in apprehending criminals and actively defeating crime?"

He laughed. "Quite frankly, no. It would not suit my temperament at all. I like adventure, excitement, and action."

There was a bench seat at the turn of the path, half hidden by shrubbery. Jack led me to it and we sat down.

My spirits were beginning to fall, following this discussion, and as I took my seat next to him, I turned to look him full in the face. "So, Mr Whitaker, is the answer for you to stay single and independent, without a wife and family?"

"Fortunately, for me, there could be an alternative. A profession on, the whole, not dangerous, but creative, in which there is still plenty of excitement and adventure. However, financially not so secure as what I do now, but with good possibilities of enrichment, if luck were on my side, as well as a loving wife."

I stiffened and raised my chin a little. "You are talking in riddles, sir. Are you going to enlighten me?"

"I will, but all in good time." I felt his hand give my shoulder a little squeeze. "My own preoccupation at the moment is to capture the arch villain, Albert Eales, possibly alias Count Valdini and put him (or them) behind bars and then I will be able to think more clearly about...other matters."

I could not help feeling disappointed at his apparent refusal to reveal his true feelings for me. Was I the 'loving wife' he envisaged? And what was the 'alternative' profession to which he referred. However, I tried to appear unaffected, as I enquired, "So what is the plan, sir?"

He took his hand from the back of the seat and leaned forward, looking at me earnestly. "I believe you have received, or will shortly be receiving an invitation from Captain and Mrs Fitzjames to go with them on their trip to Naples?"

"It has been mentioned, but I want to return to Southlands to be present when Tante Jane's time is due, which is, I believe, mid-April. I cannot think of leaving before that. She will need my love and support."

"So, what date would you see as suitable for going to Naples with the Fitzjames?"

"Probably early May."

"Good, that will fit in very well. The plan, which has been discussed with my friends, Captain and Mrs Fitzjames, is that you and I should accompany them in H.M.S. Seafarer to Naples. Captain Fitzjames will take a carefully selected crew of men he can trust. I believe you have already met Lieutenant Jonathan Baxter?"

"Yes, I knew he worked with Captain Fitzjames at the Admiralty, but I did not realise that he was a naval officer. I liked him very much."

Jack gave me a quizzical look. "Not too much I hope?"

I smiled mysteriously, but did not reply. 'Let him wonder!' I thought.

"Lieutenant Baxter will be Captain Fitzjames' First Lieutenant on the ship. I will also have a trusted assistant in Sergeant Dick Holness, the one who posed as a stable lad at Southlands and one or two other police officers I can completely rely on.

"As you know, the trip is a sort of State visit, carrying an important titled individual, possibly a Royal prince or duke, to a meeting with the King of Naples. The objective, I am told, is to pave the way for a trade agreement. In his position at the Admiralty, Captain Fitzjames has been able to get the permission of the First Lord for our secret group to be transported in the same vessel at the same time." He paused and then added, "I am sure I do not need to say that all this is very confidential, Miss Adèle."

I clapped my hands. I felt alight with excitement. "Oh, it all sounds absolutely thrilling. Do not worry, Mr Whitaker, I will not breathe a word of it to anyone else." Then I had a sudden thought. "But, how do I fit into this plan?"

"You want to visit your long-lost mother and her husband, the Count and Contessa Valdini. You will write back to your mother proposing a visit to their home, wherever that is, and when we arrive in Naples, you will make this visit, accompanied by a trusted companion. We can see how things develop from there. I promise you, Miss Adèle, that at all times you will have my personal protection and that of a group of stalwart men, who will be hidden from the Valdinis, but ready to act as necessary. At the first sign of any criminal behaviour from the count, such as trying to abduct you, or using any force against you, I will have him. There will also be someone, who will be part of our group on the ship who will be able to confirm whether Valdini and Eales are the same individual. I intend to obtain a warrant for his or their arrest on the grounds of crimes we know have already been committed and anything else will be further evidence of villainy."

I sank back against the seat, amazed and breathless.

"However," he said, looking at me intently, "Captain Fitzjames and I can do nothing without your agreement."

"I...I feel I need time to consider all of this, sir and discuss it with the Captain and his wife. I should also consult my guardian."

"Yes, I understand, Miss Adèle, but how do you personally feel about it?"

"I must confess, sir, I feel thrilled at the idea. I wanted adventure and this is exactly what you are proposing. I care less about my physical safety than you seem to think, but I am confident that you will be there to protect me."

"I swear, on my life and all that is holy, that I will!"

For just a moment I thought he was going to embrace me passionately. His arm went around me and he gripped me firmly, but then, he kissed me gently on the forehead and released me.

We vacated the seat and completed our walk around the garden in silence, before returning to the Fitzjames' home. I passed on to him the invitation to dinner that evening, but he said he would prefer to leave it until tomorrow evening, to allow me time to think about it and discuss the matter with the gallant Captain and his wife.

CHAPTER 13

At five o' clock the following evening, Diana and I were in the drawing room awaiting the return of Captain Fitzjames from his Admiralty office and the arrival of our dinner guest, Jack Whitaker.

I had said little to Diana about my discussion with Jack on our walk around the square. I suspect she had been anticipating that Jack may have been going to declare himself and make me a marriage proposal, but as I said nothing, she must have assumed that this was not the case. However, now I decided to mention the possibility of my accompanying the Fitzjames family on their visit to Naples and I queried when they were likely to go, as this would depend on the date which the 'important personage' had given.

"I think it is likely to be in early May," said Diana. "Does your enquiry mean that you would be interested in coming with us, Adèle? How delightful, I believe southern Italy is really beautiful at that time of year."

"Yes, Diana, I would love to come with you and early May would be very suitable as Tante's baby is due in April."

"Have you spoken to your guardian about it?"

"Yes, at least he knows I am keen to travel and would deem this to be a very suitable expedition for me. I will, of course, talk to him further about it when I return to Southlands at the end of the month, but I see no problems in my going. After all, he and Tante Jane want me to lead an independent life, not beholden to them, although of course my income derives from Mr Rochester's generous arrangements."

He is such a good and principled man," I continued. "Some people think him difficult and bad tempered, but I would say that this is only superficial. Beneath his crusty exterior, he is really very kind and thoughtful to others."

The door opened and Captain Fitzjames walked in. He greeted his wife with a kiss and then turned to me. "I believe you and Jack Whitaker had a conference yesterday about the trip to Italy?"

"Yes, sir, that is so. I am very keen to accompany you."

"Your guardian will not object?"

"My guardian was a little concerned to find out more about Count Valdini, sir, and I understand from Mr Whitaker that he has made some investigations and has some doubts about Valdini. Mr Whitaker has explained to me that there could be possible dangers for me on this trip, but I have thought about it carefully and I very much want to come; particularly as it will involve meeting my mother, whom I had thought had died sixteen years ago. Mr Whitaker has given me his word that I will be protected at all times.

Seeing that there was still a look of uncertainty on his face, I continued, "I have just been explaining to Mrs Fitzjames how my guardian and his wife are happy for me to travel and see the world, as long as I am with suitable companions. I am sure he will see yourself and Mrs Fitzjames in that light, and I do not think he will raise any objections. The date in early May would be suitable."

There was still a frown on Captain Fitzjames' face and he looked quickly at his wife. "However, I think it will be as well if we have a full discussion about this after dinner. There are a few matters to be considered," he said.

The door opened again and Ellen announced Mr Whitaker, looking even smarter in dark evening clothes and sporting a pale pink carnation in his buttonhole. Greeting Diana and myself, he kissed each proffered hand and his manner was easy and relaxed.

The meal which followed was a very pleasant one. Both men were in high good humour.

Afterwards, Diana and I rose to leave the gentlemen to their port, but Captain Fitzjames called me back, as I was about to follow Diana. "Miss Adèle, Mr Whitaker and I have plans to make about the proposed expedition to Naples in May. Could I call on you shortly to be present at our discussion?"

"Of course, sir."

Sitting with Diana in the drawing room, I had difficulty concentrating on what she was telling me about some little incident with the children. I was on tenterhooks to return to the dining room. Despite my assurances and easy acceptance of inclusion in their excursion to Italy, I knew that this was not going to be a relaxed or carefree trip. We were going to encounter someone who could turn out to be a dangerous villain. I was already worried on behalf of my mother, Céline. What had Valdini in store for her? I wondered why he had married her, since Jack had told me Valdini was said to have espoused women of wealth and property. Had my mother acquired any worldly riches, or was it her connection with Mr Rochester, known to be a wealthy landowner, which had tempted him? The enquiry from me must have added incentive to his plans.

Cold shivers crept up and down my spine, but I lifted my head high. 'I will go on this trip,' I said to myself, 'To save my dear mother, if nothing else.' However, I hoped I might also get her to help me prove to Mr Rochester that he was my true father. I reflected that there seemed to have been some softening towards me. I had noticed, before I left

Southlands, that the portrait Tante Jane had given him of his mother, Elizabeth, now hung in his study opposite his desk. A sign that it had meant something to him, after all, although whether he recognised me in her features, so strongly denied at first, was difficult to say.

After about half an hour, Captain Fitzjames appeared at the door. "My love," he said to Diana, "Mr Whitaker and I would like to borrow Miss Adèle for a few minutes to finalise our discussion about the Italian trip."

"Of course, dearest," said Diana, her fingers busy threading a needle.

I followed the Captain back to the dining room. Jack was sitting at the dining table, his face alight with energy and his brown eyes glowing. As soon as I had seated myself at the table, he said, "Captain Fitzjames and I have had a serious discussion about our forthcoming trip to Italy, on which you have said you would like to come. Our main concern is for your safety, Miss Adèle. We do not think it will be suitable for me to accompany you to your interview with your mother, at which it is very likely that Count Valdini will be present. I do not think Valdini will tolerate me there. He may well recognise me as a police officer, especially if he really is The Eel, Albert Eales. He and I have drawn swords in the past. A mature female companion would be more suitable. Someone we can absolutely trust and who can stay by your side at all times, ready to take speedy action if the occasion demands it."

"I see." I said in a clipped voice. Why, after all he had said yesterday, was he proposing to desert me and delegate my protection to someone, a complete stranger, a woman. Surely, she would be unlikely to give me the strong defence I might need. A horrible thought flashed through my mind. Perhaps he was thinking of asking his acquaintance, Marietta, the 'evil' one, 'dangerous as a viper' to be my companion and protector!

Outwardly, I said, coldly, "Whom did you have in mind, sir?"

I glanced at Captain Fitzjames and was surprised to see his eyes were twinkling and that a smile hovered around his mouth. Surely this was no laughing matter?

"She is a very reliable lady, a family friend I have known all my life."

"She sounds as if she might be rather elderly, sir. Could she cope with the situation, if there was any violence?"

"I assure you, she will cope very well indeed, Miss Adèle."

There was a muffled cough from Captain Fitzjames. "Something in my throat, please excuse me, Miss Adèle." He rushed out of the room.

"When will I meet this lady?" I asked rather loftily.

"She will be onboard with us when we sail, and I will introduce you then."

"I see," my tone was icy.

Jack came round the table to where I sat and took my hand, raising me to my feet. "Oh, Miss Adèle... Adèle, you are so beautiful when you are angry." He put his arm round me and drew me towards him in an embrace. "Please forgive me, dearest one," he murmured into my ear and he kissed me on the cheek. "I know I should not be so bold with you, but I just cannot help it!"

Pushing him away, I said sharply, "Mr Whitaker, you have said nothing to me, so far, to indicate that you wish to be my accepted suitor, so I cannot permit these endearments." I could imagine Madame Grevier at my elbow, as I said these words.

"Do you feel nothing for me then?" His eyes were cast down contritely, but I thought I saw the corners of his mouth twitch.

"You are laughing at me!" I cried indignantly.

He took both my hands in his and kissed them, one after the other. "Please Adèle, do not be angry. All will be revealed eventually, and you will perhaps understand."

"I hope so, sir."

"Please call me, Jack, as you used to do at Southlands."

Mollified, I said his name, "Jack."

"And from now on, as we are to be shipboard companions, may I call you Adèle?"

"Very well."

"I love you, Adèle. I know you are well above me in every way, but I adore you."

"Oh, Jack," My heart was thumping and the ice was melting rapidly. "I love you too!"

I suspect Madame Grevier would have stalked away at this point.

He took me in his arms and this time there was no resistance from me.

When we returned to the drawing room together, our heightened colour and sparkling eyes must have given us away. We were both excited and voluble, and I think our hosts probably realised that something significant may have occurred in our relationship.

Afterwards, Diana came to my room for a late night chat. "Did he propose to you this evening, Adèle?" she said in her direct way, perching on the bed.

"Not exactly," I said, truthfully, sitting up, with my arms around my knees under the covers. "But he said he loves me and I said I love him. What he told to me yesterday, in confidence, was that he wants to get this trip over and arrest Valdini, who is possibly also a man called Albert Eales. Eales is the villain behind all those jewel burglaries in wealthy houses in various parts of the country and murders too, of unfortunate people who got in the way. Once he has achieved this, he is thinking of changing his career to something else which will be a more suitable occupation for a man contemplating marriage."

"I see," said Diana thoughtfully. "But has he given you any idea that he wants to marry you, Adèle?"

"Not really, in so many words, except that he says he loves and adores me!"

"Well, please dear, be careful. Remember your reputation is at stake. Do not allow anything too intimate, will you?"

"I think he is a man of principle, like Mr Rochester, Diana, and that I am safe with him."

"But, dear, are you safe from yourself? I know how easy it is to give way to desires."

I picked up a small volume from my bedside table. "Do not forget, Diana, I have Madame Grevier's 'Little Book of Etiquette' to guard and guide me."

We both laughed and said goodnight.

After that, as my 'accepted suitor', Jack was a frequent visitor at Tavistock Square. We often took an evening stroll together and he frequently accompanied us on theatre visits and dining out in London restaurants. Some of these occasions included Jonathan Baxter and other friends of Jack's. He seemed to have a wide circle of acquaintance including members of the theatrical and artistic professions, and I found these people fascinating and stimulating.

The weeks passed quickly and then it was time for me to return to Southlands to be with Tante Jane in the last stages of her confinement.

I had hoped that Jack would see me off at Kings Cross Station, but shortly before I was about to leave, I received a message from him:

"Dearest Adèle,

I am very sorry, but something has arisen and I have to attend an important meeting of Police Officers at Scotland Yard.

I hope you will understand, my love. You see this is what the life of a Police Detective is like and why it is not very suitable for a man with other responsibilities.

Write to me and I will to you. I look forward to greeting you back in Tavistock Square in May.

I hope everything goes well for Mrs Rochester. Please give Mr and Mrs

Rochester my kindest regards and good
wishes.

  With all my love,

    Jack"

This was a blow to me, but I tried not to let it affect me, at least in front of anyone else. Diana saw me off at Kings Cross Station, and we both expressed our excitement about the Italian trip and how much we were looking forward to it.

Once again, the train pulled out of the station and carried me far from Jack and all he meant to me. I must confess that I found that journey to Fremingham a dreary one. No longer was I brightly anticipating the continuation of my stay at Southlands. My heart was aching for Jack, his lively, enthusiastic, and humorous personality, and the warm feeling in his company, that we loved each other.

At last the train drew in at Fremingham, and I alighted to find, not Jack, of course, but middle-aged, sensible William, there to take my bag and drive me to Southlands in a sedate and orderly fashion.

CHAPTER 14

The first to greet me at the front door were Fairfax and Johnny, each giving me a big hug and kiss. Behind them stood Mr Rochester with a welcoming smile, which softened his rugged features.

We all went into the drawing room where Tante Jane sat in a comfortable chair with her feet on a little footstool. I could see that her shape had altered significantly under the loose gown that she was wearing. She gave me her hand and kissed me affectionately, welcoming me back to Southlands.

Of course, they all wanted to know about my visit to London. What I had done there and whom I had met. What concerts, plays, dances, social gatherings, and art galleries I had attended, and I was able to give them a very full account of it all.

When tea was over, Mr Rochester excused himself, as he had business to attend to in his study. The children were led off to bath and bed by Rose, their nursery maid, and I was alone with Jane.

"How are you, dear Tante? You look very well," I ventured.

"Oh, well enough, but I get very tired. However, I am lovingly looked after. Dr. Brightside is pleased with me. We think the baby will be born very soon now, possibly in two weeks."

"I am so glad I am here to help you, dearest Tante."

"Now," said Jane adjusting her position more comfortably. "Something happened in London, did it not?

More than just concerts, dances, and art galleries, I can tell from your bright eyes and the glow in your complexion."

I looked down at my hands. "Well, it did, and it did not, Tante."

"Heavens, what does that mean?"

"I…met Jack Whitaker in London."

"I guessed as much."

"Yes, most surprisingly, he is a friend of Captain Fitzjames and quite a frequent visitor to their home in Tavistock Square. They knew him before they came here at Christmas. It seems Mr Whitaker and Captain Fitzjames both belong to the same club. Apparently, Mr Whitaker asked them not to reveal the connection to us as it would have destroyed his disguise, although, I believe Mr Rochester knew already."

"Well, I must confess I had my suspicions about his real identity," laughed Jane.

I clasped my hands together nervously in my lap, leaning forward and looking at Jane intently. "Tante, he and I love each other and have spent a lot of time together."

"Oh, you are affianced to him then, my dear?"

"No, no, not yet," I said with a feeling of dread, anticipating her reaction.

Jane looked at me sharply. "He has not proposed. then?"

My heart was beating quickly. "No, but the thing is, Tante, he dearly loves me, but he does not feel his present job, as a Police Detective, is right for marriage. He works long hours, is rarely at home, and there is considerable danger in dealing with often desperate criminals."

Jane pursed her lips slightly. "So, what is his solution?"

"He wants to leave his job and take up another profession, which he feels will be more suitable for us both - creative, not dangerous, but where there is a great deal of scope for success and financial reward."

"And what is this 'profession'?" Jane's tone had become rather brisk.

"I know it sounds stupid of me, but I…I am not really sure what he means." I gazed at Tante earnestly, trying to make my point more clearly so that she would understand. "You see, I trust him absolutely and I know he has something very definite in mind, but he says he does not want to go into it because, Tante, there is one last mission he wants to accomplish before he leaves the police service, and then he feels he will be in a position to consider marriage."

"Highly intriguing!" exclaimed Jane, sarcastically. "Are you going to tell me what this 'last mission' is, or do you not know that either?"

I crossed the room and knelt beside her chair. "I know it all sounds very stupid and perhaps unsatisfactory to you, Tante. Yes, I do know what the project is. You probably remember Diana telling us that Captain Fitzjames was sailing to Naples on his ship to escort a special dignitary to Naples on a state visit to the king?"

"Yes, of course."

"Well, Jack and a group of his policemen are going too, because Jack is certain that the master criminal, Albert Eales, who organised the gang of jewel thieves who stole from the families around the country, has in fact left our country and is in that part of Italy, and he hopes to arrest him and bring him back to England to face trial." Then I hurried on. "And I want to go too because, as you know, my mother, Céline, now the Contessa Valdini, is living in Sorrento with her new husband, Count Valdini, and I want to visit her there to try and prove that I am Mr Rochester's real daughter."

"It all sounds very exciting, my dear, but are there any dangers for you?"

"Why should there be, Tante?" I said innocently. I had deliberately failed to mention the suspected connection between Eales and Valdini because I knew this would make the Italian excursion seem more hazardous.

"You will be well chaperoned by Diana and Henry Fitzjames, of course, and I suppose it will give you a chance to get to know Mr Whitaker better. Perhaps you will find out what it is he intends to do when he leaves the Police," she added pointedly, but with a little laugh. "What do you want me to tell Mr Rochester?"

"Exactly what I have told you, Tante."

"I believe, though, Mr Rochester has asked Mr Whitaker to investigate Count Valdini. Do you know whether Mr Whitaker has done so?"

This last question rather confounded me. What should I say? "I…I think he will be pursuing his enquiries on Count Valdini while he is in Italy, Tante."

"Another reason for his going there, I suppose. But do you know whether he has so far found anything detrimental about the count?"

"Nothing definite, Tante." Which was true, but I felt I was bending the facts a little in saying this! "But, Tante," I continued, "Jack and Captain Fitzjames will be there all the time to escort me and everyone else."

"I am sure, dear. Well, we'll see what Edward thinks about it. Oh, one thing I was going to say, when you were telling me all this, is that Edward says he can see a likeness between you and his mother, Elizabeth, after all. He often looks at the portrait, which he now has hanging in his study, as you know. He is also very impressed with the way you have developed, Adèle, and often remarks that he has felt quite close and in sympathy with you when you have been talking together."

These words were absolutely amazing. I felt a thrill of delight, but I also felt somewhat guilty about my little deception and hoped they would never discover it. I would be devastated if Mr Rochester should change his opinion of me.

"Oh, how lovely, how wonderful," I breathed. "I just need a little more evidence to present to him and have him acknowledge me as his daughter to be the happiest girl in the world."

Afterwards, I thought I might write to Jack and tell him of this conversation with Tante concerning Valdini, asking him to make his suspicions fairly vague. After all, Jack really did not know for certain that Valdini was Albert Eales. It was just a guess at present. Otherwise, Mr Rochester might forbid me from being part of the expedition and I did so dearly want to go.

The next few days wore on. I began to feel lonely. Jane was confined to the drawing room and bedroom, and Mr Rochester was busy either in the stables or in his study, with several visits to Ferndean. The old house was now under renovation with a complete overhaul of its damp course and plumbing, to make it suitable for letting. I understood that several of the larger trees near the house, which blocked a very fine view down to the river, were being removed or lopped. He also had many matters concerning his work as a J.P. which required his attention.

The spring weather was delightful with all the glowing early flowers such as bluebells and primroses appearing in Jane's new garden and the air full of birdsong. I often walked along the path beside the river, where frequently

I met a stately mother duck with a flotilla of fluffy golden-brown babies fanning out behind her. Further along, I would come across a pair of swans shepherding their little brood of signets. All was peace, beauty and fragrance.

Unfortunately, I was far from being at peace. I longed for Jack, his reassuring electric presence and tender love. I received occasional letters from him, but these were short and written in haste. In one of these communications he mentioned that he had taken the lease on a small furnished house in Lambeth near his parents, so that he had somewhere of his own. However, he did not mention the idea of living there with a wife, which made me feel even lonelier and more neglected. It seemed he was pursuing another case about which he was unable to write in detail, for security reasons. I wrote back, of course, but forbore to mention my own sad feelings. Our lives were so different that I began to think there might be a danger of our drifting apart.

One evening, after dinner, Jane, who had been sitting covertly observing me for some while, suddenly said, "You seem restless and unhappy child. What is the matter?"

"Oh, nothing very much, Tante," I lied.

"No, there is something. Are you feeling lonely? I am afraid I am not much of a companion at present."

A sudden idea came to me. "Well, I suppose I might be feeling just a little solitary, at present, Tante. I was wondering if you would allow me to invite a friend to stay, once the 'big event' is over?"

I then went on to tell her about Annie Thomas, whom I had met in the choir at Lower Poppleton. I had managed a quick visit to their farm before I left for Fremingham and had received a warm and kindly welcome from the Thomas family in their homely but well-kept farmhouse. I had been impressed too by the whole family's united and good-humoured industry in running the farm and looking after each other and their animals, in which Annie, despite her disability, did her share. I had thought to myself then that she ought to have a holiday, if I could arrange it and that I would invite her to Southlands as soon as I saw an opportunity.

I explained all this to Jane, who was sympathetic and interested. "You say she is a merry little soul?"

"Yes, merry and pretty and brave and she has a very good soprano voice, which she ought to develop, but I doubt that she ever will because they are not wealthy people."

"It is a shame about her disability," said Jane thoughtfully. "I wonder if something could be done for her."

"Again, Tante, there is no money for expensive operations."

"There could be," said Jane musingly. "However, my dear, if you like her, she must be nice. Yes, of course, once the baby is here, by all means invite her. I expect living on a farm, she is very used to young animals. She will be able to keep Fairfax and Johnny amused." We laughed.

*****

The baby came, as they sometimes do, in the middle of the night. I was awakened by much running up and down the corridors, whispered, urgent voices, the rattle of metal pans, and by Mr Rochester's deep voice, giving commands.

I got up immediately and looked out. Mr Rochester was standing by their bedroom door in his dressing gown. Mrs Tompkins, her arms loaded with clean towels, followed by Daisy with a container of hot water, were hurrying towards him.

"Have you sent William for Brightside and the midwife?"

"William's on his way to t' doctor, sir."

"Can I do anything?" I called.

"Yes, Adèle, come here and stay with Jane. She is in labour."

I went into the bedroom and approached the bed. The covers were thrown aside and Jane lay on her back, staring upwards. Every now and then she groaned as a contraction convulsed her fragile body.

I took her hand. "Tante, it is all right. I am here."

"Dearest child," she murmured, closing her eyes.

After an interval, there was the sound of carriage wheels and Mr Rochester called to me that the doctor and midwife had arrived.

Mrs Tompkins and Daisy both appeared carrying more pans of hot water.

"Shall I leave?" I asked. But nobody answered, so I stayed in the room awaiting instructions.

The door opened and the ponderous doctor and plump, motherly midwife bustled in. They seemed to know their business, so I withdrew.

I found Mr Rochester in the corridor. He looked haggard and strained. "Be within call," he said. "I am staying here until I know how things are going."

The wait was several hours. I could not return to sleep, so I lay on my bed, trying unsuccessfully to read. I looked out into the corridor several times. Mr Rochester was sitting in a chair by the bedroom door for some while, but then, when I looked again, the chair was empty.

I crept down the stairs, meeting Mrs Tompkins, on her way up. "How is it going?" I whispered.

"Quite well, miss, I think. It's taking a long time and Mrs is suffering, but the doctor says it's all quite normal. The baby is the right way round, at any rate!"

179

"Where is Mr Rochester?"

"Doctor persuaded him to go down and take a stimulant and try not to worry. He's in his study, miss."

Something impelled me. I knew I was taking the risk of rejection, but I approached the study door and tapped. There was no response. My heart in my mouth, I tapped again and then I turned the handle and went inside.

He was sitting at the desk, a decanter of brandy and a half-filled glass in front of him. His head was resting on his hand, his black locks hanging over his face.

He looked so desolate and lonely, that I could not resist the impulse. I crept over and laid my hand on his shoulder, gently, without a word. I fully expected him to fling my hand away and to get up, ordering me out of his sanctum. Instead, he put his solitary hand over mine.

"She is my life, my all, my reason for existence," he muttered. "If anything should happen to her…."

"I know, sir," I whispered. "But it will be all right. I know it will. God is merciful."

"Can you pray for her Adèle?"

"I…I will try, sir." I raised my head, closed my eyes and spoke aloud. "Dear Lord, in your infinite wisdom and mercy, be with our dearest Jane this day. Ease her pain and help her and the doctor and midwife to safely deliver a healthy baby. Keep our darling Jane safe for us, so that she may continue to live a long and happy life with her loving husband and children. For our Blessèd Saviour's sake, Amen."

Mr Rochester uttered a wail of anguish. "I do not deserve his mercy, Adèle. I have been wicked and deceitful in the past. Please forgive me, Lord, for all my sinful behaviour."

"I know he has, sir. He brought you and Tante together again, did he not? He wants you both to continue to live together happily with your children. You will see."

There was a knock on the door. I flew to it. It was Mrs Tompkins with a beaming smile on her homely face. She looked past me to Mr Rochester, who had half risen from his chair. "The baby's born, sir, and Madam is asking for you. It's a little girl, sir, as pretty as a picture!"

Mr Rochester rushed past me. "Thanks be to God!" he cried.

I stood there in his study for some time. A daughter, Mr Rochester had a daughter. What need did he have for me? I was glad that Tante Jane was safe, but, oh the longing to be loved by him as his daughter, as well.

I had felt, for those past few moments, such an empathy with him. Had he felt it too? Was it all to be destroyed by this new little arrival? Tears began to flow down my cheeks, and I sobbed softly behind the velvet curtains.

"Adèle, Adèle are you not coming to see the new baby, my dear? What is this, tears?" Mr Rochester had returned and put his arm around me, holding me close.

If I live to be a hundred, I will always remember that moment. He did care about me, after all.

CHAPTER 15

On the appointed day in May, I was standing on the deck of H.M.S. Seafarer with a southwest wind ruffling my curls and the ribbons on my bonnet flying out behind me. My skirts billowed like the sails on the vessel, and I could taste the salt and seaweed in the cool fresh air.

The H.M.S. Seafarer was built along the lines of Mr Brunel's 'Great Britain', with sails and a steam funnel. It was quite capacious and well fitted for comfort. The Fitzjames family and myself were all accommodated in three cabins in the forepart of the boat.

We would shortly be on our way to Naples, a voyage which could take up to three weeks or more, depending on the weather. There had been a great deal of correspondence and telegraphing between Captain Fitzjames and Mr Rochester about my safety in making this trip, but at last Mr Rochester was satisfied with Captain Fitzjames' assurances and gave me his permission to go.

As the ship cast anchor, we were all in high spirits when we assembled on the deck to watch the shores and cliffs of England fade into the distance.

As I gazed at the huddled warehouses and moored ships of Portsmouth, I recalled the last few happy weeks at Southlands with satisfaction. I had quickly recovered from my feelings of being supplanted by the new baby daughter because I was definitely made to feel like one of the family.

Jane had named her new daughter Helen Elizabeth. Helen had been a much-loved school companion of Jane's at Lowood, who had died there of consumption at a young age.

It was typical of Jane to remember her sad little friend, Helen Burns, who she said had been a lovely person, with a strong Christian faith. She was very intelligent, but had been bullied and chastised by one of the teachers and had born this treatment with great patience and fortitude. After marrying Edward Rochester, Jane had arranged for Helen's lonely unmarked grave in Brockenbridge churchyard to bear a marble tablet giving her name and the word 'Resurgam'.

As Mrs Tompkins had said, Helen was a pretty baby with hazel eyes, like mine, and the promise of fair hair. Jane said she could see a similarity to me in a funny little expression she had when she smiled, which wrinkled her forehead and turned down her mouth, just like me. I must say, I had not been aware of this in myself, but I was grateful to her for linking me even more with the family's heredity.

After Helen's birth, at Jane's suggestion, I had invited Annie Thomas to Southlands for a few weeks to act as my companion and help Jane and the nurse maid, Rose, with the children. She arrived by train, looking rather scared at this honour. She was at first overawed by everything – the size and grandeur of the house, by Mr Rochester, although he was very kindly towards her, by the fact that there were servants to do her bidding and that she had her own pretty bedroom, when, at the farm, she shared with two of her sisters. She was also very nervous of our more formal meals in the dining room and I decided that, at first, she and I would eat in the breakfast room, which was more relaxing for her. However, after a few days, she overcame her timidity and her own merry little personality emerged, particularly with Jane and myself and of course with the boys, whom she adored. We were soon playing many games of hide and seek in the garden and French cricket on the lawn and our laughter rang out and cheered Jane as she recovered from the birth of

Helen. When the time came for her to depart, we all felt we were taking leave of a happy little friend.

Her disability had concerned Mr Rochester, and he said to me afterwards that he would speak to Dr Brightside about it to see what treatment or operations might be available.

My thoughts returned to the present. I looked for Jack among the passengers but could see him nowhere. Surely, he was on board. It seemed he could not get away from his police duties to visit Tavistock Square. I had seen and spoken to him as we embarked, which was our first encounter since I returned from Fremingham. He had taken my hand and kissed it, but then he had been called away by one of his police colleagues, and we had no further chance to speak properly.

Lieutenant Jonathan Baxter, the ship's First Officer, came towards me, giving me a salute. He looked very smart in his dark blue uniform with peaked cap and gold braid.

"Mr Baxter," I said anxiously, "Have you seen Mr Whitaker?"

He halted beside me. "Yes, Miss Varens, I think he is talking to the Captain on the Bridge at present. However, he asked if you would go into the saloon as there is a lady who would like to meet you. May I conduct you there, Miss Varens?"

I acquiesced and he led me along various passages and down gangways, until we reached a pair of double doors. Then he stood aside to allow me to pass through.

A tall female figure was standing in the centre of the saloon, and she swung round quickly as I entered.

"May I introduce Miss Edwina Foskit, Miss Varens," said Lieutenant Baxter with a wave of his hand.

"How do you do?" cried the woman, curtseying deeply. Her voice was high-pitched and shrill. "Ai am a distant relative of Mr Whitaker and his family, deah."

I too gave a quick curtsey, as I studied this apparition. Indeed, she was a strange-looking woman. Somewhat taller and broader than the average female, she wore a deep bonnet, under which was a mass of grey curls, shadowing her face. However, her complexion was pink and unlined, and I could see that she had brown eyes and a nose, not unlike Jack's. When she opened her mouth to speak, I saw a row of uneven discoloured teeth. She wore a snuff-coloured crinoline trimmed with scarlet, which matched the red ribbons in her bonnet. Around her shoulders was a black shawl, which concealed her upper half and her hands and arms were encased in black lace mittens. I could see, however, that her hands were quite large. Black shiny boots protruded from underneath her voluminous skirts.

"It is nice to meet you, my deah," she chortled. "I am to be your companion on the voyage and I am sure we are going to get along very well!"

I was not so sure of this and began to wonder how this strange creature would be able to protect me against the possible machination of Count Valdini.

"I hear you sing, my deah," she said. "I have a good voice myself. Would you like to hear it?"

She gave a shriek, which practically deafened me. "That is my top C deah. I heah you ca-a-a-alling me," she sang, or rather shrieked, the words of a well-known ballad. "Perhaps we could sing a duet to entertain the company," she cried.

I heard a sort of muffled choking sound behind me and looked around to find that a small audience had formed in the saloon. Captain Fitzjames, Diana and their children, as well as Sergeant Holness and Lieutenant Baxter were there, together with several others. Some were bent double with laughter, while those, like Diana, held a discreet handkerchief to their lips.

I turned back to Edwina Foskit, to find to my amazement, that the lower half of her costume had descended to the floor. The bonnet and shawl had been discarded, and there stood Jack in shirt and breeches, brandishing a pistol.

"Oh, excuse me a minute, Adèle," he said, as I stood in utter astonishment. He turned from me, bent his head, and then faced me again giving me a flashing white smile and holding in his hand a set of discoloured uneven teeth.

"Jack!" I exclaimed and then joined the others in their laughter.

When I had recovered a little, I gasped, "Is this what you meant when you said I would be accompanied by a female family friend to my meeting with the Count and Contessa Valdini?"

"Yes, you see, if Eales and Valdini are one and the same person, then, as I think I've said before, I have had dealings with Eales in the past and he would undoubtedly recognise me. This seemed the best solution to the problem. I would then be in a good position to take him completely unawares, if the occasion required it." He looked at me a little anxiously. "I do hope this little charade has not upset you. I thought it was a good way of testing my disguise. If you, who know me well, did not twig, then I doubt if Valdini will."

"I certainly was fooled, Jack. You were extraordinary!" I addressed the others. What did you think, everyone? Do you imagine he will get away with it in front of the count?"

"One criticism, Mr Whitaker, if I may," said Diana. "I think your voice is too loud and shrill. Most women, when they meet people for the first time, are fairly restrained and quiet, and if you kept your voice at a lower pitch, it would make your other characteristics less noticeable."

"Other characteristics?" said Jack, with his eyebrows raised in a wicked chuckle.

"For one thing, you are much taller and broader than the average lady. A quieter manner would make you more acceptable," I interjected.

"I take your point, ladies." His voice took on a genteel whisper, "Like this, perhaps? I am so looking forward to this voyage, Miss Adèle."

"Yes, Jack, gentle and humble, like that. Otherwise, you are quite convincing."

Unfortunately, a few hours into the voyage we encountered some very rough weather, with a very choppy sea. A number of passengers, unused to sea travel, became sea sick, including Diana and the children. I seemed to be unaffected, but I did my best to administer to them. However, they kept to their cabins, and I was frequently on my own on the deck.

Jack, like me, was not affected by the problem and we were often the only passengers able to brave the weather. In view of our feelings for each other, this was to our advantage.

We found a quiet, sheltered place on the deck, behind several tarpaulin-covered lifeboats, aft, where we could sit together on piles of coiled ropes and talk. While we talked, we watched the ship's wake foaming away from us, like a great tail and the turbulent waves creaming around us.

I told Jack all about my background in Paris, explaining my mother's connection with Mr Rochester and how he had difficulty in recognising me as his daughter when I was born; this attitude enhanced by my mother's betrayal of him with another. I explained how he had cast her off and how she had, eventually, formed a relationship with an Italian singer, with whom she had run away, leaving me, a tiny child, destitute, at the mercy of the villainous landlord and his wife. Then, I described how Mr Rochester had rescued me and made me his ward. I told him that I deeply admired and respected Mr Rochester and his wife, and that I had the hope that one day he would regard me as his true daughter, which I feel I am.

I said all this into his apparently sympathetic and understanding ear, but then, after we parted for the night, I began to have grave doubts that I had done the right thing, particularly in emphasising my illegitimacy. Another man might well cut me off for such a confession.

However, when we met again the following evening, still in our nook behind the lifeboats, he was at pains to assure me that he felt nothing but love and sympathy for me, as someone who needed his protection.

"But, what about you, Jack, dear? I am bursting to know about your early life and background. You seem to be such an inscrutable person."

He leaned forward his chin in his hand. "Well, let me see," he said thoughtfully. "Shall I tell you about my job as an assistant lion tamer? Or about how I walked a tightrope fifty feet up, with no net? Or, again, how I learned to ride two wild Arabian steeds, with a foot on each, as they galloped?" He said all this in a most matter of fact, off hand sort of way, as though it was nothing.

I reeled back against the lifeboats in amazement. "Jack, please be serious. I want to know all about your real background, dearest."

He cocked an eyebrow at me and grinned. "Sorry, my love, but that is my real background, or at least part of it. Can you not guess from that, the profession in which I and my family might have been engaged?"

"Do you mean…? No, I really cannot guess, Jack. You tell me."

"It was the circus, my darling! Have you ever heard of Modbury's Circus? No, probably not - the name was changed about thirty years ago, and you are far too young. Well, my father worked at Modbury's. At first, he was an acrobat and did all sorts of amazing things. Then he became a trapeze artist, which is how he met my mother. They did a double act together, which would have made your pretty hair stand on end if you had seen it. However then, because he showed such talent and intelligence, Mr Modbury promoted him to be Ring Master. By then, he and my mother had married and babies began to arrive, so my mother decided to retire."

He laughed. "My earliest memory of my father is of him wearing his black shiny top hat, scarlet coat, white breeches, and highly polished top boots, holding a whip and exchanging bandinage with our two clowns, Aleppo and Fingini. He was the 'straight man' for all their jokes. He had a fantastic presence of his own though. It was he who built up Modburys. When Mr Modbury passed away, he took over and renamed it Whitakers Circus. You see, he and his brother, Ted had by then inherited their father's pawnshop business, but my father had no interest in running it. So, he sold his share to my uncle Ted and used the money to improve and develop the circus."

"A circus background!" I remembered what I had read about J.D. Whitaker in the 'Magic Forest' poster. "Jack, is your father J.D. Whitaker?"

"He is, my love. What happened was that, as time went on, he became more interested in the theatre than the circus. He felt it had more future and scope. He still retains a considerable interest in Whitakers Circus, but it is now run by my cousin Tom and his family. As you know, from having seen 'The Magic Forest', which he wrote, by the way, as well as directed and produced, he has had considerable acclaim. He has also had several previous successes before that and has become very well known. But he is always seeking to find new shows which will interest the public."

"All this is so exciting and almost unbelievable," I gasped, "But how do you fit in Jack?"

"Well, at present I don't, but I think I will." He paused and looked keenly into my eyes. "You see, dearest, like many only sons – I have three elder sisters – I did not want to follow in father's footsteps. I wanted to be independent and develop my own talents in my own way. So, I decided to join the police force, and I worked my way up to my present position."

He looked away across the heaving waves and then back at me, with a rueful smile.

"I think Pa was initially very disappointed in me. But I believe he is beginning to see my logic. If I decide to join him now, I will bring with me a great deal of knowledge and experience, of which we can make use in future productions. I think my understanding of the criminal mind and my ability to solve strange cases, which I have done, will be a great asset. I am also an accomplished singer and have acted in some of his productions. So, I think the time is ripe."

"And presumably, this is the alternative creative career you were talking about?"

"Yes, you have it, my love." He took both my hands and gazed at me earnestly. "I now know that entertainment is my first love, and I suspect you feel that too."

He paused for a moment. "Tell me, when you sing in front of an audience, do you experience a kind of power and connection with those people?" He held out his hand and cupped long fingers. "Do you feel you hold them in your hand and that you could sway their emotions one way or another, by the tone of your voice?"

"Well," I said thoughtfully, "I have certainly felt a kind of exultation. When I was singing solo in 'The Messiah' I felt as if I was floating upwards amongst the stars. But then my experience is very limited compared to yours."

"That is certainly part of what an entertainer feels and it is a wonderful sensation. I also like to think that I am giving pleasure and a memorable experience."

"Yes," I said. "From the comments I received in my one public performance, so far, I was conscious of the pleasure and delight which I had created."

"I knew it!" he said, taking my hands again. "You and I are so much alike. I have known it from the first moment I saw you." Then he paused and his hands grasped mine even tighter. "But if you are unhappy about all I have told you concerning myself and my background and want to get up from that rope coil and end our romance, I shall be devastated but I will accept your decision."

There was a silence. I looked deeply into his warm brown eyes. The wind quietened, and the waves too seemed to abate as if they were listening.

Then, I took courage. I must make him finalise things with no more uncertainty. "Decision!" I said at last. "What decision are you asking me to make? Do you realise that you have not asked me the most important and fundamental question about our relationship for me to give you a definite answer?"

He gave a little chuckle, and before I could move or speak, he had put his hands on either side of my waist and lifted me up to one of the lifeboats, seating me gently upon a flat tarpaulin-covered area. He then took off his cap and went down on one knee.

"Dearest, adorable, beautiful Adèle. Now that I have told you everything, I am asking you to join me in the great adventure I contemplate, which is to make a career in the theatre. Will you be my wife, my inspiration, and my helpmate in this undertaking, through thick and thin? It may not be an easy life I am offering you, but you are the girl I choose, above all others, to be by my side."

"Oh, Jack, darling, Jack. You are the man I believe can make a success of anything he undertakes. I shall be proud to be your wife and helpmate."

Jack reached into a pocket and produced a small grey velvet box. Then he got up and moved towards me. He opened the box and inside, reposing on a nest of black velvet, was a beautiful ring, a glowing ruby, surrounded by sparkling diamonds, in a heart shape.

I gasped. "Oh, Jack, it is absolutely lovely."

"It belonged to my grandmother, Elena, the intrepid bare-back rider, a remarkable lady." He took my left hand and placed the ring on my finger, saying solemnly, "With this ring I pledge our betrothal."

Then, he lifted me gently down from the lifeboat into his arms. The wild wind and white-capped waves echoed the depths of our emotions. We were lost in each other.

CHAPTER 16

My happiness was short-lived, however. As I walked down the passageway to my cabin, after parting from Jack, with many a goodnight kiss, a door opened as I passed, and a woman looked out. As soon as she saw me, she withdrew and closed the door firmly, but I had recognised her. It was Marietta. My joyous feelings vanished and alarm, uncertainty, and fear took their place. Marietta, whom Jack had described as evil and treacherous. What was she doing on board the Seafarer?

I remembered that he had said she was useful to him as an informant and would be able to identify Albert Eales and Valdini, if they turned out to be the same person, but I had imagined this would be after Eales or Valdini had been arrested and returned to England, as part of evidence in an English court of law, rather than in Italy. I trusted Jack's motives, but nevertheless, I could not help my feelings being a little tinged with jealousy. After all, she was very beautiful, and I still had memories of seeing them together at the theatre.

The following day, as soon as I had an opportunity, I tackled Jack on the subject.

His brown eyes looked steadily into mine as he said, "Do not worry about Marietta, dearest. She will be no threat to you. She asked me if she could come on the voyage, and I agreed. It occurred to me that, if I do manage to corner Count Valdini and we need immediate proof about his true identity, she is the one person we can rely on to confirm it because of their close association. At present, she is convinced of who

Valdini really is, and she is full of vengeance and hate against him for marrying your mother."

"Oh dear, does that mean that my mother is also in danger from her?"

"I do not think so. She knows about Valdini's or Eales' other victims and how they met their untimely ends and I would imagine that she would regard your mother in that light, as a victim and not as a rival or enemy."

I sincerely hoped he was right.

Jack and I decided that we would not tell the others about our engagement until his mission was accomplished. It was difficult to conceal my feelings of excitement though, and I was often conscious of Diana's gaze resting on me speculatively. I kept my beautiful ring in my jewel box, hidden from sight, but every evening, before retiring, I put it on for a few minutes and kissed it before hiding it away again.

After several days, we reached Lisbon, where the party went ashore to look at the city and some of the beautiful churches and places of interest. Jack and I did our best to behave normally, just like good companions, but I think the others suspected that something special had occurred between us.

As for Marietta, her cabin door remained firmly closed during the day, and she did not mingle with the rest of us. However, late in the evenings, when most of us were retiring to our own cabins, I often glimpsed her strolling on a quiet part of the deck, attended by Sergeant Holness. I was not quite sure what his role was. Perhaps he had been detailed by Jack to act as her guardian, especially in view of the allegedly treacherous and dangerous side of her nature.

The 'Important Personage' had come on board quietly, just before we set sail from England. He arrived with a retinue of staff, and they all occupied a suite of the best cabins in the centre of the ship. We glimpsed him occasionally, strolling alone, or accompanied by an attendant. He was a thin, pale young man, immaculately dressed, with a rather superior expression. Only the Captain had any dealings with him. Rumour had it that he was a royal prince, but we never did discover the truth. His staff kept him well away from the other passengers. The purpose of his visit to Naples was also shrouded in secrecy, but it was thought to be in connection with some form of trade negotiation and that he would be visiting the King in the Royal Palace.

After Lisbon there were several further ports of call; Gibralter, Barcelona, Marseilles and, at last, Naples, which we reached on a beautiful morning of sparkling sunshine. The vista across the bay to Mount Vesuvius was breathtaking. We had all heard about the terrible eruptions which had occurred from time to time over the centuries and about the one in Roman times, which had totally engulfed the towns of Herculaneum and Pompeii. Excavations had been taking place there since the last century and human remains had been found. The idea of cities buried with all their inhabitants, lent a certain macabre thrill to the scene.

This part of Italy is truly beautiful. There are lovely trees and luxuriant flowers and shrubs everywhere. However, we found Naples itself somewhat malodorous and not very safe for ladies to walk unattended through the streets. So we stayed on board. However, as soon as the Royal Party had disembarked and driven off in four carriages, with royal crests on their doors, Captain Fitzjames' initial responsibility was completed. His orders were that he must return in three weeks to transport his special passengers back to England, and we were able to continue on to our final destination,

Sorrento, where we would find the villa of the Count and Contessa Valdini.

As we sailed along the coastline, we were able to admire its picturesque qualities. High up on the craggy cliffs we could see white dwellings surrounded by the green of exuberant foliage. We saw small villages and palatial residences, all gleaming in the brilliant sunshine, with the sea below in hues ranging from palest turquoise to deepest indigo.

We entered the port of Sorrento with its steeply layered geography. Tiers of houses in pastel shades soared upwards. Across the bay we could still see Mount Vesuvius, crouched like a sleeping monster, slightly obscured by mist.

The Valdini villa was called the Villa Romero and enquiry revealed that it was situated on a rock, high above the town. There had been correspondence between myself and my mother and when we had moored in Sorrento, a messenger had been despatched from the ship to confirm our arrival. I had received a reply from the contessa giving me a day and time for my visit.

Once more Jack, dressed as Edwina Foskit, paraded 'herself' before me so that I could check on any little oversights which might give 'her' away to the beady gaze of Count Valdini.

At last we were ready to leave. I was naturally extremely agitated and nervous at the thought of meeting my long lost parent. Diana, who had been informed of our visit, came to me and kissed me. "Do not be fearful, my dear. You are going to meet your own mother after a very long time. My wishes go with you that the interview will be a very happy one for you both."

A carriage had been ordered and the two of us, 'Edwina Foskit' and myself, climbed inside. Our coach driver was Sergeant Holness, dressed appropriately for the part and ready to come to our assistance, if needed, with a pistol hidden in his waistband.

The road we followed climbed upwards through the town and soon we were looking down on the beautiful bay of Naples of deepest blue, with the sky above a matching azure.

Shortly afterwards, we came to a high wall in which was a small wooden door, bearing the name 'Villa Romero'.

Descending from the carriage, Jack dropped swiftly to the ground and fluffed out his skirts. Then he helped me down. "I'll just ring the bell, deah!" 'she' exclaimed, in her high-pitched voice, assuming her role.

We heard a faint tinkle on the other side and, after a few moments, the upper half of the door was opened. A dark-haired, surly individual looked out. "Si, signoras, who are you?" he enquired gruffly in Italian.

"Miss Edwina Foskit and Miss Adèle Varens to see the Contessa Valdini, by appointment, my good man," my companion said sharply, in English.

The man studied us for a further minute and then bent down and undid the bolts of the gate, opening it wide.

Beyond him we could see a shady pergola covered in deep red bougainvillaea, leading to a magnificent garden, laid out with paths and formal flowerbeds. Alabaster statues were placed here and there and we could hear the cool musical sound of water splashing into stone basins.

I gasped at this elegance and beauty. "It's like paradise!"

'Edwina' sniffed disapprovingly. "A bit too foreign and colourful for me, deah. Give me Battersea Park, any day."

The man stood aside to let us through, indicating to our driver that he and his vehicle must stay outside the wall in a special area reserved for carriages.

We followed him along various paths and under several arches, until we reached an emerald lawn in front of an imposing mansion. Built in the Palladian style, it resembled an elaborate birthday cake with its pale pink walls and white stucco decorations.

Before the house was a raised terrace, with a flight of steps leading up to it. A group of people sat there on elegant white chairs around a long white table, on which refreshments were arranged. I had already had the sensation, as we walked through the glorious garden, with its bird song, splashing water and scents of many flowers, that I was in a delightful dream and the people before me enhance this sense of unreality. They were all sitting silently, in various attitudes, as though posed for the start of a theatrical performance.

At the head of the table was a man of medium height, portly and rotund, wearing a pale cream suit with a red gardenia in his buttonhole. His skin was swarthy and his hair an oily black, worn quite long. He sported a large, glossy black moustache, carefully groomed and waxed. At the other end of the table sat a lady of about forty, her figure rounded, but still elegant, wearing a pale cream gown. She was bonnet-less, with her golden hair piled elaborately on top of her head, like a crown. Her face was thin and nervous. I noted bags beneath her blue eyes. She had once been very beautiful, but her attractions were beginning to fade.

The other members of the group were a youth of about nineteen or twenty years, with dark hair and eyes, who fiddled incessantly with a spoon on the tablecloth and two other men of swarthy appearance, well muscled, who looked as if their dark suits were too tight for their bulging forceps and thick thighs.

I involuntarily broke the silence. "Maman, is it you? Maman?" I stepped towards the lady, who started and turned her head nervously. "It is I, your daughter, Adèle!"

The lady half rose and held out her arms. "My little Adèle, my little girl," she whispered.

I rushed towards her and we embraced. This was not the time for reproaches or recriminations. All I felt at that moment was a tremendous sense of love, as her arms surrounded me, after all those weary years.

"This is most touching." The voice was harsh, tinged with sarcasm. The count spoke in English with an Italian accent. "May I introduce myself? I am Count Valdini and thees," he indicated the youth, "ees my son, Alfonso." He waved to the other two men. "These gentlemen are my associates. Welcome to the Villa Romero, Mees Adèle. Could we know the name of your companion?"

"Edwina Foskit, count," that 'lady' announced in 'her' piercing voice, leaning on 'her' parasol. "Pleased to meet you all, I'm sure!"

"Count Valdini," I said gently. "Would it be possible to have a private talk with my mother? There is so much we have to say to each other after all these many years."

"By all means," said the count. He turned to his wife. "My dear, why do you not take Mees Adèle to the rose garden? We will entertain Mees Foskit here."

I looked at Jack, but he seemed completely at ease. He seated himself at the table. "How about a cup of tea, count? I'm nearly parched on such a hot day as this." 'She' waved a large black-feathered fan in front of her face and 'her' grey curls bounced.

The count picked up a small bell from the table and rang it. Almost immediately, a maid in white cap and apron appeared, as if she had been waiting behind a bush. "Some Eenglish tea for the lady," he commanded.

The contessa took my hand and led me down a winding pathway. Soon the terrace was out of sight. We passed under an arch and emerged into a beautiful area full of roses in bloom. In the centre of a smooth lawn was a lily pond where a fountain played with a soothing plash. My mother led me to a seat on the far side of the pond and we sat down together.

I looked at the contessa's profile, as she studied the water, trying to recall her face. It was difficult to recognise the young, vivacious woman who had been my mother in this faded, languid person at my side. "Maman?" I said at last.

She started, as though her thoughts had been far away and turned to face me. Then she began to speak very quickly, almost gabbling. "I did go back to Paris to find you. I did. But when I got there, you had gone."

"Yes, that must have been several weeks after you left me, I suppose, or maybe it was longer? Mr Rochester came at last and collected me. But they were horrible people, Maman. You did not leave any money for my support, and you had not paid the rent for several weeks before that. They made me work like…like a slave in the house, doing tasks that were too much for me at four years old and hardly giving me anything to eat." I felt my voice had begun to take on an accusing note, but I could not help myself. All my unhappy thoughts and feelings over the years tumbled out. I was sobbing like the tiny child I had once been.

"But…but I left money with that woman to pay the rent and enough to keep you for at least a month besides."

She put her hands to her head. "At least I think I did, but my memory these days is not so good as it was."

"But unfortunately, she was not to be trusted, Maman. She told that man, her husband, that there was no money."

"Oh, I am so sorry my dearest child!" She put her shaky arms around me and held me close, weeping softly.

As our tears continued to flow together, I felt my anger and bitterness towards her begin to dissolve, leaving only sadness and regret.

We stayed in our mutual embrace for some time, as the water tinkled gently beside us. Then I released myself and dried my eyes. "I think the best thing, Maman, is to forget the past and be joyful that at last we have come together."

"Forget the past," she said sadly. "That I find hard to do, my dear. I have wasted so much of my life in frivolous, worthless things, and now I am in greater trouble than ever!"

"Trouble, Maman? But you have recently married a wealthy titled man and are now the Contessa Valdini, living in this beautiful place."

My mother looked around her and shuddered. "It may seem beautiful to you, my love, but it is a prison and the count is the jailer!"

I stared at her in horror.

"He restricts my movements and watches me continually. Those two men he called his 'associates' are his bodyguards, and when he is absent, which is very often, they take over the job of spying on me and preventing me from leaving the villa, unless they accompany me. No doubt they report everything back to him when he returns. I am wretched, Adèle. Often he…."

"My dear…" the count's voice was so close behind us that we both started.

I looked around. The bushes behind us had parted, and Valdini was standing within a foot of our seat, looking down at us. Had he heard what his wife had just said?

"Eef you have had your leettle chat, perhaps you will return to the terrace." This was spoken like a command, rather than a request.

Obediently we both arose. In the distance, I notice that 'Edwina' was standing under the archway, 'her' hand shielding 'her' eyes from the sun, observing us closely.

"Come and have some tea deah. I've poured it out for you. Not that they can make proper tea in this country. Then we had better go." 'She' took my arm firmly.

We resumed our seats at the silent table, where the other occupants did not appear to have moved or spoken since we left.

"Deed I hear you say you had to go?" enquired Valdini.

"Yes, I'm afraid we have an evening engagement," said 'Edwina' tossing 'her' bonneted head and making the curls and feathers nod, as though in agreement.

"Well, I inseest that you come again and bring the rest of your party. You are all invited to a soirée here on Saturday evening. There will be some of my friends and acquaintances from the town. I hope you will do me the honour of accepting?"

'Edwina' looked at me, and I thought 'she' nodded slightly. It would certainly give me another opportunity for further talk with my mother, and perhaps she would be able to give me some proof that Mr Rochester was indeed my father.

"We would be delighted to come, sir. At what time?" I replied.

"At eight o'clock. There will be refreshments, and dancing on the terrace."

"One thing about Italy," said 'Edwina' who had now risen ready to depart, "You don't have to worry about the weather. I've got my feet wet so many times at fêtes and the like out of doors in England...Well, ta,ta, count and contessa, we'll look forward to Saturday."

The count and his son gave us a formal bow in farewell, and we followed the surly gatekeeper back to the entrance gate and our carriage.

CHAPTER 17

When we returned to the ship, we were met by a welcoming committee, intent on hearing how we had fared.

"Did they rumble you, Jack?" enquired Captain Fitzjames, with a laugh.

"He was marvellous," I cried. "I am sure they did not guess anything."

"No need for your firearms then, I hope?" asked Diana anxiously.

"No," said Jack. It was all very peaceful. They sat around a table on a terrace like a lot of stuffed sheep." He then went on to describe the scene in the garden.

"Did you speak to your mother?" enquired Diana, drawing me to one side, while the men continued to talk on other matters connected with our visit.

"Yes, I did. When we arrived, she was sitting at the end of the table looking very tense and anxious and so much changed from the beautiful lady I remembered."

"Well, my dear," sighed Diana. "Sixteen years is a long time and I do not suppose she has had an easy life."

"No, and I think she feels some remorse for having deserted me. But the interesting thing is that she said she gave that horrible woman in Paris enough money for her back rent and to keep me for some weeks. But the woman denied all knowledge of the money to her husband. It was only Mr Rochester's arrival that saved me from being thrown out on the streets."

"Yes, I have heard some of your story from Jane," said Diana sympathetically.

"Anyway, I requested of the count that he allow me to talk to my mother in private, which he did, and we were able to resolve our differences. I found that my feelings of anger and indignation at her treatment of me were banished by the realisation that I was actually talking to my long-lost mother, who seemed in a very unhappy state. She is very upset about her marriage and implied that the count is treating her badly. She feels like a prisoner, not allowed out of the villa without his permission and he or his henchmen watching her every move. She would have told me more, but the count appeared behind the seat where we were sitting and more or less ordered us back to the terrace to join the others."

"What was the count like?"

"In appearance, plump, fairly short, long black hair, fierce and shiny black eyes, a large drooping moustache, and an oily manner. I am afraid I did not like him at all. Strangely enough, though, he reminded me of someone, but I cannot think who."

Diana shivered. "I do not like the sound of him, Adèle."

"No, I felt a sense of considerable repulsion when I was anywhere near him."

After dinner that evening, everyone concerned with our venture was asked to gather in the saloon for a council of war.

Jack addressed us all authoritatively. "All the passengers on the ship have been invited to a party at the count's villa on Saturday, but we think it advisable that only those people on this list should attend." He produced a paper on which names had been written and passed it around.

This immediately produced a reaction from Diana. "Jack, what is this? Captain Fitzjames is going, and Adèle's name is on the list, but I am excluded, why?"

"It is because we feel there is danger of abduction. Adèle has to go, because she is part of our plan, but she will be carefully guarded at every moment. However, in your case, Mrs Fitzjames, Captain Fitzjames naturally wants to protect you. There are others not on the list, but that is because we want to keep a body of armed men outside the villa, particularly my own policemen, to act as our back up in case of trouble."

"I am sorry," said Diana firmly, her cheeks flushed with annoyance, "But I do not agree. Do you seriously think anything of that sort would happen to me? I would like to go to the ball and see this beautiful villa and its gardens."

The Captain took his wife's hand. "I hope you will understand, dearest. We are dealing with what we suspect is a vicious criminal, capable of anything, whom Jack wants to bring to justice. I suggest you write a polite letter to the contessa, explaining that you are unable to attend, which we will send by messenger. You could say that you are feeling unwell, or make an excuse about not wanting to leave the children for so long."

"And what about Adèle?" cried Diana. "From what you say, Jack, she is in much more obvious danger than myself."

"Adèle is particularly vulnerable, I agree," said Jack. "But it will be simpler if I only have one lady to protect. Also, it would look very odd if Adèle did not go, because she has sought the count and her long-lost mother out, and obviously they would expect her to accept the invitation. If she did not appear again, it would look as if she thought there was something to be feared and we do not want to create that impression."

"Adèle, what do you think about this?" enquired Diana indignantly. "Jack seems almost to be using you as bait to trap this man Valdini."

"Jack knows he has my full trust and support over this," I said passionately. "With him to guard me, I do not feel I will be in any danger. However, Diana, none of us want to risk you, the mother of two children."

"How about the father of two children?" exclaimed Diana. "Perhaps Captain Fitzjames should stay away as well!"

"Now my dear. Please be sensible about this. Like Jack, I am a man of action and well able to look after myself."

So, the plan was accepted, although reluctantly by Diana, and on the following Saturday evening, Jack and myself, Captain Fizjames and Jonathan Baxter entered the carriage bound for the Villa Romero, driven, as before, by our trusty Dick Holness. Several other men, a mixture of policemen and trusted members of the Seafarer's crew, followed behind in a separate vehicle.

Jack was still in his role as Edwina and wore a black evening dress of Diana's, suitably altered to fit his much larger frame, with a black lace shawl to hide such masculine traits as muscular male shoulders and arms. 'She' also wore her black mittens. Shoes were a problem. There was none sufficiently dainty in Jack's wardrobe, and mine or Diana's were far too small. So 'she' ended up by wearing the same black boots as before, to which we attached black velvet bows.

In spite of the potential dangers we were facing, the dressing of Jack in this outfit caused us much hilarity, particularly the boots.

Captain Fitzjames and Lieutenant Baxter wore the evening version of their naval uniforms. I was in white, with pink roses at my bosom and in my hair.

It was a beautiful calm evening. The western sky was a blaze of glory and a crescent moon and stars were beginning to appear in the blue firmament above the dark misty outline of Mount Vesuvius.

We followed the same winding upward road as before and reached the small gateway to the garden of the Villa Romero. This stood open to receive the guests and several servants were there to direct the visitors and to tell their drivers where they could leave their vehicles. The space was already becoming quite crowded.

From the gate, we took the pathway through the pergola and emerged onto the wide lawn in front of the villa. This was thronged with people, all talking volubly in Italian. I could not help noticing what a flamboyant crowd they were. Most of the men wore the type of tight black suit I had noticed favoured by the two 'associates' of the count. I thought that their faces had a shifty, crafty look, their black eyes darting around and their mouths pinched, taut and unsmiling. They were, in many cases, much older than the women, who wore elaborate gowns in bright colours, with very revealing necklines and ostentatiously feathered headdresses.

"Should think he's raided all the bordellos and low dives in Sorrento to get this lot together!" whispered Jack in my ear, as we smiled warmly at our host and hostess.

The Contessa Céline was quite modestly and quietly attired in black lace and pearls and her husband looked much the same as we had last seen him, with a white rose in his buttonhole.

On the terrace above us, an orchestra began to play a waltz.

We greeted our hosts, and the contessa expressed her disappointment that Mrs Fitzjames could not attend the party. We were then ushered up to the terrace. The count followed us and bowed to me. "May I have the privilege of this waltz, Signorina Varens?"

My heart sank, but realising that I could not avoid it, I smiled politely and murmured, "Si signore," and was whirled away into the dance.

He danced well, but held my hand in an almost vicelike grip and pulled me much closer to him than I cared to be. Again, I was reminded of something similar, but I could not quite remember what it was. At close quarters, I was looking into a pair of long black steely eyes.

I made a few comments in Italian about the beautiful evening and his lovely garden.

"Ah, you speak our language," he said in English.

"Yes, signore, I learned it at my school in Geneva."

"I believe you have a guardian, signorina who lives in England?"

"Yes, that is correct, signore. He lives in Woldenshire."

He then began to ask me several questions about Mr and Mrs Rochester, some of which concerned their social position and wealth. I began to find this intrusive, and I changed the subject to our voyage here and what an interesting experience it had been.

"How long do you intend to stay in Sorrento, signorina?"

"Oh, only for about three weeks. Captain Fitzjames is due back in Naples to collect an important ambassador from our country who is visiting the King."

"Very interesting, very interesting," he commented. "And why is this person here?"

"Oh, that I do not know. We have not been informed."

"Would you be able to stay longer, signorina, on you own? I am sure your mother would like it."

"Unfortunately, I could not signore. My family are expecting me back by the end of June."

"Perhaps you can be persuaded to change your plans."

He said this very softly in my ear, but I sensed the power of his will behind these words.

At this point, the waltz finished, and I returned thoughtfully to 'Edwina' who was now sitting down on a bench, and had been watching us closely.

"Phew, it's hot 'she' said in 'her' high piercing voice, waving 'her' black-feathered fan in front of her face. "How did you get on with the count?" Jack muttered from behind the fan in his normal voice. "You look a little pale, are you all right?"

"He is pressing me to stay on here alone in the villa." I whispered, as I took a seat beside him.

"What did you say?" said Jack, keeping his voice low.

"I made an excuse about being expected back at Southlands, but," I shivered. "I think he may pursue it. I, I, think I would really like to leave now, Jack." I leaned back, passing my hand across my brow.

"All right, my love. But didn't you want to have a few words with your mother before we go?"

"Yes, I do, Jack. Have you seen her?"

"I think she is sitting somewhere on this terrace. Let's go and find her."

After a short search, we saw my mother sitting with another lady, also in black. My mother's companion was rather plump and covered in sparkly jet jewellery. I was immediately reminded of Madame Blanche, the brothel keeper, who had lived next door in Paris, all those years ago.

"Maman!" I exclaimed. "Could I have a private word with you?"

"Of course, my dear." She arose. "Let us take a turn about the garden." She addressed herself to the other woman. "Will you excuse us, signora? This is my daughter, whom I have not seen for a long time, we have much to talk about." The woman nodded with a slight smile.

"I'll keep you company signora," cried 'Edwina', taking the vacant seat. "How do you do, Madame? I am Edwina Foskit, the companion to Signorina Varens."

As we walked away, I turned around and saw that 'Edwina' and the lady were having an animated conversation.

My mother and I crossed the lawn, threading through the crowd of people still conversing there, and took a seat in an alcove. The garden was illuminated by coloured lanterns and the moonlight cast a silvery radiance over everything, but our corner was in deepest shadow.

"Maman," I began urgently, knowing that we could be interrupted at any minute by the vigilant count. "I wanted to ask you last time, but I did not have the opportunity."

"Yes, dear?" My mother turned to me, a weary resigned expression on her face.

"I want to try and prove to Mr Rochester that I really am his daughter and not just his ward and I wondered if you could tell me anything that would help me. Was Mr Rochester your only gentleman friend in the months before my birth?"

The contessa sighed. It is so long ago, my dear. I can hardly remember it." She thought for a few minutes. "Yes, I think it is true. I did not meet the man Mr Rochester had the duel with until you were about six months old. When you were born, he was away, and on his return, I presented you to him. However, he said, at the time, that you did not resemble him in any way. I remember I was very upset by his attitude. I was sure that he was your father. When you were little, you bore no look of him, but now I can see you as a grown-up young lady, I think I can find something of him in your personality, if not your appearance."

"You will be interested to know, Maman, that Mrs Rochester, his wife, whom I call Tante Jane, has discovered a portrait of Mr Rochester's mother at the age of eighteen or so, which looks very much like me. She had different colouring to mine, but her eyes and her face are very similar."

"Eh bien, people do not always take after their parents. They often leap a generation, and you obviously favour the female side of your family facially, although you have inherited my golden hair." She touched her gleaming tresses self-consciously. "Was this not proof enough for him?"

"He would not admit it, in his perverse way." I laughed a little as I said this. "He kept saying he could see no likeness, but Tante Jane said so, as well as Mrs Tompkins, the housekeeper, who at first, thought it was a portrait of me."

"Eh bien, chérie. There you are."

"But still, Maman, I feel I need something more - positive proof."

My mother sighed. "I can think of nothing else that will help." She patted my knee. But from what you say, and from what I know of Edward Rochester, I predict that he will eventually acknowledge you. How do you get on with him, my dear?"

"When I was little, he was always rejecting me. I suppose I tried too hard to be loved. He did not approve of anything I did to try and please him; my singing or dancing, or liking pretty clothes, which all reminded him of you."

My mother sighed. "I think I hurt him very badly, didn't I?" A tear slid down her cheek.

"Yes, I am afraid you did, dear Maman." I put my arm about her and gave her a hug. "But, as I have grown up and particularly after my time at the finishing school in Geneva, I have begun to feel a greater closeness to him, and the last time we spoke together, he was so kind and understanding that it was just as if he saw himself as my father."

"Perhaps, then, it does not really matter if he does not acknowledge you formally as his daughter, if he treats you as if you are?"

I looked down at my hands and I too sighed. "Maybe not."

We both returned to the house, and my mother gave me a kiss and disappeared down a corridor.

There was a commotion on the terrace where the dancing was still in progress. To my amazement, I saw that 'Edwina' was dancing a polka with a swarthy little Italian, considerably shorter than 'herself'. 'Her' skirts were flying, revealing the velvet bow-decorate boots and several inches of striped black and yellow stocking, but they were obviously both enjoying it and 'Edwina' kept exclaiming "Allez oop" in a loud voice at the start of every gallop, just as though she was riding a horse.

The rest of the dancers had formed a circle around them and were clapping in time to the music. It was all so highly ridiculous and funny that I could not help joining in the laughter, but I also had an underlying dread that 'she' would reveal too much and be discovered. Supposing the pistol she was carrying should fall? This would really give her disguise away. I looked for the count and found him gazing at the scene in an inscrutable way. There was no smile on his face.

The dance came to an end and 'Edwina' collapsed in a clumsy heap onto a small gold chair. "Phew",," she said, fanning herself vigorously. "I'm hotter than ever now."

"May I bring you some cordial, signora?" asked her attentive little partner.

"That would be lovely, Alberto, duckie," 'she' cried. 'Edwina' winked at me as soon as Alberto had disappeared. "I think I'm getting off with him," 'she' giggled.

"Jack!" I exclaimed. "Do be careful."

"It's all right my love. I know what I'm doing."

We were joined by Captain Fitzjames. "Do you think we can make our excuses and leave now?" he muttered.

Alberto returned with a glass of cordial, which Jack quaffed at almost one gulp. "Oh, that's much better!" 'she' exclaimed, wiping 'her' mouth on the back of 'her' black mittened hand.

"Really, Edwina!" I exclaimed in mock horror. "Have you no handkerchief? Where are your manners?"

'Edwina' laughed at me mischievously.

"Would you care to dance again, signora?" enquired Alberto.

"No thank you, Alberto, duckie. I will just sit here and recover. Why don't you ask that pretty young girl over there for a dance, and I'll see you later."

Alberto, bowed politely and strolled off.

Jack got up. "Yes", he said to Captain Fitzjames. "I think it's time to go. I have learnt a few things about the Valdini set up by talking to various other guests. How about you Henry?"

"Yes, I have gleaned a few facts as well." He laughed. "I think Jonathan may be reluctant to go. He seems to have found a rather charming young English lady, here with her parents, but I believe they are just leaving themselves."

"And, Adèle, how did the chat with your mother go?"

"Oh, quite well, but she cannot really give me any further proof, except from her memory of my birth. However, she has given me some advice, which I will mull over."

"Let us talk about it all on the Seafarer when we get back," said Captain Fitzjames.

We all stood up and Captain Fitzjames signalled to Count Valdini that we were about to go. We gave him our thanks for the evening, and he bowed his acknowledgement. The contessa was nowhere to be seen.

"Perhaps you will visit us again before you leave Sorrento?" enquired the count.

"I think we will have to see count." squawked 'Edwina', rearranging 'her' skirts. "Thanks for the offer, anyway."

The sullen gatekeeper was at our side, having been summoned discreetly by the count, and we all bowed or curtseyed to Valdini before following the servant through the garden to the gate.

It was very dark in the area beyond. I could see several conveyances standing close together with their horses. The gate was shut firmly behind us and what little light there was, came from a small flickering lantern high up on the wall.

"Where's our carriage?" cried Jack. "Dick, Dick, where are you? We're ready to leave."

"I'll see if he is round the other side of this enormous coach," volunteered Captain Fitzjames, and he disappeared through a gap.

We waited for about two minutes and we could hear Henry's and Dick's voices. There seemed to be a problem extracting our carriage.

"Wait here, Adèle. I'll see if I can help," ordered Jack. "I won't be long."

He also disappeared through the same gap.

I stood in the dim light looking across the sea to Vesuvius and breathing in the sweet scents all around me.

Looking around, I saw that Jonathan had passed through the gate with a very pretty girl and an older couple, obviously her parents. Jonathan waved his arm at me and then turned to say Goodbye and shake hands with the gentleman and bow to the ladies. His back was towards me.

Suddenly, I felt myself seized from behind in a strong grip. I opened my mouth to scream, but a gag was quickly inserted between my lips and tied at the back of my head. A strong rope was whipped around me, tying my arms, and at the same time, a thick cloak was flung over my head. I was lifted bodily from the ground and carried a few paces, and then I heard, what sounded like a carriage door creak, and I was thrust into the interior.

I heard shouts, and I think Jonathan had rushed forward. I also heard Jack's voice. But a whip cracked, and the vehicle began to move away at great speed.

I lay on the carriage seat, faint with shock and horror, in complete terror and bewilderment.

Chapter 18

The journey was fast and violent over a rough road. As my arms were tied, I had no means of saving myself and was flung hither and thither. The material of the cloak covered my face. I could see nothing, and I was almost choking with the smell of the dusty garment. There seemed to be another presence in the coach and whoever it was, did not seem to be restricted as I was and could hold on when the carriage bumped over lumps in the road. Once, when I nearly rolled onto the floor, hands pushed me back into a sitting position, and I smelt a faint whiff of perfume.

After a while, I sensed that we were climbing a hill, and the pace slowed down considerably. Straining my ears, I was certain that another carriage was behind us. I heard the crack of a whip, the snort of horses, and voices shouting.

The upward motion continued for a good amount of time, with frequent turns to the left or right on what must have been a very winding mountain road. I began to lose consciousness and fell into a troubled sleep.

I came to myself to find the carriage had stopped. There was a rumble and clank of a heavy chain, as though a gate or bar had been opened or lowered, and the carriage moved forward slowly, traversing what felt like wooden planks.

By the ringing echoes from the carriage wheels and jingle of harness, I guessed we were in an enclosed courtyard, surrounded by what must be lofty walls.

The carriage door opened and strong rough arms lifted me out. To my horror, I was flung over a sturdy male shoulder, with my head hanging downwards and my face bumping against my captor's back at his every movement. He paused, while he adjusted the skirts of my voluminous ball gown, which must have blocked his vision somewhat, and then he walked up steps into a building, and the echoes were deadened. We began to climb stairs; a muscular hand gripping my waist. We stopped. He walked forward. I was faint with terror. A door creaked open inwards, and I was thrown down on my back onto a soft surface, which I assumed to be a bed or sofa.

There were a few muffled words in Italian between the man who had carried me and someone else, whose voice was harsh, but almost certainly female. Heavy boots stamped out, and the door was banged shut. A key turned in the lock.

Hands pulled the cloak from my face, so that I could at last breathe properly, and the same hands untied the kerchief which had gagged me. My mouth felt sore and strained.

I looked about me fearfully. The chamber was almost in darkness, but I had the impression that it was large, with a high ceiling.

I was conscious of someone bending over me. A candle flame sprang into life, and in its weak light, I gasped in terror as I saw the flash of a large pointed knife.

"Do nota fear, leetle one. I am nota going to harma you. I willa cuta your bonds." My companion spoke in English, but with a heavy Italian accent.

The rope which had bound my arms fell away, and I thankfully moved my aching limbs and shoulders.

"Where am I? And…who are you?" I demanded weakly.

"You are in Valdini Castle in the mountains, and I am Marietta, a friend of Jack Whitaker's, who came with you on the boat to Italia."

My stomach gave a lurch. Marietta, the 'treacherous viper', as described by Jack!

"I do not understand. How did you manage to get here?"

"I came in the carriage with you, leetle one. It was a rough ride for you, I am afraid. I knew what Valdini was planning, so I left the ball and installed myself in the vehicle I knew they intended to use to abduct you, without Valdini's knowledge. I told your captor that Valdini had sent me to look after you."

"Whose side are you on then?"

She gave a bitter laugh. "My own; I have been helping Jack Whitaker and have given heem some useful information to help heem arrest Count Valdini, who is also Albert Eales, amongst other disguises." She ran long fingers through her night-black hair. "Thees man was my lover, but he betrayed me by marrying zat Céline Varens. I know Valdini still trusts me. He does nota know my true feelings."

"Céline Varens is my mother."

Marietta nodded. "Youra mother ees a weak, tired creature. She will not last very long."

I gasped in horror. "What do you mean?"

"He weel extract from her all the money she has and then…" She drew her hand across her throat and brandished the knife.

"Oh, no, my poor mother! She has been lost to me for sixteen years and I will not allow it to happen. I will save her!"

219

Marietta's face, hidden in the gloom, seemed to be smiling. "You weel nota be able to save her on your own, leetle one, but you can witha my help."

"Where is Jack?" I cried, shrinking from the expression on her face.

"Jack and the Capitano Feetzjames are two very brave gentlemen. They hava followed your captors to the castle and ara outside. There is a drawbridge guarded by one of Valdini's men." I heard a rustle as she rose from the bed. "I intenda to distract heem" She gave a purring sort of laugh. "Once he isa removed, I can raise the drawbridge, give them a signal and leta them in."

"Valdini, where is he?"

"I expecta he and the contessa, with Alfonso, are on theira way hera now. Thata was Valdini's plan."

"Do you know why he abducted me?" I asked fearfully.

"I can guess. You ara the ward, or is it daughter? of a very wealthy Eengleesh gentleman, Mr Rochester, who will pay Valdina handsomely for your freedom and safety. Valdini will threaten to either forcibly marry you off to hees son, Alfonso or...knowing heem as I do, faced with your youth and beauty, he will marry you heemself."

"Marry me!" I cried in a mixture of disgust and horror. "But he is already married to my mother." I shuddered.

"Oh, that weel be no problem. As I have said, your mother will 'fall ill' and die. Eet will be given out that she had a fever, or consumption, or some other fatal illness, and then he will be free."

"Does he think Mr Rochester will pay him, just like that? My guardian is a powerful man in our country. He is a

J.P., a man of influence. He will raise the whole country and its police force against a villain like Valdini and rescue me!"

"You do nota know what influence Valdini has hera. Many politicians and heads of police ara in his pay. He can maka it extremely difficult for Mr Rochester to save you. This castle is a stronghold. There are secret rooms and dungeons whera people and bodies can be hidden fora years."

In spite of the feelings of horror Marietta's words had created in me, I sat up straight on the bed and raised my head proudly. "Well, I have a great deal of faith in Jack. If anyone can save me, it will be him."

"Yes, and he also hasa me too on his side. So do nota fear."

"I won't, Marieta and I am sure my guardian will want to show you his gratitude."

"Gratitude? I do nota want that. As I hava said, I do thees for myself, nota for you, or Jack or youra guardian," she spoke sharply.

"I…I…am sorry."

"I am going to leave you now, leetle one. There is a guard outsida the door. I weel lock eet, but eef alla goes as I plan eet, Jack weel soon be at youra side to release you."

She glided out and I heard the key turn in the lock.

The room was very dark, but Marietta had left me the candle, flickering on a nearby table. High up on the wall was a tiny window, like an arrow slit and the cold white light of the moon shone in an oblong on the floor, like a piece of silver. I glimpsed tapestries on the walls and there were velvet hangings on the bed on which I lay. The light caught the gleam of sumptuous gilded furniture. However, I could also hear scurrying sounds in the corners of the room and realised these might possibly be from rats.

I drew my feet up, until I was in a crouching position, with my skirts tucked tightly under me, listening intently for any other sounds from outside. However, the thick walls kept all noises at bay. I felt very cold....

The key turning in the lock startled me into wakefulness.

"Adèle?" It was Jack's voice.

"Jack, oh Jack. Tears of relief were running down my face.

His arms were around me and he lifted me off the bed and set me on my feet. "Quick, dearest, there is no time!" He pulled me through the door and out into the corridor. Captain Fitzjames was standing with a cocked pistol pointing at the man who had been guarding me. The man had his hands in the air and was shivering with fright.

"Shove him into the room and lock the door." said Jack.

Fitzjames followed these instructions. The door was slammed shut and locked and we were just about to descend the winding staircase, when Marietta appeared at the other end of the corridor.

Her dark eyes flashed in her sallow face. "Jack, Valdini ees here and he ees just abouta to come upa thesa stairs to viewa his capteeve." She pointed urgently back along the passage from where she had come. "There ees another way outa down through the kitchen and into the great hall. Follow me, pronto."

Jack, Fitzjames, and I raced after her and down a second staircase, which was equally narrow and winding as the first. We rounded a corner and found ourselves in a vast kitchen.

A long deal table ran down the centre and the walls were lined with an assortment of copper pans. A bright fire burnt in the range at one end, on which a large pan was simmering. In front of it, a man in a white apron and tall white cap sat dozing.

We crept past him silently, following Marietta, who led us through a heavy oak door into another passage and thence to the great hall. We ran across this and out through the door. We were now in the courtyard and there was the gateway with the drawbridge down. True to her promise, Marietta had managed to 'distract' the gatekeeper enough to lower the bridge. He was afterwards discovered lying senseless in a corner, where she had knocked him out with a large handy stone.

Our way to freedom lay before us. Jack seized my hand and together we ran across the courtyard and onto the drawbridge. I could see our carriage waiting and the driver, ready to whip up the horses at a word from Jack.

We had reached the middle of the bridge when we became aware that it was slowly moving upwards. Jack turned round, and there at the castle gateway was Valdini with an evil smile on his face, turning the wheel which raised and lowered the bridge. The slope under our feet increased. There was no way we could leap across to safety.

Suddenly, a shot rang out from the courtyard behind, and Valdini crumpled and sank to his knees clutching his arm. Marietta was standing in the courtyard, her head thrown back and her eyes glittering. She held a pistol, still levelled at Valdini. "You vile deceiver and betrayer, you scum, you...." Then she dropped the pistol and producing a dagger from her bosom, she was about to race forward to Valdini, no doubt with the intention of finishing him off, when a figure behind her, which had been moving cautiously and silently towards her, suddenly seized hold of both her arms and pinioned her, so that she could not move. It was Dick Holness. He took the dagger from her imprisoned hand, and she turned towards him burying her face in his broad chest and sobbing bitterly.

From the way he embraced and soothed her, it was obvious to me that there was rather more to their relationship than a shipboard acquaintance. But I was too preoccupied with what was going on in front of me concerning Valdini to give it much thought at that moment.

Fitzjames moved forward and rewound the wheel, so that the bridge returned to its former flat position. He then stood guarding the gateway with his pistol, so that there could be no further attempts by any of Valdini's men to stop us.

Jack left my side and walked back towards Valdini's huddled form by the gate. I followed him, shaking in every limb. Reaching Valdini, he bent down, pulled back his head and ripped at the glossy moustache. It came away easily from his upper lip. Jack grasped the long oily black hair and that too came off. Underneath was a neatly cut head of dark hair.

I moved forward and stood beside Jack, looking down at Valdini, who was glaring defiantly up at us both.

Then I started. There was the face I detested: The long steely dark eyes, the cruel mouth, and the fat well-fed countenance of...James Boulding. "Mr Boulding!" I gasped.

With a quick glance at me, Jack walked over to Marietta and Sergeant Holness and whispered in her ear. She shuddered, but then she nodded her head and came forward to stare triumphantly at Valdini. "Yes, thata is the man known as Albert Eales, who poses as Count Victorio Valdini," she cried.

Jack produced a document from his pocket. "Count Victorio Alfonso Valdini, real name Albert Eales, with many other identities, including James Boulding, as identified by Miss Adèle Varens. In the name of Her Majesty Queen Victoria of England and His Majesty King of Naples, I have a warrant for your arrest for many crimes committed in England and in Italy, a list of which will be read to you at the prison in Sorrento, and for the abduction of Miss Adèle Varens, your most recent crime, for which I have ample witnesses, I am hereby taking you into custody forthwith."

Several men in dark clothes appeared from the shadows. These were part of the force Jack had gathered to help him, and I heard Jack instruct them to ransack the castle and arrest anyone who resided there.

Sergeant Dick Holness, came forward with a pair of manacles, which were placed around Valdini's wrists.

Valdini glared at Jack and myself. "I will get even with you all. Never fear."

"Do you hear that, Captain Fitzjames and Sergeant Holness?" said Jack. "Threatening a police officer and witnesses in the course of his arrest. A further charge to be added to the long list."

There was a cry from the courtyard, and the figure of a woman appeared. She had a wild look. Her hair was hanging about her face, and she was draped in several fluttering gauzy scarves over her black dress. She ran forward, tottering slightly, towards me. "Adèle, Adèle, what is happening? Where is my husband, the count?"

Jack indicated Valdini, who was now standing unsteadily between two of Jack's men. Blood was seeping from the wound in his arm and he looked as if he was about to lose consciousness.

The contessa rushed to him. "Victorio, what has happened? What have they done to you?"

"He is under arrest, madam," said Jack quietly. "And he has been shot trying to prevent your daughter and myself from leaving this castle. His wound will be treated, but he will then be imprisoned in the jail in Sorrento and then taken back to England to face trial as a criminal for a list of crimes, including suspected murder and robbery and the attempted abduction of your daughter, Adèle."

The contessa looked around wildly and clasped her hands. "I do not understand." She staggered, as if she too was about to faint.

Jack put his arm around her and led her to me. "Please take your mother back to the Villa Romero, dearest. The coach is over there." He indicated with his arm. "Try to explain to her how things stand, if you can. I will join you there later, once we have sorted out matters at the jail."

Alfonso came forward timidly "Can I return to the villa with the contessa, signor?"

Jack looked at him appraisingly. "I suppose so. At present we have nothing against you. But I will want to ask you some questions later. I will instruct one of my men to accompany you to the villa. He will ensure that you do not leave it until I have given you permission to do so."

We climbed into the coach he had indicated, and this took us down on the winding rocky road to the Villa Romero, which we reached about an hour later.

All the guests had gone, and I noticed several uniformed Italian police officers were in the grounds. The gate to the garden was opened by one of these. Jack's man, who had accompanied us, explained who we were, and we were allowed to enter the villa.

The contessa immediately took my arm and led me up to her bedroom. Alfonso, rather uncertainly, followed behind us and disappeared into his own room.

CHAPTER 19

The contessa's bedroom was a beautiful chamber in pastel shades of pale blue, pink, and silver-grey. An enormous canopied bed with gauzy curtains stood in the centre and long windows gave onto a balcony overlooking the garden and the bay, still glittering in the moonlight. The sweet fragrance of jasmine and many other scented flowers wafted through the open casements.

Céline sank down onto her bed, in complete exhaustion, resting her head on the pillows and weeping sadly.

I sat down on the bed beside her and took her hand. "Is there anything I can get you, Maman?"

Céline removed her handkerchief from her streaming eyes. "There is wine on the table over there, my love. Could you pour me a glass?"

I did as she had requested and brought her a goblet of red wine and a plate of macaroons.

She sat up and began to sip the wine and nibble a biscuit. "I am sorry," she said. "I am in a state of shock, that is all, because, really, I cannot feel very distressed about the count. I knew, from the first few weeks of our marriage that I had made a mistake. He was not the kind, considerate husband I had expected. In fact, he was very sinister, and I felt very frightened of him most of the time. I had imagined I was going to have a pleasant life and move in the social circles of the town, with occasional visits to friends or to Paris, Rome, or Venice, but instead, I felt like a prisoner, as I have already told you. Everything I did was questioned.

Valdini looked at all my correspondence. Nothing was private. He used to go away for quite long periods, I have no idea where and leave those two men in charge of everything, including myself. It was really intolerable. I longed to leave him."

She grasped my hand. "And then we received the letter sent by the tutor at your school. Valdini wanted to know all about you. I told him about my having to leave you in Paris and about how my ex-lover, Mr Rochester had taken you to England and made you his ward. Valdini then wanted to know all about Mr Rochester, his position in society, and his wealth. I did not know a great deal about him, but I told Valdini that he was a gentleman with an estate in England. He told me to reply to the letter via the tutor as we did not know your address."

"Your letter was very cold and distant, Maman," I said gently. "I was really very put off by your apparent lack of feelings for me."

My mother turned and looked me full in the face. "Then I achieved the effect I was hoping for, my child. I did not want you to come and visit me. I felt sure that Valdini had some sinister plan in mind. So, I thought I would make the letter as cool and off-hand as possible."

I smiled sadly. "I did feel all that, Maman, but I had a strong desire to see you and I also felt you held the key to my birth and whether I am Mr Rochester's daughter or not. As you know, we have discussed this and you have given me some advice about it. I was a little upset, although of course, pleased for her, when his wife, Jane, gave birth recently to a baby girl, a little daughter for him, but then was encouraged by his kindly and loving attitude towards me afterwards."

There was a pause and then my mother sat up in a purposeful way, rearranging her pillows. "But now my love I need some advice from you. I am not sure where I stand. Valdini has been caught red handed in his attempt to kidnap you and has been arrested by that English policeman, to be taken back to England to face trial for a long list of crimes he has committed, including murder. Where am I to go? How am I to live?"

"Do you have any money of your own, Maman? Or are you entirely dependent on Valdini for support?

"Money? He took everything he thought I had. I would be penniless, except for my own commonsense." She smiled to herself and then looked at me, as if trying to decide on something. "I hope I can trust you, Adèle, not to breathe a word of what I am about to tell you?"

I looked at her in surprise. "Of course you can trust me, Maman."

"Well, for several years, here in Sorrento, before I met the count, I was running a little business as a dressmaker."

"A dressmaker!" I was very taken aback. Somehow, I could not equate the glamorous lady I remembered as a child with such a practical undertaking.

"Yes, as a matter of fact, I have always had the skill of being able to sew very well and it was very useful, even in Paris, when I lacked engagements in the theatre. But, I finished with the theatre years ago and when Guiseppi left me, I had to do something, so I started up this trade. I had quite a distinguished clientele of ladies in the end, and eventually, I employed several staff who did most of the hand sewing, although I always put in the finishing touches. I designed the gowns, coats, hats, etcetera myself, using the beautiful materials which we have available in Italy." She paused and took a sip of wine.

"After some time, I had the idea I should like to be married to some wealthy gentleman and lead an entirely different sort of life, like the ladies who were my clients. I appointed the most reliable and long-serving of my dressmaking staff to be the manageress of the business. She has proved to be very efficient and completely trustworthy. I opened a special bank account under a different name, into which all the profits of the business were paid, once all the running costs and wages had been deducted. I was then able to wear the fine clothes, designed by myself of course, and posing as a widow, I entered into the social life of the town. It was not long before I became acquainted with several gentlemen, all of whom sought my hand in marriage. The one I chose, because of his title, was Count Valdini. He, of course, knew nothing about my business and thought my money came from my deceased husband's estate.

She sighed. "When he appropriated all of this, I began to realise I may have made a big mistake. As it happened, my manageress approached me secretly one day and asked if I would be interested in selling the business to her. She had received some financial backing from someone and named quite a handsome sum. I would have been tempted, but for my doubts about my husband, so I left the matter in abeyance. However, now that this has happened, I think the sensible thing to do would be to accept my manageress's offer and start a new life somewhere else. I should have quite a useful sum at my disposal." She gave a sad laugh. "I might even start up another dressmaking establishment, although not of course in Sorrento and probably not in this country at all."

I sat beside her silently, thinking about what she had told me. It seemed to me that my mother was a very resourceful lady. She was not, by any means, the faded, fluttering, nervous creature I had thought her when we had been reunited. Was all that an act? After all, she had been an actress and she had successfully deceived Edward Rochester in the past. She was definitely a survivor, with her rather hard-headed business plans. But, perhaps we were alike. I was not the sort of person to sit down and suffer persecution either. In her situation, perhaps I would have acted in the same way.

My mother patted my hand. "I can see I have surprised you my love. Let us not worry about this anymore tonight." She gave a discreet yawn. "I am very tired. I need to sleep. We can discuss things further tomorrow." She settled herself more comfortably on the bed and closed her eyes. "Stay with me here until the morning. That young English policeman will be here soon. Will you deal with him for me?" Her voice was becoming more and more drowsy as she fell asleep.

I moved from the bed and sat down on a sofa, which faced the long open windows, with its back to the bed. I leaned my head against the cushions, and I too slept.

*****

There was a light tap on the door. I had locked it, shortly after we had entered the room. We had not wanted any of those tough-looking Italian policemen to disturb us.

I went to the door and put my ear to it. "Who is it?" I whispered in Italian.

A familiar Cockney voice answered softly. "It's me, Jack. Are you both all right?"

"Yes, Jack, we are. But Maman is asleep." I opened the door and fell into his arms.

Between kisses, I murmured, "Oh, Jack, what a terrible night it has been, but thank God we are both safe and now together." Closing and relocking the door, I led him to the sofa and we both relaxed against the cushions, our arms around each other.

"How is the contessa?"

"She was very shocked by what happened, but she was very unhappy in her marriage to the count and not really surprised to discover his true villainous character."

"Did he treat her badly?"

"Yes, he tried to restrict and control her. She felt like a prisoner." I then told him more of what she had told me concerning her relationship with her husband.

"But one of the almost unbelievable things, Jack, is to discover that James Boulding, the Director of Music at Wolden Cathedral, was one of Albert Eales' aliases, a pillar of respectability, even though a pompous bore. I can still hardly credit it. I mean, how could he have maintained such a role for so many years?"

"I suppose that was part of his many talents, if you can call them that."

"But why, what was the point of it? How would it benefit him?"

"Well, do not forget that he was the leader of a criminal gang, but he needed a respectable cloak, a personality which nobody would think to challenge. He actually does have a knowledge of music and is an accomplished musician. In organising these concerts which he put on, he had to travel about the country and even abroad, finding suitable performers. Count Valdini was often away from Sorrento for longish periods. So that is when he was in Wolden, or liaising with his gang."

Jack laughed. "You will be interested to hear, love, that the Dean of Wolden is seeking James Boulding's whereabouts. I had a communication from my office in London. He disappeared with all the money from his last concert and has not been heard of since. With his gang disbanded, he was obviously short of money and saw this opportunity for some ready cash."

I gazed at Jack in amazement. "When was he last seen by the Dean, then?"

"Sometime in mid-February, I believe, after the concert. That would have been the one in which he invited you to participate, wouldn't it?"

"Yes, it would, and what you do not know, Jack, is that he called in at Southlands on Mr Rochester's birthday, the fourteenth of February and made me a proposal of marriage."

Jack gave a laugh, which he quickly suppressed, giving a quick glance at the bed. "Well, the cunning old…individual. That would have been when he had left Wolden with the money and was on his way to Sorrento to resume his life as Count Valdini."

"But, Jack, I do not understand. Supposing I had accepted him?"

"Well, probably he thought he would have a shot at linking himself to you in marriage. A lady with a rich guardian could have had good possibilities for him. If you had accepted him, he would probably have turned around and gone back to Wolden and resumed his life as James Boulding. It is very likely he would have returned the money he had stolen, but demanded a substantial dowry from your guardian, and do not forget that, as your husband, he would have been entitled to any other money which might have been settled on you."

"But what about the fact that, as Count Valdini, he was married to my mother?"

"Yes, well, he has been able to manage the two personalities quite successfully up to now, spending time at

Wolden and time in Sorrento, so he may have continued to do so, for a while. However, I think he had plans to rid himself of your poor mother anyway."

"Yes, so Marietta told me."

I looked quickly at the bed, afraid that my mother had overheard, but was reassured to find that she was still breathing peacefully in sleep.

"About your mother, dearest, has she any thoughts for her future? Does she want to continue living here in this villa?"

"We have discussed this, Jack, and I have the impression that she wants to leave here and start a new life somewhere else. It seems that she may have the necessary funds to do so, but I would rather you talked with her about it."

"Of course, my love." Jack gave a yawn. "I have just realised how tired I am." He settled himself more comfortably on the sofa. We kissed and I nestled beside him, our arms about each other. The perfumes of the night continued to drift in on the soft breeze, which billowed out the gauzy curtains, and we slept.

*****

I awoke some hours later to find myself lying on the bed next to my mother, with the morning sun streaming across the room.

There was a knock on the door, and in came Jack, bearing a tray on which there was a plate of hot rolls, butter, preserves, cups, and a steaming coffee pot. He put the tray down on the bedside table. "Your breakfast, contessa and signorina," he said, flourishing a napkin on his arm.

"You seem to have reverted to your previous footman's role, Jack," I said with a sleepy little laugh.

Jack smiled at me. "I will wait for you both downstairs. Join me when you are ready, and we can have a further discussion about the situation, particularly regarding your mother."

He bowed, kissed his hand to me, and withdrew.

The contessa awoke at this point and raised her head to see Jack disappearing through the door. "Oh, the young policeman and what a delicious aroma of coffee! How are you this morning, my dear child?"

"I am very well, Maman," I said brightly, "but there are a few things I need to tell you."

My mother sat up and, taking the cup of fragrant coffee I handed to her, began to sip it appreciatively.

I began to butter the rolls for our breakfast. "That 'young policeman' you have recently met at Valdini Castle and saw disappearing through the door is Detective Jack Whitaker of Scotland Yard, London, Maman, and he is my fiancé."

My mother gave me a quick glance of surprise.

"Yes, Maman, we became engaged secretly on the voyage out here from England. There is a lot more I have to tell you about him and will do so later."

"Does your guardian know of this engagement?"

"No, not at present. But he knows Jack, who used to work for him in…another capacity, and he likes and respects him. I think Jack is in a position to help you, Maman, if you want to leave Sorrento. Have you had any more thoughts about your future?"

My mother sipped her coffee silently for a few minutes and then gave me one of her quick appraising looks. "You are returning to England by boat, are you not?"

I nodded.

My mother played with a teaspoon thoughtfully, "How would you feel if I said I would like to come with you?"

"Oh, Maman, I think that would be a lovely idea. But where would you live and what would you do in England?"

"Well, as I told you last night, I have funds available and could probably settle my affairs here quite quickly, within a few days. I would have enough to find a small house, possibly in London, and I may decide to start up another dressmaking establishment in that city."

I clapped my hands. "I…I think it could all work out very well, Maman. Jack has a small house in Lambeth and you could probably find something close to us, once we are married."

"Yes, that is a possibility," said my mother thoughtfully. "But how would your fiancé, Jack, feel about it?"

"Oh, I am sure he will agree, Maman. But he is waiting for us downstairs to discuss your situation and plans. Let us make ourselves ready and go down and see him."

The thought that I might have my very own mother living near me, after all these years of longing for her, had filled me with irrepressible joy.

Once we were dressed, we made our way downstairs to Jack, who was sitting at the white terrace table, a cup of coffee before him, busily writing notes.

As soon as he saw us, he rose and gave a little bow. "And how is the contessa this morning?" he said brightly

I could not keep the news from him. I was so excited. "Jack, Maman has asked if we could take her to London on the Seafarer. She has money available and the means of supporting herself."

Jack gave us both a quizzical look from his bright brown eyes. "Perhaps the contessa would like to tell me more?"

My mother then told Jack the same story that she had told me, about her dressmaking business in Sorrento and how she had continued to collect money from it, unbeknown to the count. She also touched briefly on how unhappy she had been in her marriage and how frightened of her husband and how he had treated her. She then explained about selling her business and the idea of starting up something similar in the West End of London.

Jack listened to her carefully, asking the occasional question, as she told him her plans. "Dressmaking, hmmm…you know, I think it could be an excellent idea, and it has given me another idea of my own, which, in time, I might discuss with you, contessa."

He turned to me, "Er, beloved, have you told your mother about us?"

"Yes, I have Jack, dear. I… I think she is pleased. Are you, Maman?"

"I hope I will be, dear, but it is so much to take in at once. However, I really feel you should tell Mr Rochester."

"We will do so in the very near future, contessa," cried Jack, getting up and giving us both a hearty kiss. "And now, I suggest we drive down to the harbour and make everything known to our companions on the Seafarer."

CHAPTER 20

Before we left Sorrento, I celebrated my twenty-first birthday with all my shipboard friends. The chef made a lovely birthday cake and a delicious array of delicacies for my birthday party. On this special occasion, Jack and I announced our engagement, and I was able to show everybody my beautiful diamond and ruby ring and receive their heartfelt congratulations.

Not everybody on board was equally happy, though. Albert Eales, alias Count Valdini, having spent a few days in the Sorrento jail, was taken onto the ship quietly, at night, whilst everyone slept and installed in a cabin near the hold. Probably far from pleasant place to spend the weeks before we reached England.

I had been concerned about his son, Alfonso, who had not seemed to me to be a wicked character like his father. However, my mother had spoken to Jack about him. It seems he wasn't really the count's son. His mother had been the count's mistress, and thinking to advance her son's prospects, she had passed him off at the age of about fifteen to Valdini as the result of their previous union; whereas, in fact, Alfonso knew who his real father was. However, Valdini, in need of a son to one day become second in command in his criminal schemes and because Alfonso was a pleasant, good-looking youth, had accepted his mother's story. But Alfonso was far from happy. He did not like the environment into which he had been thrust and disliked Valdini intensely. He spent most of the time looking for a safe way to escape.

My mother told Jack that he had been a very supportive help to her, because he had taken coded messages back and forth between herself and her dressmaking manageress, Lucilla, about her secret business. Otherwise, being constantly under surveillance, she would have been unable to communicate. She tested him out with one message to Lucilla and found that he had delivered it faithfully and brought back a reply, so she began to have complete faith in him. She knew of no criminal activities that he had been involved in, and Jack concluded he was innocent. Which has proved to be the case. Alfonso was extremely helpful in arranging for the transaction between Lucilla and my mother in the sale of the business, and Céline's financial affairs were satisfactorily concluded within a few days, as she had hoped.

It seems that Lucilla and Alfonso had decided to form a partnership, and he is now helping her run the business by acting as a salesman and procuring new clients. It is on the cards that this partnership may well become a marital one as well, and my mother told me that she felt happy for them both.

A few days before we were due to return to Naples, Captain Fitzjames received instructions that the 'Important Personage' whom he had transported to Naples had finished his business there but had decided to stay on for several more weeks. The personage had also decided to return on H.M.S. Sea Queen, a sister ship of H.M.S. Seafarer, which we gathered had even more luxurious accommodation than our ship, and this would enable him to travel in the company of several of his friends, returning to England.

On hearing this news, Diana, so full of fun, verve and ideas, ran into my cabin. "Why don't you and Jack have a shipboard wedding? My husband, the captain is legally entitled to marry you and it would be so romantic. You could use the Royal Suite for your Honeymoon." She gave a little laugh, "I must say it was very nice of the Prince, or whatever he is, to decide not to come back with us. His quarters would be ideal."

At first, I was dubious. Would not Mr and Mrs Rochester be upset or annoyed that we were not to have our wedding from Southlands and at St. Mary's Church, Fremingham?

I expressed these concerns to Diana, but she, so full of alternatives, suggested we had a Blessing at St Mary's, when we returned to England, to be followed by a reception at Southlands for all our other relatives and friends.

Jack and I decided to write to my guardian from Sorrento, giving our news about the engagement, and asking for his permission to marry. We also mentioned Diana's suggestion about the shipboard ceremony and having a Blessing and reception at Southlands on our return. Dick Holness volunteered to take the letter by a fast packet ship leaving Sorrento that day, bound for Portsmouth, and to arrange for its urgent delivery to Southlands. We would also request that Mr Rochester should send his reply to the harbourmaster's office in Lisbon where we hoped we might find it on our arrival there in several weeks' time.

Dick and Marietta had both decided to travel back together on the packet, and we waved them off at Sorrento that morning, with many expressions of thanks for Dick's friendly assistance and for Marietta's help to Jack in saving me. We also gave them both our good wishes because they told us they planned to marry soon themselves.

I must confess I felt rather dubious about their chances of a happy marriage. She was such a spitfire, and he so solid and reliable. I said as much to Jack, but he did not agree.

"I think it is a case of the attraction of opposites." he said, putting his arm about my waist. "He will be very good for her. He seems to know how to calm her down, and she will regard him as her rock in a difficult and dangerous world. I think they'll get along very well."

When we reached Lisbon in about three weeks, Jack went straight to the Harbourmaster and was very pleased to find a letter addressed to him in Mr Rochester's bold hand.

He ran back to the Seafarer and together we hastily read its contents.

"My dear Mr Whitaker,

Mrs Rochester and I were delighted to receive the news about your engagement to my ward, Miss Adèle Varens, and I am pleased to give my permission for your shipboard wedding to be conducted by Captain Fitzjames.

If I say I assume 'feathers' are affordable, I think Adèle will know what I mean.

We are touched that you wish to return to Southlands for a Blessing in Fremingham church and a reception here at Southlands for all your friends and will look forward to hearing from you, when you reach England.

241

*I trust that the other matter has
been satisfactorily resolved?
I am sir, yours most sincerely,
Edward F. Rochester"*

"Feathers affordable, what does he mean?" exclaimed Jack.

I giggled and took his arm affectionately, "Oh, just a little joke between us. All to do with your rather reckless driving when you and I first met. I got flung sideways in the carriage, and the feather on my bonnet got bent. Do you remember?"

He gave me a mischievous look. "Yes, I well remember. I was a bit put out by your imperious manner, my sweet. I'm afraid I didn't really enjoy being a servant."

"I think that was obvious dearest. But what I imagine he actually means is that he assumes you can afford to support me, in the style to which I am accustomed, not of course, just in new feathers."

Jack looked serious. "I really feel I should write to him again and explain myself fully. That is, on how I see our future and my change of plans. We certainly won't starve. Initially, I will have my police pay, but then, after that, I have prospects which I think could be very lucrative."

"I think that is an excellent idea, Jack. I am sure he will appreciate it. I cannot help feeling that we have been a little bit too casual about things. At present, as his ward, I receive the interest on a sum of £3,000, but he has reserved the right to withhold this, if he is unhappy about the man I want to marry. He arranged it like this to confound fortune seekers. He knows you, of course, and I do not think he has any reservations about your character, but if you write and tell him your plans, particularly about leaving the police force and going into the theatre, it would be helpful to him."

Accordingly, Jack drafted a letter to Mr Rochester, which he showed to me for my approval. It read,

"Dear Mr Rochester,

Thank you for giving your permission for my marriage to your ward, Miss Adèle Varens.

She has explained to me the remark in your letter about feathers.

Events having happened so quickly, we are at present on board HM Seafarer and hope to be married here shortly and there has been no chance for me to explain to you how I see our future, from a financial point of view. As you know, I am a detective, working for Scotland Yard. My present salary is more than enough to support a wife and I have taken a lease on a small furnished house in Lambeth where we will live when we return to England.

My father is J.D. Whitaker, who is a well-known theatrical manager and producer and has many successful productions to his credit. I took shares in the last one, 'The Magic Forest' and this has been very profitable, so I have a reasonable sum put by. My father has asked me to come and work with him as a partner and assist him with future productions. There is a new play scheduled to start at Christmas, of which we have high hopes. I am therefore confident that, if I leave the Police Force, we will have ample means.

I hope this will be to your satisfaction, but if you have any queries, I will be pleased to discuss them more fully when we next meet at Southlands.

As to your query about 'the other matter', yes, all has now been resolved, and I will report to you about that as soon as I reach England.

I am, sir, your obedient servant,

John Richard Whitaker"

"Yes, that seems fine to me," I commented. "I hope it will put his mind to rest. The only thing is, dearest, I feel that perhaps I should also write a brief letter to them to enclose with yours, giving my thanks for his agreement to our plans and saying how happy we are – also perhaps sending my good wishes to Tante Jane and Baby Helen."

"Yes, darling, that would be a good idea." He smiled. "And at least they'll know you want to marry me and that you are not under any duress to do so!"

"Oh, Jack, don't be ridiculous." This exchange promoted a prolonged and loving kiss.

I then wrote my note and Jack enclosed it with his, and we sent it off on its journey to Southlands.

Later that day, as we took an evening stroll around the deck, I reverted to my allowance and said I felt sure that Mr Rochester was unlikely to withdraw it, particularly on receiving Jack's letter.

Jack shrugged. "Well, if he does, dearest, it will not be the end of the world."

"Perhaps I can get involved in the theatre, too." I said hopefully.

"Only if it is your choice, my love. However, there is a tradition in our family that, if a wife should work and earn money, for example, when my mother continued on as a trapeze artist after her marriage and later went on the stage in pantomime, any money she earned was hers to do with what she wanted. My father did not grab it as his, like our friend, Valdini!"

"That seems very enlightened, Jack – as long as you do not expect me to be a trapeze artist!" We both laughed.

*****

Whilst we were in Lisbon, Jack obtained a special licence for our shipboard marriage, and there were flowers and other ornaments to be bought for the ceremony.

My mother had a lovely idea for my wedding dress. She adapted a white ball gown of mine (*not the one I had worn when abducted!*). It had a rather low neckline, which we felt was unsuitable for a blushing bride, so my mother created a little gauzy cape which fitted over my shoulders and was much more decorous

When all our arrangements had been completed, H.M.S. Seafarer put to sea again. The wedding day passed in a dream of love and joy. My mother gave me away and Diana acted as Matron of Honour. We had a reception on board in the saloon, to which all on board ship were invited – with one notable exception, of course, the prisoner below decks.

After our wedding night in the glamorous surroundings of the Royal Suite, I know we both felt that we were now one, and were 'bone of my bone and flesh of my flesh'. I had not imagined that a marriage between two people as suited physically and mentally as we were could produce such a wonderful feeling of completeness and sense of belonging. We were on a nightly voyage of ecstasy and discovery and I felt I was living in a totally different dimension.

When we reached Portsmouth, the prisoner, Albert Eales, was removed to a closed waiting vehicle, which drove to the local jail to await further proceedings. Again, this happened in the early hours of the morning and none of the passengers was aware of it. Jack said he thought that, if found guilty of even one of his crimes, and there was plenty of evidence, he would certainly be executed.

CHAPTER 21

We said goodbye to our shipboard companions, promising to meet them again in London soon and accepting all their repeated good wishes for our marriage. The Fitzjames family were going to visit friends near Portsmouth, so they would not be returning to Tavistock Square for a few days.

Jack and I, accompanied by my mother, took a train to London and then a hansom cab to Jack's house in Lambeth, where it had been agreed between the three of us that my mother would stay with us temporarily, until she had found a suitable property of her own.

The house proved to be one of a terrace, in Drayton Way, a respectable street. Built in the 1820s, it had several rooms on each floor; a basement kitchen and scullery and above, at street level, two interconnecting rooms divided with double sliding panels which were dining room and drawing room. Upstairs, a main bedroom to the front and two smaller ones behind and, on the upper floor, several attics for storage and one suitable for a maid.

Jack told me though, that he did not think of this house as being our permanent home. As soon as our fortunes improved, he said, he planned we should move to a much more fashionable district, north of the river, perhaps Kensington or Chelsea.

When we arrived, a small, rather untidy little maid opened the door to us. She looked at us in dismay, particularly when we asked for tea and something to eat. My mother immediately took charge and got little Effie organised, and the necessary refreshments were eventually produced. Effie was then packed off to the market, which was in a nearby street, with the strange name of The Cut, with a list, and an adequate supper appeared on our table that evening, partially prepared by my mother who, it seems when she chooses, can be a capable organiser.

My mother, Céline, had been a different person since she had left the influence of her dominating and controlling husband. There was a sense of purpose and energy about her. Gone was the weak, clinging, tearful woman. Even her skin looked smoother and more youthful. Her blue eyes were brighter, her blond hair sleeker, and she had taken to wearing plain but elegant clothes rather than the gauzy floating creations she had favoured at the Villa Romero. No doubt our English climate had something to do with this. I felt much happier about her future here than I did when we had first agreed that she come with us to England.

I could see that Jack, who had no doubt suffered from Effie's inefficiency in the past, appreciated my mother's skills as a manager. As we ate a rich beefsteak pie from the local pie shop, served with hot potatoes and vegetables, he commented that he could see that he would be 'well looked after' and smiled appreciatively at us both. "Still," he said, "I think we will have to look out for a suitable cook."

"Yes," I laughed. "I am afraid my finishing school did not think it necessary to include cooking on its list of subjects. I suppose Madame imagined we would all go back to homes with a full staff of servants.

"And marry husbands who could supply them?" asked Jack ruefully.

I touched his arm, tenderly. "I would rather be here with you in this dear little house in Lambeth than anywhere else in the world, darling Jack."

That evening, as we snuggled down together in the double bed in what had previously been his room, the large chamber at the front, he said, "I telegraphed Ma and Pa from Portsmouth, when we arrived, my love, and I would like to take you to meet my ma tomorrow afternoon for tea. I am sure she is dying to see you."

I stroked his cheek gently, pushing back a lock of his chestnut hair as I murmured, sleepily, "Of course, Jack, I would love to meet her, but what about your father?"

"My father works long hours in the theatre, so he won't be available at home, but we can probably go and see him there in a few days."

Jack's parents lived in a small terraced house, very similar to his, in a nearby Lambeth street. As we approached, I could see it was all very trim and well kept.

His mother answered the front door herself. She was tall, like Jack, with similar colouring. Her chestnut hair was curly, like his, and framed her face, but drawn into a bun at the back. She had the same bright brown eyes and her face was rosy with a merry expression, which frequently broke into a smile, showing strong white teeth. Her figure was matronly and rounded, but supple. I guessed her age to be somewhere in the fifties. She had a Cockney accent and spoke in a low, fairly deep voice.

Jack introduced us, and immediately after she saw me, I was drawn into a warm embrace. "Jest call me Edie, love, everyone else does," she said, and then she led us into the front room, which was all very neat and well polished. There was a snowy tablecloth and pretty pink and white china, laid out ready for tea. The room was full of mementoes of the circus and theatre. Over the fireplace was a portrait of Jack's father, J.D. Whitaker, burly and commanding. He was probably in his thirties then, with dark hair, dressed as a

Circus Master in white trousers and a scarlet jacket, flourishing the traditional circus whip.

We had a very merry tea together.

I described Jack's disguise as Edwina Foskit and Edie went into peals of laughter, especially when I told her about his doing the polka with the unsuspecting young Italian and the boots with velvet bows.

Holding her sides, she exclaimed, "Oh, Adèle, wot a wonderful picture you've painted. I can jest imagine it. Jack is such a character. D'you remember, Jackie, 'ow you played Dame Betty Bloomers in 'Jack and the Beanstalk' at the Theatre Royal, Stockton?"

Jack was laughing too. "And you played the Principal Boy, Ma."

Edie looked down modestly "Yes, me legs was better then. I could get away with it." She flexed her ankles under her skirt.

"You still could, Ma, you're as young as ever."

"Well, there's lots of younger talent coming along," she said. "Not much call for old stagers like me."

"You'll never be old, darling!" cried Jack, giving her a smacking kiss.

"And wot about you, Adèle? Are you in the profession too?"

"The profession?" I gave her a startled look.

Jack laughed. "Ma means the theatrical profession, Adèle." He glanced proudly at me. "Ma, Adèle has a lovely soprano voice. She sings at concerts in churches and cathedrals and you would think she was an angel from heaven if you heard her."

Jack's mother expressed her surprise and pleasure at this news, but then started asking me more about my background. I told her about my past, and about my mother

Céline, and our life in Paris, and then about how Mr Rochester was my guardian, and about Tante Jane and their home in Southlands, Woldenshire.

"Youre a reel lady, then?"

"No, I am not a lady, Mrs Wh...I mean, Edie," I said firmly. "My guardian, although I love him dearly, will not acknowledge me as his daughter, which I feel I am, but in any case, I am the natural product of his liaison with my mother, Céline, an opera dancer, as I told you previously. My mother left me in Paris when I was very young, and, as I explained, that is how I came to be Mr Rochester's ward.

"However, our trip to Italy on H.M.S. Seafarer with Mrs Rochester's cousin, Diana Fitzjames and her husband, the Seafarer's captain was, from my point of view, to be reunited with my mother after many years. I had thought she was dead, but then I heard that she had married an Italian count, Count Valdini." I glanced at Jack. "I met your son, Jack, when he was working at Southlands, in his job as a Scotland Yard Police Detective, disguised as the Rochester's coachman and footman." I stopped at that point as it all seemed rather complicated to explain, but Jack took up the story.

"You see, Ma, I took that disguise in order to investigate the activities of a gang of thieves operating in that area, and I was asked by Mr Rochester to also investigate Count Valdini's background before Adèle travelled to Italy to meet her mother and the count. I then discovered that the count was very likely an imposter, and his real identity was that of a villainous criminal, head of the gang of thieves I had been investigating."

Jack's mother threw herself back in her chair in amazement. "Well, I never, Jack. It all sounds so complicated and dangerous."

"Yes, it was, Ma. But that's my job, and I'm often in that kind of danger. Adèle, of course, had no idea of the peril she might be in. So, I warned her that if the count was the person I suspected he was, she could be abducted and held for ransom." He glanced at me fondly. "But then Adèle, being the brave girl that she is, saw it all as part of an adventure and was prepared to run the risks, particularly as she began to be fearful for her mother's safety, with good cause, I'm afraid."

"But, as you're both 'ere safe and sound, it all worked out all right in the end, did it?" Jack's mother was looking a little pale and concerned as our story had unfolded.

"Yes, it did, Edie," I said soothingly, putting out my hand to touch hers. "I'm afraid I was abducted and driven to the count's castle in the mountains, but I was rescued by Jack and his team of policemen and members of the Seafarer's crew, and the count was identified as the man Jack thought he was and arrested. Valdini came back to England on the ship with us, in the hold and is now in prison awaiting trial."

"Well, thank The Lord for that!" Edie exclaimed. "Could you pour me out another cuppa, dearie? I feel quite faint."

I did as she requested, and she sipped the hot liquid quietly.

In an endeavour to change the subject, I enquired whether Jack was her only child.

She looked at Jack and they both smiled. "Jack is my baby, dearie. He is the youngest in our family and our only son. He has three sisters, all now married and living round and about, and we all spoil him terribly. But I'm so glad he's found you. I think you'll be very good for him. I am sure you won't stand any nonsense. You'll keep him in order!"

"Ma, really. I'm not that difficult, am I?"

I looked at Jack fondly, and he put his arm around my waist. We all laughed.

"So, what's happened to your ma, dearie? Is she safe now?" pursued Edie.

"Yes, she is, ma. Safe as houses. She has come back to England with us and is living in my, or should I say, our house in Drayton Way," said Jack.

"She has money of her own from the sale of her dressmaking business in Sorrento and she plans to start up another such business in London," I added.

"I should think she might do very well in the West End," said Edie thoughtfully. "Perhaps I can meet her, dearie, particularly as she's so close to us 'ere."

"Oh, I'll bring her over to see you!" I exclaimed. "It seems as if she'll be helping me keep house for a bit, but she is looking for a suitable property for her business."

"Well, perhaps I could give 'er some ideas about where to look," Edie said reflectively.

"Oh, by the way Edie," I said "I don't suppose you know anyone who is looking for a job as a cook. We are trying to manage with our little maid Effie's efforts at cooking, but she is totally inexperienced."

Before his mother could reply, Jack came in with, "Sorry, love, I omitted to tell you. I think I've found someone suitable."

We both looked at him questioningly.

"Yes, her name is Mrs Christa Pergamena. She has been working in a West End restaurant kitchen and is very experienced. But she has a large family and is looking for a local job in Lambeth. She only lives a few streets away from us."

"Goodness, that is excellent news, Jack. Will you arrange for me to meet her?"

"Yes, of course, darling. Only one thing, though, I thought I should mention it. She happens to be Marietta's elder sister."

I gave him a startled look. I had a sudden vision of Marietta wielding her dagger and about to rush at Valdini and stab him to death. There were plenty of sharp knives in our kitchen!

As though he read my thoughts, Jack added hastily, "But don't worry, love. She's nothing like her sister."

CHAPTER 22

We began to settle down in our new home, with my mother and I sharing the duties of housekeeper and training little Effie as we did so. The latter had become much neater and had begun to take a pride in her work. The house was beginning to look more attractive and homely, with fresh curtains at the windows, ornaments either discovered in drawers and cupboards or purchased in the local market, and fresh flowers placed on windowsills and tables. I had also arranged for a gardener to clear the rubbish from the rear yard and make it look more presentable. I thought it would be a pleasant place to sit on warm summer days.

Marietta's sister, Christa Pergamena, called one day to discuss working for us as our cook. She seemed much older and plumper than Marietta, but not nearly so dramatic or excitable. She was very quietly spoken, but with the same Italian accent as Marietta. Her experience in a West End restaurant had given her the ability to cook a variety of dishes, both Continental and English. Because of her family (she had four children), she would not be able to live in. However, we came to a satisfactory arrangement about her hours, and the wage I offered her seemed acceptable, and we agreed that she would start the following Monday.

We had been in touch with Mr Rochester and Tante Jane at Southlands, and a date had been fixed for our Blessing at St Mary's church, Fremingham. Invitations for the reception at Southlands were to be sent out by them, in accordance with a list which I had sent them.

A few days after our tea with Edie, Jack returned home after his day's work at Scotland Yard and suggested that we should visit his father the following day at the theatre, where 'The Magic Forest' was still running and where he had a temporary office.

I felt extremely nervous at the prospect of this encounter with the great J.D. Whitaker. Jack had told me he was an impressive and strong personality, but very little else about him.

We arrived at the stage door of the theatre in the mid-afternoon, while a matinee was in progress. A bent, elderly man ushered us up a flight of steep uncarpeted stairs to a door with 'J.D. Whitaker' painted across the glass and, opening it, ushered us inside.

We were in a dusty, untidy room with desks and stools on which sat two young men scribbling furiously with quill pens. Jack knew them both and introduced them to me as Bill and Oliver. They rose from their stools and bowed courteously.

A very loud sonorous voice could be heard coming through a closed inner door. The voice sounded angry and there seemed to be an argument in progress.

"This is no damn good to me!" said the voice.

There was a muffled response.

"Excuses, excuses, I've heard enough of them to last me a lifetime. Come back tomorrow with what I want, or I'll look elsewhere. Now get out, sir!"

I looked at Jack fearfully and whispered, "I think we have come at a bad time, Jack dear. Perhaps we should...."

Jack squeezed my arm, "It's all right, darling. It's all right. His bark is definitely worse than his bite!"

The door was flung open and a pale, thin young man, carrying a sheaf of papers, fled out and through the office to the stairs.

"Wait here, dear," said Jack confidently. "I'll have a quick word and then I'll introduce you."

"Will you have a seat, Mrs Whitaker, ma'am?" said Oliver. He wore a dusty green velvet jacket but there was a bright smile on his long, expressive face.

I sat down on one of the stools. "What are you doing?" I enquired, mainly for something to say. Inside, my stomach muscles were clenched with dread.

"Copying out parts for the next play." said Bill. "We go into rehearsal soon."

"What is the next play?" I asked.

"Not sure what it's called yet. Don't think they've given it a title so far."

The inner door suddenly opened and a bulky man, like a bulldog, stood framed in the doorway. Because of the sunlight behind him, he looked enormous. He was enveloped in a cloud of tobacco smoke from a large cigar clenched between his teeth, and I could not see his face clearly. Then he removed the cigar and I was conscious of bright black eyes looking me up and down appraisingly.

Behind him, I could see Jack grinning at me and making comic gestures with his hands, which made me almost laugh.

"By God, she's a beauty!"

Jack came forward quickly past his father and made the introductions.

"My wife, Adèle, Pa," and then to me, "Dearest, this is my father, Jeremy Whitaker, known to all as 'J.D.'"

"Come in, come into my office, darling. So, you are my daughter-in-law."

J.D. waved an outstretched arm encouragingly back towards his office, and I slid past him, nervously. I know I was blushing furiously.

"Please sit down, my dear. Well, well, so you've done it at last, my boy and done it very well, I can see that!"

He resumed his seat behind the desk and waved Jack to another next to me. Jack sat down and grasped my hand reassuringly.

The man before me was a giant in many ways. His face was craggy and red with a protruding nose. His eyes, small, black and keen, like a ferret's; his lips red and bulbous, his hair dark with some grey, as was his close-cut beard. Nobody could have described him as handsome, but I could feel an electric energy radiating from him. I was reminded that I had felt this about Jack, when I had first met him, but whereas Jack's personality is light, debonair, and airy, this man was forceful, arrogant, and dominating. I suppose he made me think also of Edward Rochester, but Mr Rochester was more sardonic than arrogant and always courteous and a gentleman. Jeremy Whitaker had been brought up in a much tougher and rougher school and had fought his way through to the top by the sheer strength of his dynamic character.

"How's 'The Magic Forest' going, Pa?" asked Jack lightly, probably to break any ice that might be forming.

"Very well, my boy, very well. Still packing 'em in. Our lease on this theatre runs out in about a month, but I'm planning to take it on tour." He looked at me with those keen little eyes. "What's your background, Mrs Jack? Are you on the stage?" He lit another cigar and blew out another cloud of smoke.

"Oh no, Pa, Adèle isn't an actress, but she has a lovely soprano voice."

"Yes, I think Edie mentioned it to me," He gave another puff. "Any interest in the theatre, Mrs Jack?"

"Well, my mother was an opera dancer in Paris, and I have performed in public myself in church with a choir. We did 'The Messiah', and I took a solo soprano part. I was extremely nervous at first, but then I felt a wonderful thrill. I could feel the audience responding to me..." My voice trailed away. Had I said too much? I glanced nervously at the great man.

"Sounds like you could be a trooper, if you wanted to be."

Jack intervened. "I didn't marry Adèle to put her on the stage, Pa. If she was interested, she could try it out, but she and I would need to discuss it together."

"All right, my boy, all right. Anyway, my darling, glad to have you in the family. We must celebrate. How about dinner in the West End next week after the show?"

*****

When Jack and I were alone together that evening, my mother having retired early, I seated myself on his knee, stroking his chestnut curls and giving him a loving kiss. He put his arms around me and we sat quietly for a few minutes looking into the flickering fire and reflecting on the events of the day.

"Dearest Jack," I said softly, "If I told you I would be interested in trying out a part on the stage, would you be unhappy?"

"Well, darling, I certainly wouldn't be unhappy, if that is what you really want. I suppose you could try out a minor part in 'The Magic Forest'. He thought for a few minutes, and then he said, "I happen to know that one of the young ladies playing a fairy is leaving the cast because she's in the family way, and I very much doubt that she will want to go on tour with the show in a month's time."

"Oh, that sounds ideal! Does it involve any singing?"

"It could do. At present the girl in the part doesn't sing solo. She merely joins in the choruses with the rest of the cast, but we could give you a song or two. You would need to learn the part of course. She is the one who gets turned into a mouse."

"Oh Jack, it sounds great fun. I should love to do it." I jumped to my feet in my excitement.

Jack got up too and took me in his arms again. "How would you feel about going on tour though?" he whispered into my hair.

"Where are we likely to go? And would you be able to come too?"

"I think J.D. is talking about the South Coast towns, but as to whether I could accompany you does depend on my supervisor at Scotland Yard. As it happens, I have recently satisfactorily concluded another minor investigation, and I know they are very pleased over the Eales affair. I am entitled to some leave soon, in any case. So, I think it would be possible. The South Coast in September would be very pleasant."

"Of course, we will have our trip to Southlands and the Blessing and reception first, won't we? And it could be like a working honeymoon for us on the South Coast."

"Of course it could, darling." He thought for a few minutes and then said, "I'll talk to Pa about it. I expect he'll want to audition you first, though."

My spirits took a tumble at this. 'But, after all' I told myself, 'I've done auditions before and I have been successful. So, I do not suppose it would be too terrible.'

*****

The following week, we had a lovely evening with Jack's parents at a very elegant restaurant in the West End, after the performance. My mother was invited as well, and she came looking really ravishing in black lace. She is one of those people who can change, like a chameleon to fit in with her surroundings, by putting on the right dress and altering her hairstyle and her manner.

I could see that J.D. was very taken with her, and he said what a lucky man he was to be dining with two such beautiful women. He was in great form. Despite his rough personality, he can put on the demeanour of a gentleman and was particularly charming to Maman and myself. I can see, however, that he and Edie are a very happy couple and fit each other like a pair of gloves.

Prior to this, Jack had brought me a sheaf of papers which was the script of 'The Magic Forest' and my part, which was that of a fairy called Ariadne. He also brought the music and lyrics of two songs he thought I could practise.

There was a piano in the sitting room of our house, and I was able to accompany myself and try these pieces out. We had a mock audition one evening, with Jack and Maman as my audience. Afterwards, my mother gave me a fond embrace and exclaimed, "My darling, clever daughter. I think you will be lovely in the part!"

The audition at the theatre took place shortly afterwards. As always, I felt petrified. My legs were shaking so much, I could hardly walk across the stage. I noticed the young lady I was replacing had joined the rest of the cast in the wings to look and listen and undoubtedly judge my performance. She was giggling with another two girls beside her. I wondered what they were saying. Were they laughing at me? I felt I was going to faint.

Then that thing happened, as before. Oliver, whom I had previously met in J.D.'s office, was my accompanist at the piano. He gave me a sweet smile and just before he played the opening bars, he whispered "Good luck" and this warm gesture made all the difference. I no longer felt like a silly impostor. I went into the song, uncertainly at first, but then gathering strength and confidence. I could see Jack standing in the wings watching me, as he had done that evening when I had sung in the drawing room of Southlands. I started to 'act' the song, which required a lively jaunty manner, and when I finished, there was a round of applause

"Try the other song, darling," said J D. He was sitting astride a wooden chair, leaning on its back, the inevitable cigar clamped between his teeth.

Oliver turned over the music and gave me a wink and another smile, as he led into the piece. I was singing now, as the little mouse, with various squeaks and hand actions, like stroking my whiskers and feeling for my tail, all of which I had rehearsed at home. I heard a few titters from my audience which encouraged me to play up even more and when I reached the last note, there was hearty applause all round and cries of 'Encore' and 'Bravo'. Even two stage hands, standing on a plank near the ceiling above our heads, joined in.

As soon as this favourable reaction had died down, J.D. got up. His face was expressionless. He motioned to Jack and said to me, "Yes, I think we can use you, Mrs J. Come into my office, both of you."

Once inside that sanctum, he said enthusiastically, "You've got good potential, Mrs J. I think you could be a star, my dear. You've got the part when we go on tour, if you want it."

"*If* I want it, J.D." I said, excitedly, "I most certainly do. When does the tour start?"

"We start in Brighton in a month's time." He looked at Jack. "Does that suit you, my lad, in your newly married life? Can you bear to lose this lovely young lady for a month or so?"

"I don't think I shall have to, Pa. I've got several weeks' leave from Scotland Yard, so I'll be coming too."

"Well, that's great, my boy. We can certainly use you." He drew on his cigar. "However, I've got another idea, as well." He looked at Jack. "There's another part I think Adèle could be very suitable for. She's got the looks, the accent, and the voice. What about Lorraine?"

"Lorraine!" exclaimed Jack, "You mean the leading role?"

"Yes, I think she'd be good."

"Do you mind telling me what you are both talking about?" I said, with a touch of indignation.

"I'm sorry, sweet," said Jack, giving me a squeeze with his arm. "One last thing you don't know about me is that I'm a writer, as well as all the other things, and I've written a play with music. Pa's seen the script and he is prepared to back it. It's about a French émigré, called Lorraine, rescued from the Terror of the French Revolution. We both think you would be great for it."

CHAPTER 23

The following week we took the train down to Fremingham for our church blessing and the reception at Southlands. On the way, we had to decide how we were going to explain my new career on the stage to Mr Rochester and Tante Jane.

We considered together what would be their possible objections. I remembered my conversation with Tante the previous Christmas when she had implied it would be unladylike for a respectable girl to be 'ogled' on the stage by the men in the audience who would offer their unwelcome attentions at the stage door afterwards. But I was not really sure that would be Mr Rochester's main objection. I suspected that his principal feelings were prejudiced about my mother's infidelity and the insults he had overheard about himself, which might possibly make him think that all actresses, even myself, could behave in the same way.

Jack took the view that, now I was a married lady, people would respect me on and off the stage. The part I was about to play in 'The Magic Forest' did not carry any particular glamour which would attract the stage door hangers-on and in 'Lorraine' I would be playing a serious and partially tragic role, which would generate sympathy rather than anything else, with delight for the final happy ending. He said that he would do everything possible to protect my reputation from any slurs. Men hanging around the stage door with flowers and invitations to dinner would be totally banned by him, as my husband and also by J.D.

Mr Rochester's feelings about my mother would have to be dealt with carefully, without upsetting him. We decided we would mention that my mother had travelled back to England with us but was staying with us only temporarily and that she had needed our support as she had been in a troubled state of mind, following the arrest of her husband, the count, and the discovery that he was an impostor. We would also tell him that she had means of her own and, when she was fully recovered, was hoping to start up an enterprise in London.

Our greetings and congratulations at Southlands were rapturous. Of course, the boys rushed up and flung their arms around me. Tante came forward with a warm embrace and behind her came the nursery maid carrying little Helen, now over three months old. She had the same very dark eyes and hair as her father and chuckled at us happily. Mr Rochester shook hands enthusiastically with Jack and kissed me on both cheeks, calling me, "dear child".

We dined alone with Mr and Mrs Rochester that evening. Our Blessing was to take place on the morrow, when all the guests would arrive.

During the meal, there was no shortage of conversation. Mr and Mrs Rochester wanted to hear about our adventurous Italian trip. Between us, Jack and I gave a lively account of it. Once again, the story of Jack dressing up as Edwina caused much mirth, particularly from Jane.

We then told them about my abduction and temporary imprisonment at Valdini Castle and how Jack and Henry Fitzjames had rescued me with the help of Marietta and how the count had been finally vanquished and arrested. However, I did my best to play down the fear and horror of my capture and what the consequences might have been, had I not been rescued.

Our listeners were absolutely amazed and stunned to hear of these adventures, and Jack and I received much praise for our bravery in placing ourselves in such a dangerous position. But Mr Rochester added a few words of reproof and reproach to us both for not telling him of the potential risks.

"I assure you, Guardian, that Jack and I had no idea that Valdini would really attempt such a thing. And it was really only a fluke that I was left unattended for about a minute in the dark area where the carriages were standing, so that the abduction was able to take place."

And then I gave him a pleading look. "Please do not be angry with us, guardian. If Jack had realised that, despite all his precautions, this might really happen and told you, Guardian, you would have forbidden me to go on this trip to Italy, and I did so want to."

Mr Rochester gave a short laugh. "Yes, Adèle, you have a reckless streak, I can see that. Very much like myself at your age. But now that you are safely married, I expect you will settle down to a quiet life, looking after your husband and children, when the latter begin to arrive."

I glanced at Jack at these words, and he gave me one of his winks. I somehow did not think a career on the stage was what Mr Rochester had in mind with this forecast of my future.

We told them about Valdini's other disguise as James Boulding, the Director of Music at Wolden Cathedral. They had already heard from Mary Wharton about his disappearance with the money from the cathedral funds and particularly the takings from the concert.

"I know I did not like the fellow, when he came here to ask for your hand in marriage, Adèle." grunted Mr Rochester. "And the fact that he did so whilst actually married to your mother under a different identity, fills me with utter abhorrence and disgust."

"Yes, Guardian, if I had accepted him, then my mother would have had little chance of survival as his wife. I am very sure that he had grown tired of her and would have found some way of disposing of her. Marietta told me as much when she helped me. There is a long list of ladies whom he has married for their money and then got rid of, which are some of the crimes of which he has been accused."

"So, Mr Rochester," interposed Jack, "Adèle and I decided to invite the Contessa Valdini back to England with us. She tells me she has money and has the idea of starting up an enterprise in London, similar to one in which she had been engaged before she met Valdini in Sorrento."

"At the moment, she is living with us." I added, looking at my guardian anxiously and trying to gauge his reactions, "but that is only until she is able to find a property of her own in which she can start up her business. She also needs time to recover from the knowledge that her husband married her under a false identity and is in fact a criminal."

"And what, pray, is her business?" Mr Rochester's tone had taken on a scornful note.

"That of a dressmaker. She has talent in that direction, both in design and execution. She has already made a few things for me which are lovely. I understand her Sorrento business was successful. She sold it to her manageress for a sufficient sum to finance her in something similar in London."

Mr Rochester was silent, but his brows had drawn together in a frown.

"If you could see her now, sir, you would hardly recognise her as the feather-brained and flighty individual you once knew. She has matured considerably and now seems very quiet and sensible." In desperation, I threw into the continued disapproving silence, "I have grown very fond of her."

"Despite the fact that she deserted you when you were a tiny defenceless infant and left you to the mercy of her landlord and his wife in Paris?"

"Yes, I know that seems a terrible and irresponsible thing to do, and I have talked to her about it. She was a little vague, but it seems she was under pressure to leave me for financial reasons and go with her Italian lover to Italy. But she said she remembers leaving some money – enough for my upkeep for a few weeks – with the landlord's wife. The woman, of course, decided to keep the money from her husband and tell him my mother had left none. I have accepted her story, sir, and have forgiven her."

"I suppose it was very likely," said Jane to Mr Rochester. "Such a woman could well have been kept short of money by her husband, who sounds as if he was a very unpleasant and rough sort, and the temptation for her to keep the money Céline had given her would have been very strong."

"And she did take my part, a little," I interjected, "Because she prevented him from beating me and tried to find me work that was within my strength to do."

"Just as well I did eventually receive Céline's letter then and was able to rescue you," said Mr Rochester dryly. "But what about that cold impersonal letter she wrote to you when you suggested visiting her and the count?"

"Yes, I did ask her about that when we met and she told me she had made the letter deliberately unfriendly and lacking in the warmth of motherly love because she was being supervised by Valdini, who read all her correspondence. She suspected he had some wicked plan in his mind about me, and she wanted to put me off visiting her." I smiled at my guardian. "She nearly achieved her objective, as you know, but the desire to see my own mother after all those years was too strong." I took a deep breath and looked Mr Rochester firmly in his dark eye. "You see, Guardian, I wanted to find out as much as I could about my parentage, particularly who was my true father, and from what she told me, I feel sure that there could have been no other father but yourself, sir."

We had now finished our main course and sat in silence after my last statement. I was trembling at my temerity and stole a look at my guardian. He was sitting with his heavy black brows once more drawn together, and he was staring into space.

Robert entered to clear away our plates and serve us with our next course and then withdrew discreetly.

It was Jane who broke the silence. "Adèle, I am sure you remember little Annie Thomas from Wolden, whom you invited down to stay with us after Helen was born?

"Of course, Tante. How is she getting on?"

"Extremely well, my dear. As you know, Mr Rochester arranged for her to have an operation on her foot which was completely successful."

"Yes," I said eagerly to my guardian. "I have not had an opportunity to thank you for that, sir. It was a wonderful thing that you did for her. I am sure it must have changed her life."

"It certainly did, my dear," said Jane smiling at her husband fondly. "I had a letter from her two days ago, accepting my invitation to the reception and asking if she could bring her husband-to-be, Mr David Browning. Annie explained that he was a young farmer, whose land adjoins theirs. I wrote back at once and sent our congratulations and said we would all love to meet the young man."

"Oh, I am so pleased for her!" I said, clapping my hands in delight. "That is really lovely news, Tante. She is such a sweet lively girl, and she made us all so happy when she was staying here with us. I am really very fond of her."

When the meal had finished, we all adjourned to the drawing room. Robert served the coffee, and we settled down in front of the fire.

"Incidentally, Mr Whitaker, what happened about that reward for £200 for the capture of the master criminal, er...what was his name?"

"Albert Eales, sir, also known as Count Valdini, James Boulding, and a whole string of aliases from the past. I received it, sir, but I have distributed most of it to those of my fellow police officers who came with us on the voyage in the Seafarer. Especially to Sergeant Dick Holness who played such a crucial part in his capture. As he has recently married the lady who was my informant and helper in the matter, a donation of £50 was very welcome to them both."

"Very good and generous of you, sir. By the way, thank you for your recent letter about your plans for the future and the fact that you intend to leave the police force and go into partnership with your father. But I feel you know much more about the financial possibilities of a venture like this in the theatre than I do. Has Adèle told you about the sum I set aside for her, and her allowance, which is the interest on this capital sum?"

"Yes, she did mention it, sir. As I explained in my letter, I feel I can fully support Adèle, as my wife – and pay for all her feathers," he said with a smile. "So, I leave it entirely to your discretion what you decide to do about the allowance and the capital sum."

"I will continue the allowance, Adèle," Mr Rochester said, looking at me, "and I will see how your plans go. But I will probably pay over the capital in a year or two, when I feel that such a donation might be needed."

"Oh, that is very kind and thoughtful of you, Guardian," I exclaimed. "I am sure that Jack feels the same."

"Yes, most certainly, sir, although I very much hope it will not be needed," said Jack.

"So, Edward," said Jane picking up her embroidery and threading a needle, "How do you regard your ward now? Do you still feel that you are only her guardian or do you sense a stronger bond between you?"

Mr Rochester opened his cigar case and offered one to Jack, who thanked him but politely declined. He lit the cigar and blew out a cloud of fragrant smoke. "My love, I appreciate your interest and concern, but I must have time to think the matter over. I agree that there are various things which point in the direction you envisage: The portrait of my mother, Adèle's own personality, and certain similarities in our ways of thinking and acting. But I need to come to terms with the situation."

And that is all he would say on the subject, which we were obliged to leave in abeyance.

Jack and I still had no opportunity of mentioning my stage career, but we hoped we could somehow introduce the subject before we left Southlands.

*****

The Blessing at St Mary's Church in Fremingham was a very happy occasion. It was conducted by the vicar, who handled the service sensitively, and afterwards, I felt well and truly married in the sight of God.

All our friends and relatives who had not been at the wedding ceremony on the Seafarer, filled the church. There were a number from Lower Poppleton choir, together with the choirmaster, Mr Pinto. Of course, there was my dear little friend, Annie, all in pale blue, accompanied by her fiancé, Farmer Browning, his tall, bulky frame looking a little out of place in a smart blue jacket and cream trousers. No doubt his bulging muscles were used to a much rougher garb.

Annie told me they planned to marry in the spring, and I promised that, when time allowed, I would come and pay her a visit, once she was settled into her new life.

The reception at Southlands was equally happy and memorable. Jane's new garden was looking radiant and colourful on this brilliant July day, and everyone was able to promenade outside and admire its beauty.

Stephen and Mary Wharton together with their children were staying the night, but it was late evening before the rest of the guests departed with many congratulations and good wishes. The table in the hall was piled with cards and wedding gifts.

Jack and I had told The Whartons all about our Italian trip and our various adventures, including my abduction. Mary Wharton was amazed to hear of the true identity of James Boulding. "He seemed such a respectable man at first," said Mary. "Although, as you know, I never liked him."

"I think he must have been desperate for cash," said Jack, who was part of this conversation over dinner, that evening. "His gang had been imprisoned and all the money and jewels he had acquired through their robberies had been confiscated. We were closing in on him, and he felt himself to be on the run. Probably his abduction of you, Adèle, dearest was a last wild act to generate more money. He obviously had the idea of blackmailing Mr Rochester."

"What a lucky escape you have had," commented Mary.

"I hope the Dean has also learned the importance of enquiring more fully into the background of the next Director of Music at the cathedral before he appoints someone else," was Stephen Wharton's caustic comment. "I am going to suggest Cedric Pinto for the position."

"Oh, what a good idea!" I exclaimed. "I am sure he would be an excellent choice."

At last it was time to say our goodbyes and return to London. We had decided to let things out gently about my plans. I told the Rochesters that Jack's father, J.D. Whitaker, whom by now they understood was a prominent man in the London theatre, had talked about a small part for me in his current production and that I was 'thinking about it'.

"A very small part indeed, sir," interjected Jack, hurriedly. "Adèle would just sing a couple of songs on the stage, all very seemly and respectable, I assure you."

My guardian made little comment, but he looked at us both keenly. "I am sure Adèle will only do what she considers to be suitable, and I trust her judgment. I expect she will have every protection from you, Mr Whitaker?"

"Of course, sir, of course." said Jack reassuringly.

CHAPTER 24

Reader, a year has elapsed since I began to write this account of myself. Once again, it is December. I am sitting in my dressing room at The Theatre Royal, Drury Lane, waiting to be called for the first night of Jack's play, 'Lorraine'. What amazing twists and turns life has in store!

When we returned to London, it seemed to me that I was immediately caught up in a whirl of events.

I was given the chance of a few weeks to understudy the part of Ariadne, and then the lease of the theatre was up, and the whole company travelled down to Brighton where we were due to open within a few days. We were there for two weeks, and then we moved on to Eastbourne, Hastings, Bognor, and finally Worthing.

It was a completely novel experience for me, to arrive at an unknown theatre on a new stage and have to give the same performance night after night for a week or more. J.D. came to Brighton with us and directed me in my initial appearances. He was a hard taskmaster and expected perfection. I was completely unused to that sort of work. My studies at the Finishing School in Geneva had certainly not prepared me for this. I couldn't help wondering what Madame Grevier would make of it. But in spite of the hard graft, I enjoyed it and felt I was really making use of my talent in a meaningful way. Of course, it was wonderful to have the support of my dear husband, Jack. He gave me every encouragement, particularly when I felt weary at the end of a long day.

We had Sundays off and took the opportunity to relax and enjoy ourselves, spending the time exploring the Sussex countryside and walking on the Downs. We often had an alfresco lunch at a viewpoint, or discovered a pretty village, where we could refresh ourselves at the local Inn.

My performance in 'The Magic Forest' did not go unnoticed. At several towns, following a generally favourable local newspaper review of the play, there were remarks like "we particularly enjoyed the charming performance of the fairy, Ariadne, played by Miss Adèle Varens". Or comments equally complimentary and implying that the writer hoped to see more of me in future productions. This was of course very encouraging.

However, I had been worried that the rest of the cast might feel that I had got the part of Ariadne, purely on the strength of my marriage to Jack. Well, that was true in a way, but if I had failed the audition, that would have been that, as far as I was concerned. I doubt if I would have had the courage to pursue it further. Still, I had noticed one or two spiteful looks from the two girls playing fairies, who had been giggling with Maria, the girl who had left the cast to have a baby. I decided to get an independent opinion from Oliver, someone whom I regarded as a friend and supporter.

His answer was very definite. He looked down at me from his gangling six-foot height, crossed his arms, and smiled. "In this profession, Mrs Jack (They all call me that now), it's all down to audience reaction. From what I can see you've got real talent. Very few people get the cast applauding them like that after an audition and I've seen the audience reaction down here in Sussex, after your songs, particularly the mouse one – utter delight and laughter and hearty clapping. Also, have you seen the notices in the local papers?"

"Yes, I have. I thought them very gratifying."

"Very unusual too. They don't normally pick out someone in a minor part for praise. Don't you worry, Mrs Jack you're all right, and most of the cast love you. You're so kind and considerate to us all."

"I try to be."

"As for Phyllis and Greta who are the ones you are concerned about, they don't have much talent themselves, and they're just jealous. J.D. doesn't think much of them, and I suspect they'll be out of the cast for the next production."

*****

Back in London we found that my mother, with Edie's help – the two had met and got on extremely well, both having a theatrical background in common – had found a suitable premises in a small quiet road near Oxford Street, where she had taken rooms, partially for her own accommodation and one which she intended to convert into a work room. She planned to advertise her business locally.

Then, Jack had the idea that perhaps his father could make use of her services in the next production. After all, it was partially set in Paris, so her advice on locations and scenery could be useful. Also, she may have more information about the costumes of Parisians in the late eighteenth century. Maman was very enthusiastic about this and offered her services as a costume designer and costume maker for the production, which Jack readily accepted. Her advertisements and cards, left in the wealthy houses in the district also produced a response from various ladies of fashion. She was soon so busy that she had to hire a small team of seamstresses, and a flourishing business began to develop.

The plot of 'Lorraine' is very dramatic and full of intrigue and suspense. Lorraine is the daughter of the mayor of a small French town. At the Chateaux nearby, live two brothers. The elder is a Marquis. Both are attracted to the beautiful Lorraine, but one loves her for herself and the other, the Marquis, has dishonourable intentions and plans to make her his mistress. Not realising this, she falls in love with the Marquis. Set against the background of the French Revolution and The Terror, the story is one of heartache, betrayal, and intrigue, but with a happy ending when Lorraine finally realises the depths of the villainy of the Marquis and the value of his brother. The music and songs are often sad and soulful, but there are some very beautiful love duets, which I sing with Pierre, the 'good' brother.

The rehearsals for 'Lorraine' were extremely hard work for me, under the direction of J.D. but I began to get a good 'feel' for the part. It reflected some of my own unhappy experiences of desertion and loneliness in Paris.

Now, of course it is the evening of our First Night. My usual nerves are affecting me, but I am just hoping that I will receive that wonderful inspiration and confidence which has carried me through since my very first performance in the drawing room at Southlands, almost a year ago.

"Five minutes, please, Miss Varens," calls a voice outside my door.

My stomach is doing a somersault. I check my reflection in the long mirror. I am wearing a drab brown dress with white frills at the neckline and a frilly little white cap, ala the late eighteenth century. Feeling I am walking on pins and needles, I shakily make my way to the wings of the stage.

The scene is a gloomy garret in which stands an old tattered couch and a table and chair. I take my seat at the table. Soft music plays and the song of a blackbird is heard

277

through a small window (We had found a useful man who can imitate bird calls).

The curtain is rising. A short pause, and then I begin to sing my sad little refrain.

*****

It is all over! My excitement and happiness know no bounds. The play is a great success. There are at least five or six curtain calls and enormous bouquets of flowers, roses, lilies, and others, are showered onto the stage by my enthusiastic audience.

But, best of all, oh the very best!

We had sent Mr and Mrs Rochester tickets for a box for the First Night. I was dubious that they would come, but no doubt, with Tante's gentle persuasion, Mr Rochester had agreed. They are staying at a hotel in the Strand for a few days.

As I returned to my dressing room and sat down in front of my mirror, there was a tap on the door and Jack ushered them in.

Mr Rochester came forward, his arms outstretched to embrace me with the words, "My lovely, Adèle, my very own child. I now have two daughters, little Helen, a tiny bundle of mysterious possibilities, still to be discovered, but you, my love, are my very own clever and talented daughter." Saying this, he clasped me to his breast.

"Your daughter, do you really mean it? Can I call you Father? Dearest Father, dearest Papa!" I replied, through tears of joy.

My cup is full. I can write no more.

Acknowledgements

Firstly, I would like to acknowledge how much contemporary Victorian novels have influenced me in the writing of this book, in particular, the novels of Charlotte Bronte and her sisters, Emily and Anne as well as the works of Charles Dickens.

I would also like to thank my husband Colin for his help, encouragement, time and computer expertise in the production of this book.

I would like to thank S.F. Bennett, a local author and lecturer, for her interest and help and for reading and proofing the early chapters of 'Not Forgetting Adèle'. Also for giving me very useful historical guidance about the period.

My information about The Detective Department at Scotland Yard in the mid-Victorian period came from 'The Story of Scotland Yard' by Sir Ronald Howe, Head of The Detective Department and later Superintendent and Chief Constable of the C.I.D.

ABOUT THE AUTHOR

Julia Harbour was born in Watford, Hertfordshire. She was educated in Harrow, Middlesex, where her family lived. When the family moved to Devon, she continued her education there. She achieved good 'O' level grades but there was no money to go further and she left school at 16.

After doing a variety of secretarial jobs in London, she joined the BBC and worked in several departments, both production and administrative, before achieving promotion and becoming a BBC Appointments Officer. The work was recruitment in all its forms. She also became interested in recruiting the less fortunate disabled applicants and established a scheme of work experience for them. To raise awareness of this in the world of the media, she successfully organised and hosted a conference with representatives of the various Broadcasting companies, subsequently held on an annual basis.

Eventually she decided pursue her more artistic side. When Julia and her husband Colin moved to Devon she became involved in painting with a group of artists who meet weekly and hold an annual exhibition of their work. For some years she attended a Creative Writing class. She is also an avid reader and has been organising a Book Group.

After reading Jane Eyre, for the umpteenth time, she had a very strong feeling that she would love the book to continue. So she decided to write her own sequel, using the character,

Adèle, whom she had often felt got a rather poor deal from Mr. Rochester. The title of the book follows on from Jane's remark at the end of the novel "You have not quite forgotten Adèle, have you Reader?" And the novel 'Not Forgetting Adèle' came into being.

Belanger Books

Made in the USA
Middletown, DE
27 April 2022

64833447R00159